Q UATTROCENTO

Doubleday

New York   London   Toronto

Sydney   Auckland

Quattrocento

A NOVEL

James McKean

PUBLISHED BY DOUBLEDAY
a division of Random House, Inc.
1540 Broadway, New York, New York 10036

DOUBLEDAY and the portrayal of an anchor with a dolphin are
trademarks of Doubleday, a division of Random House, Inc.

This book is a work of fiction. Names, characters,
businesses, organizations, places, events, and incidents
either are the product of the author's imagination or are
used fictitiously. Any resemblance to actual persons,
living or dead, events, or locales is entirely coincidental.

Cataloging-in-Publication Data is on file with
the Library of Congress

ISBN 0-385-50319-9

Book design by Maria Carella

PRINTED IN THE UNITED STATES OF AMERICA

August 2002

First Edition

1   3   5   7   9   10   8   6   4   2

For Charlie and Jack

Acknowledgments

This book would not be in your hands if Bill Thomas, editor in chief of Doubleday, had not taken such a risk and shown so much faith in an incomplete manuscript by an unpublished writer. I can't thank him enough for his constant support and encouragement. My agents—Chris Calhoun, at Sterling Lord Literistic, Agnes Krup, and Jody Hotchkiss—transformed a dream into a reality, and a writer into an author. My family and friends—Jane, Betsy, both Charlies, Tricia, Claire, Jack, George, Sandy, and Julie McGowan, David Lusterman, Mary VanClay, Jovanina Pagano, Yung and Chao-mei Chin, Andy and Rachel Kuhn, Mark and Lorna LaRiviere, Bob and Nancy Mazzoli, Fiona Pixley, Guy Rabut, and Jamie Dettmer—were unstinting in their enthusiasm and belief in this endeavor during the many long years before it came, at last, to fruition. Dr. Eric Canel deserves a special thanks for so patiently explaining the concepts of quantum physics to me; I still have the restaurant napkins with his sketches illuminating how it could be possible that Schroedinger's cat both did and didn't die. The Greenwich Public Library, in the depth of its collection and the always friendly and helpful staff, afforded everything I needed in my research, while the Metro North Railroad has over the past fifteen years provided me with the best office in the world— safe, dependable, and with conductors who were quite understanding as to how on occasion a laptop might be remembered but a ticket left behind.

Lastly, it is with the utmost gratitude, admiration, and affection that I thank my editor on this book, Amy Scheibe, who helped me center the note.

QUATTROCENTO

chapter 1

Blue. Darker than the sky, as deep as the sea, a blue so rich Matt could almost taste it on the breeze that rippled across the field of asters. Shading his eyes from the hot Umbrian sun, he watched the manticore lope down the field and leap into the sky with a stroke of its powerful wings. A harsh cry and it was gone, circling away over the trees, while below the faint silvery call of trumpets sounded amidst the high tenor yelp of dogs on the hunt. How could he have forgotten?

It was cool under the trees, the air fragrant with the scent of hemlock and mountain laurel. Led on by the neighing of horses and shouts echoing out of sight ahead, Matt forced his way through the underbrush, thick leaves and branches breaking against him like waves, sweat running down his back and into his eyes. It's not too late, he thought. Gone before they were seen, the sinuous outlines of hounds slipped through the shadows, followed by the figure of a man, a flash of red and yellow with a tall black stave in his hands, and then another.

Matt's horse followed, tossing her head as he urged her on, twisting and turning through the underbrush. Bursting into a clearing his mount reared and Matt was drifting through the dappled air, sword sailing from his hand as the trees spiraled around him, their crowns sparkling with sunlight far away. The ground slammed into him, hard under the thin layer of leaves, knocking the wind out of him, sliding away from his hands as he scrabbled to find a purchase, the dirt cold on his cheek.

"Orlando," he gasped, chest burning. The boy, he had to find the boy. He forced himself to his knees, and then with a groan to his feet, staggering as the trees circled him like hawks in the sky, his arm throbbing as though it would burst. His blue doublet crusted with dirt and dead leaves, one knee shining whitely through a jagged tear in his hose, he searched the ground around him for his sword. Orlando, his sword, it was all wrong. A trunk moved, detaching itself from the rest that stood in a silent rank around the glade. Black armor, gigantic, gleamed dully like water under the moonlight, the cuirass emblazoned with a double eagle and another eagle, bronze, nodding from the helmet, wings raised and beak opened in midcry. A sword, flat and broad, rose in its gloved hands, as the figure advanced toward Matt across the glade.

Holding his arm, Matt swayed as he tried to keep his balance. The blade drew closer and closer, settling at last on his chest. The sharp point probed, digging through the linen of his doublet and then his shirt, thin and wet with sweat, finding the soft hollow under his sternum, pushing him back step by step

until the broad trunk of a tree stopped him. Turning up, the tip
of the blade lifted him onto his toes, pressing him back against
the unyielding tree.

"You don't belong here," a voice, disembodied, came from
behind the burnished visor, the slit for the eyes an empty black
gash. Another point of steel was next to Matt's eye, the blade of
the knife cold against his skin, flattening his cheek. "Do you?"
the man whispered. "Do you?" he shouted, and began to laugh,
louder and louder, as the sword against Matt's chest dropped
away and a massive hand, gloved in leather and chain mail,
jammed around his throat, slamming his head back against the
rough bark of the tree and lifting him higher and higher until
he floated, the soft light of the clearing darkening and turning
red and then black, exploding with pinwheels of vibrant color as
the laugh rang through him, changing into a single note,
discordant and harsh, resonating from deep within, crushing
him with its power, the wolf tone—

chapter 2

"Poplar?" Sally asked, turning the small painting over so that she could see the wood panel of the back. She stroked the surface, as smooth as old ivory and almost black with age, the raised grain like the carved veins of a marble statue under her fingertips.

"Lombardy poplar," Matt replied.

"Oh. Lombardy poplar. That makes all the difference in the world."

"Well, it does," Matt said with a faint smile. "Go ahead and laugh."

A harsh tattoo of rain pelted against the window, the storm gaining as the late-November day faded into evening. Water streamed down the glass, dissolving the shadows from the light that, pearl-like, barely reached the back of the cluttered office. "Well, I just don't see it," Sally said, examining the darkened painting. "I can barely make out that it's supposed to be a face. There's something decidedly creepy going on here," she added with a frown. "It makes me think of Ophelia. Floating in the weeds, forgotten by Hamlet. You think you can bring her back to life?"

"I think it's worth a try."

"You're being awfully noncommittal," she said, giving him a sharp glance. "I know you. You're on to something, aren't you? What is this? A lost Leonardo?"

"Dream on. The odds are better than even that I'll never be able to put a name to it." He ran his hand through his hair, pushing it away from his forehead but it fell back again. He couldn't blame her, he thought, for he was just the same. Even though he knew arriving at who painted a picture should be the last step in a very long journey, it was impossible not to start thinking of it right away. Like walking down the street. A person in the crowd catches your eye; is it something singular about the face, or is it someone you know? For him, as an associate curator of Italian paintings at the Metropolitan Museum, it was also a professional reflex, and after five years he had to force himself to look for its own sake.

"Seems like a lot of work," Sally commented. "How long will it take you?"

Matt shrugged. "Hard to say. It depends on what's been put on it over the years. But it's not that big. It shouldn't take me more than a hundred hours. A hundred fifty, at the outside. Maybe two, if some clever restorer way back when came up with some varnish I've never seen before."

"Two hundred hours! Is it worth it?"

"I don't know. I never thought of it that way before."

"You're too much." Sally laughed. "How else would you look at it?"

"I forgot. In the legal world, time is the measure of all things. Two hundred hours would be . . . what? Forty thousand dollars? A minor brush with the SEC?"

"Eighty thousand, but that's not what I meant, and you know it. It's a lot of time out of your life, no matter how you count it. And you're the one who is always so suspicious of anything that pretends to be old. How do you know this isn't a fake?"

Matt took the picture from her and leaned back against the edge of the workbench. Crowded behind him was a jumble of books and tools that had been shoved aside for projects awaiting his attention. At the back of the bench, next to a rainbow of jars shadowed by a forest of brushes bunched together in coffee cups and old cans, stood a small brass clock under a dome of glass. The finely machined works spun and turned in an intricate dance, sparkling in the light of the lamp. The minute hand slipped upward, moving as it edged into perfect alignment with the hour hand, transforming the two into a double-ended arrow. The clock began chiming the hour. A soft counterpoint to the irregular drumming of the rain on the window. As it stopped, the minute hand fell to the right, breaking the arrow. Matt finally stirred, his face relaxing into a faint smile.

"So?" Sally asked. "What's the verdict?"

"It's the real thing," he said, propping the picture back

against the ruined fortress of books that tumbled to one side of the workbench.

"What makes you so sure? Tell me what you see."

"I see what you see. A lot of dirt, a lot of work. It's what I don't see that counts."

Sally glanced at the clock. "We should get moving. This thing ends at seven."

"Good point," he replied. "Why don't we just skip it and go have dinner?"

She laughed and handed him his jacket, an old tweed that had seen almost every party he had attended since graduation from college eight years before. "You just told me Charles has been working on this for fifteen years. Come on."

"It's a permanent installation," he protested, shrugging his arms into his coat. "We can see it anytime. He won't even notice."

"Yes, he will," she said, guiding him out the door. "What do you mean, it's what you don't see that matters?"

"The eye sleeps until the spirit awakens it with a question," Matt replied. The door to the stairwell closed behind them with a hollow slam as they walked down the short flight of stairs from the conservation lab to the ground floor of the museum. "That's what my old professor down at NYU always said to us, and he was right. I've had her right next to me for weeks now. Half the time I look at her I don't even realize I have."

"So?"

"No alarm bells. When you look at a picture, you see what

you're looking for, or what the painter wanted you to see. It's when you aren't looking that something that doesn't fit will jump out and grab you." They could hear the sounds of a party as they came out into the first-floor galleries of the museum. As they turned the corner into the vast medieval hall, dominated by the three-story carved and gilded rood screen from a cathedral in Spain, the hum of conversation and laughter grew louder. "Do you remember Saint George?"

"I've never been. Where is it? The Caribbean?"

"*Saint George and the Dragon.* It was a painting attributed to Luca Signorelli, so let's say around 1500. One day while I was talking on the phone I reached across and moved the panel to find a pad of paper and realized right then that it was completely wrong."

"What did you see?"

"Can't say, really. It was the angle. Saint George suddenly looked very much like he belonged in a Manet. One of those suspendered bourgeois gents at a river café enjoying a glass of wine on a Saturday afternoon. The thing is, once I saw it, it was so obvious and crude I couldn't believe I had been taken in. Speaking of a glass of wine?" he asked as they began edging through the crowd.

"Sure," Sally replied. Matt disappeared into the pack around the bar set up next to the massive table that had once graced the dining hall of the Farnese Palace in Rome.

"I had no idea this was such a big deal," Sally remarked, as Matt squeezed his way back to her.

"What's the big deal?" a voice said out of the buzz of

conversation as one hand appeared on Matt's shoulder, another on his arm.

"You. You're the man." Matt greeted Charles, his immediate superior, with genuine warmth and affection. "Who's the man?" he asked Sally.

"Charles," she replied with a laugh, and held up her glass. "Congratulations. Everybody's here."

"Don't I know it," Charles said, rolling his eyes. A smile gleamed through his beard, a well-trimmed thick black speckled one with just the beginning of white. A head taller than Matt, he was as solidly built as an old armchair upholstered in sturdy wool. "I'm completely stressed," he added. "I need a drink. No, I can't," he said, as Matt offered his untouched glass. "I'm working. But later—there's a whole case of Moët waiting. I told Kent to make sure it's cold enough to freeze the bubbles."

"I didn't see him. Where is he?"

"Oh, he's not here. He called and said he had some people coming by the gallery and wouldn't be able to make it. You know how he is. Plans are made to be broken. He'll be at the apartment later, though. You are coming, aren't you?"

"Of course."

"And, Sally, you're ravishing. No, you are, don't make that face. Your friend here is looking mighty trim, too. Matt, you've lost weight," he added, leaning back for a better look, his hand still on Matt's shoulder.

"Charles, you've been working too hard," Matt said with a laugh. "You see me every day. I'm just the same as I was this morning."

"I guess I'm just getting fatter. And grayer, and don't try telling me I'm not, you're the worst liar ever born. Something's different. You look so fit."

"It's the fencing," Sally said.

"Swordplay?" Charles asked. "Have you taken that up again?"

"I needed the exercise," Matt replied.

"I've got to run," Charles said. "I'll see you at the apartment," he added with a parting squeeze of Matt's shoulder. They watched as he dodged his way through the crowd and, with an effusiveness that betrayed no sign of stress, greeted the two men who had just walked in. The taller of the two, a man with an air of urbanity derived from equal parts of aristocratic features, expensive tan, and Italian suit, was the curator of the Department of Renaissance Art, Silvio Petrocelli.

"That must be Klein," Matt said, looking at the man Petrocelli was guiding by the elbow. As impeccably refined as the curator, he was younger, with straight black hair that had none of the silver that was the primary reason for the word "distinguished" that had begun appearing before Petrocelli's name in the press. Whether it was the thin titanium frames of his glasses, or the handkerchief in his jacket pocket arranged as precisely as the part of his hair, Petrocelli's guest had a Continental air to rival that of his escort. Talking to Charles they looked to Matt like emissaries from a European law firm that had taken no new clients since steam had replaced sail, sent to the New World to find him, the last descendant of an ancient family gone native, a brown bear with a well-trimmed black beard.

"Who is Klein?"

"He's the one who paid for all this." Matt had never seen the mysterious donor who had provided the small fortune that had funded the restoration of the studiolo, a project that had consumed countless man-hours over a span of twenty years. It was almost inconceivable that one man would have paid for it all, but in its acknowledgments of support the museum bulletin had just one name: Dr. Johannes Klein, of the Fleigander Foundation, in Prague.

"What does he do?"

"I don't know that he really does much of anything. Charles says he's 'in acoustics,' whatever that means."

"He's a musician?"

"No. Something to do with vibrations. Or was it resonating frequencies? I'm really not sure. He consults. Charles says the space shuttle would still be a little plastic model without him. Apparently Boeing pays him a ton of money just so he won't talk to Airbus. Like most people, he has a personal computer. His just happens to be a Cray."

"Not bad," Sally said. "I'd sort of like to see what his largesse has bought. Can we take a peek?"

"Sure."

The two of them followed a knot of guests leaving the reception through the small exhibition gallery that led back into the great medieval hall. To one side was a tall doorway, flanked by columns and crowned by a wide lintel, with heavy wooden doors that had been hooked open.

"Very impressive," Sally said as they approached the doorway. "It looks like the entrance to the Supreme Court." She came to an abrupt halt just inside the doors. Not much larger than a walk-in closet, the room was decorated with trompe l'oeil imaginary cabinets made to look so real that at first it seemed much larger than it was. "What is this?" she asked, looking around in amazement.

"The studiolo from the ducal palace in Gubbio, in Umbria. It's one of the glories of the Quattrocento."

"I assume you are referring to that period of the fourteen hundreds in Italy that was the foundation of the early Renaissance."

"The very same one," Matt replied, in a deadpan tone to equal hers. Sally, as she was putting smoked salmon on a toasted bagel the morning after the first night they had spent together, had told him that she had liked him right away at the dinner party where they had first met, and so she had decided that his somewhat pedantic explanation of the term (in their very first conversation, she reminded him, when he denied having explained anything) had been more earnest than patronizing. It was a reflection of his enthusiasm, she said; sort of cute, the way he assumed everyone would find it as engrossing as he did, if they only knew. Pedantic, he was willing to admit (he knew he tended to go on, once he got started); patronizing, he didn't like at all, and as for cute—even though he wasn't overly thrilled by the word, he knew that women thought of it as the highest compliment.

"Glorious is one way to put it. I'm astounded. I never imagined anything like this could even exist. What was a studiolo?"

"A study, but in the real sense of the word. It was a room

for contemplation, a place to reflect." Matt was surprised to find himself as overwhelmed as she was. He had already seen most of the room, disassembled, as it was being restored. It had been standing next to one of the panels that he had first met Charles, brush in hand and working glasses halfway down his nose. But seeing the separate panels, stripped down and laid bare to the bright overhead lights of the restoration lab, had not prepared him for the power of the space once inside it.

"There were only three like this ever built," Matt said. "The pope had one and Federico, the duke, had the other two. This one, and another in his palace at Urbino. That one was done by Botticelli."

"You must be joking. This guy had Botticelli doing room decoration? Where did he get his money?"

"He was the greatest of the Renaissance condottiere. Mercenaries," he explained, answering her glance. "Soldiers for hire. Florence wants Volterra? Talk to Federico, the deal's done. He was unique for the time because he never went back on his condotta—his contract. Others would switch sides at the drop of a hat, but when you hired Federico, he was yours for the duration. But he was also one of the leading humanists of the day. Scholars traveled from all across Europe to read his collection of books and manuscripts, many of which couldn't be found anywhere else. They became the core of the Vatican library."

Sally stepped forward, trying to gain a sense of the true dimensions of the room, and then turned in a slow circle. The imaginary latticework doors of the cabinets had been left ajar, affording tantalizing glimpses of shelves crammed with the everyday life of the Quattrocento. Candlesticks, an inkwell, a pair of eyeglasses carefully folded and put away in their case, in the warm glow of the subdued light it was all as real as a waking dream. Books abounded, along with manuscripts, one left unrolled as though the reader had just been called away and would be back at any moment. Musical instruments were everywhere, from the delicate bodies and fretted necks of lutes and citterns to a tambourine and drum. A crescent ivory horn chased in silver hung from a hook, ready at hand for the next hunt, while for a dance, a pair of cornetti and a rebec had been left nearby. On the next shelf lay a harp, the fine thread of an errant string curling upward, while hanging beneath it a thoughtful hand had provided a tuning key, its tiny shadow just visible on the wall behind.

One cabinet had been stocked with armor, a brutal reminder of the source of the wealth that had made the room possible. A mailed glove had been thrown carelessly on shin greaves and spurs with a mace propped up next to them, its graceful execution giving a deadly beauty to the barbs and sharp ridges of the heavy iron head. In the shadows an eagle perched on a helmet, its wings raised defiantly and its beak open in a silent snarl, a shield clutched in one taloned foot.

Sally found a birdcage tucked inside a cabinet to one side of an alcove barely large enough for a small window. A parrot, its feathers the pale green and red of dried flowers, perched behind the delicate tracery of the bars that held it captive. She leaned in for a closer look.

"Wood," she said, and looked around the room, astounded. "This isn't painted. It's all wood."

"Intarsio," Matt said. "The Florentines were famous for it."

"It's simply amazing." She circled the room again and then turned to him. "We should go. Could you hold this for me?" she asked, handing him her coat. "I'll be right back."

Matt drifted around the room, gazing at the panels, Sally's coat draped between his clasped hands. A couple looked in the door but left, leaving him in solitary possession of the still room. The wooden paneling dampened what was left of the sounds of the reception outside, making it seem worlds away. Going from panel to panel, he ended up at the long wall across from the alcove. Staring at one side, he found the cabinets slightly distorted, as though seen out of the corner of his eye. He moved step by step toward the center of the wall, and then backed away. Finding that he had gone too far, he moved slightly in again and then stopped, transfixed by the sight. The wall vanished, the world beyond revealed as clearly as though he had thrown open a window. The shelves receded in front of him, the cabinets to each side, the inlaid shadows as real as though cast by the light from the window behind him. The books, a tour de force of marquetry before, now waited for him to pick them up, the candle to be lit, the harp to be tuned and played. Matt had found the vanishing point, the spot where all the lines of the perspective converged. He closed his eyes and then slowly opened them, enjoying the slight vertiginous rush as the wall between him and the cabinets again dissolved. The scene had been executed so perfectly that the imaginary pilasters framing the doors and the bench that ran below the cabinets seemed to extend right out into the room toward him.

Lying on the bench directly in front of him was a

checkered circle, a faceted octagon the size of a man's head. A mazzocchio, the wooden form around which the men of the day had wrapped the material of their elaborate headdresses, Matt could see now that the builders had placed it precisely on the vertical axis of the inlaid scene. But where was the horizontal axis? It should be at eye level. He looked back up at the panel in front of him. There it was. Not the middle shelf, as he had first thought, but just under it. Suspended from a hook, centered on the horizontal axis as the mazzocchio was on the vertical, was another circle, much smaller. Made to appear as though it had been worked in cloth, the circlet was looped and buckled with a dangling tail capped by a tiny pearl that seemed to gleam translucently against the dark background.

Of course, Matt thought; what better for the vanishing point than the symbol of the Knights of the Garter, the most elite of the honorary orders of the Renaissance? Appointed a member by King Edward IV of England, Federico had considered it the highest honor of his career. But something was wrong. Looking at the Garter Matt felt off balance, as though he were trying to look around a corner. He glanced down at the mazzocchio, and then back up at the circle of cloth. There was the same sideways tug. The Garter was out of true. How could it be? The builders of the room, masters though they had been, had misplaced the focal point of the entire wall. Or had they? He leaned closer, like someone trying to make out the bottom through the surface of a pond. There was something else, something on the wall behind the Garter. An echo of the cloth circle, its shadow could just be seen, black against the dark under

the shelf. The shadow was the true vanishing point. But was it
even a shadow? Staring at it, now that he saw it, he wasn't sure.

It stood out from the wall, sharply etched, the Garter next
to it now the double image, a new moon and a full, both rising.
He looked from one to the other, seeing both at the same time.
Light and shadow, circling, almost merging, one black, one light,
patterns against the shadows, black and white, squares—the
mazzocchio. Odd, he thought, he had been looking at the
Garter, but here now was the mazzocchio. The black and white
squares mapped the circle, echoed in its own shadow on the
bench. There was a bench, and on it a mazzocchio, and on the
wall, behind the wall, inside the cabinet, hanging from a hook
was a Garter, he could see it; with a pearl and a silver buckle
and there was the shadow, black and sharp, looking back at him,
regarding him with a steady, unblinking gaze.

He remembered once sitting by a window, waiting for his
train to move, his gaze on the cars next to his, also motionless,
squares of light against the black night, people reading, talking,
staring into space, one looking back across at him. His thoughts
elsewhere, he had noticed that the other train had begun to
move, only to discover that his was the one that was drawing
away, the bright squares vanishing behind as his train swayed
and bumped, picking up speed, the flashes of light faster and
faster, like the sun sparkling through the canopy of trees high
overhead. Shadows and light, a raised sword, a harsh laugh
changing into a deep discordant howl, like a wolf—

"Ready?" Sally walked back in. "Matt," she said, taking
him by the arm.

Matt, tense and rigid, relaxed. He looked at her. "What is it?" he asked.

"Are you all right?"

"I'm fine."

"Something's bothering you. What is it?"

"Nothing. It's just a dream I've been having."

"What's it about?"

"The usual thing. You're running and you can't get away."

"We both need to get away. I can't wait for June. It will be here before we know it."

chapter 3

Leaning against a gust of cold rain, Matt and Sally dashed the short distance from the curb into the quiet lobby of Charles's apartment house. As they waited for the elevator Matt shook out the umbrella, still soaked from their long search for a cab outside the museum.

"Are we going to see Gubbio?" Sally asked, combing the tangles out of her hair as she examined her reflection in the brass doors.

"I hope so," Matt said. "It's not far from Assisi, and June would be a lovely time to be there. There's no art worth seeing, but you'll love the town. Most of it's medieval," he added, following her into the small car. He pressed the button for Charles's floor. "All stone and narrow winding alleys, and above it on the hillside the palazzo where the studiolo came from. There's an old Roman amphitheater outside the town that's one of the best preserved in all of Italy," he added, thinking of the last time he had been there. He had wakened before dawn one early morning from a vivid dream. Unable to get back to sleep, he had decided to do what he had been thinking of for the past week, to climb up to the hillside above the town and watch the sun rise over the valley. It had been a cool night, and with the rising mist the old city and the ancient amphitheater would be a sight that he would remember forever; it was why he was there, he told himself. He had second thoughts, though, stepping from the warm house into the damp cold. The ancient cobblestone alleys, slick underfoot, disappeared in the impenetrable black, uninviting and vaguely threatening. But dark as it still was, there was the indefinable feeling in the air that morning had begun, so he had set off to find his way out of town.

Once walking, he began to enjoy the stillness of the early morning, fresh with the scent of the wet stone and the poplars by the river that cascaded down a narrow ravine through the town. He was well up the hillside with the houses barely taking form against the blackness when he heard the sound of hooves coming down toward him, echoing off the stones of the alley and the silent houses. Soon an old peasant appeared out of the shadows leading a donkey laden with packs. The donkey had his head down, and the old man never looked at him as he passed, but riding on top and holding on with both hands as if he were on the largest elephant in the world was a little boy. He gave Matt an enormous smile. Matt hadn't looked back to watch them go after they had passed, feeling that it would have been a betrayal. He had gone on, and as he left the town behind, the sun had greeted him, the warmth flooding through him as he climbed the steep hillside, winding along a path through rugged olive trees and grass, yellow, with delicate wildflowers that he couldn't identify. The mist lay in the valley below, obscuring the old Roman ruins and the town, any sign of human presence, and he had felt a wonderful freedom, walking in the brilliant sunshine of the early morning.

"Medieval?" Sally asked. "Do they have indoor plumbing?"

"Don't worry," Matt said. "They even have television in the rooms. But, still, that's the sense you get of the whole area, that it hasn't really changed since Roman times. They still hunt wild boar up around there. I saw a wolf, once, when I was hiking in the hills above the town. When I got back to the hotel and told them, they said that wasn't unusual."

"Maybe not for them. No, thank you. I don't care how cute people think they are, to me they just look hungry."

When they reached the apartment Matt recognized the woman who opened the door, but couldn't place her. At first envious of the wide circle of friends and acquaintances that Charles had acquired, he now wondered where he found the stamina, much less the time, to keep up with them all.

A glass of wine in her free hand, the woman waved them in. "There's no food yet," she said, "but corks are flying. You haven't seen our host, have you?"

"He's doing some last-minute donor stroking," Sally replied. "He said he'd be here soon."

The apartment was comfortably crowded. In the kitchen, bustling with activity, all the burners on the stove were being used and the door to the refrigerator was opened again as soon as it was shut. Dishes clattered, a cork popped, everyone and no one was in charge.

"Here, Renaissance man," a thin woman with short blond hair and bony wrists said to Matt, handing him a flute with bubbles cascading down the stem. She wore a black jacket with its sleeves turned up, rayon shimmering blue and green in the bright kitchen lights. "You look like you could use this." She began to fill another, cupping the glass in the palm of her manicured hand. She stopped pouring just as the bubbles surged to the rim, and then smiled as they ran over and down the side. "And for you," she added, handing it to Sally.

"I'm Sally," she said, taking the glass.

"Karen," the woman replied, watching the wine as she filled another glass, this one for herself.

"So how are things at the gallery?" Matt asked. He had last seen Karen at the opening of a show that she and Kent had collaborated on a few months before. The artist, a Buddhist from Los Angeles who divided his time between Fez and New Mexico, had achieved a certain renown by arranging wood in circles on the floor. Kent, with some sharpness, had corrected Matt when he had referred to it as firewood. That was not what it was at all. In a heuristic sense, perhaps, since it called upon the communal memory of fire that is within all of us, but the installation was about displacement. The artist had lived with the Pueblo Indians, who as Matt knew—yes?—had left their art outdoors, not so much exposed to nature as in recognition that it was a part of it, inseparable, and that its transience as a discrete object was illusory in the greater context of permanence. It was all about what was there before and what would be there afterward. It was about eighty grand, Matt remarked, reading from the list he had picked up. The artist supervises the installation, Kent told him, adding that it had been acquired by the Whitney.

"We've got a group show opening in a week," Karen replied. "Recent work of the Chicago women's cooperative. I'll send you an invitation. Aren't they beautiful?" she asked, studying the thread of bubbles floating upward as she held her glass against the light. "Like a waterfall to the sky. The laws of gravity have been repealed."

There was a loud round of laughter from the living room, a voice rising above the others, and then Kent appeared around the corner. He slipped through the crowd, a gazelle leaping through tall grass. "All this food," he exclaimed, reaching Karen and giving her a kiss on the cheek. "Hello, Matt," he said, "Sally." He took the glass that Karen had filled for him. "Really, Karen," he said, transferring the glass to his other hand and shaking the sparkling wine from his fingers, "this drip thing is cute, but it's been done. Jackson Pollock, anyone? Does the name ring a bell? Alton, take this." He passed the glass to the young man who had followed him through the crowd and now stood by his side. His skin dark enough so that his short dreadlocks didn't seem affected, Alton still had a reassuringly prep school air. Dealer and artist, they were like a place setting in a museum gift shop—a knife and a fork, stylish and readily identifiable. Alton eyed the platter of penne with basil and olives on the counter next to him. "Man, I'm hungry," he said, with the faintest trace of an English accent. "I haven't eaten all day."

"Eat?" Kent asked. "What would you want to eat for? All it does is fill you up."

Karen, laughing, steadied herself with one hand on Matt's shoulder and the other holding her glass away so that it wouldn't spill on her.

"Food is so inefficient," Kent continued. "What do cars run on? Or airplanes? Liquid is the way to go. Solid food just slows you down."

"Rockets use solid fuel," Sally said.

"Yes, but they're going to outer space," Kent returned. "What's that all about? That's like moving to the suburbs. Start eating solid food and next thing you know you'll be in Scarsdale in a split-level. Mowing the lawn and spending Saturday mornings in a station wagon on Route One."

"There's Charles at last," Matt said.

Seeing him at the same time, the crowd in the kitchen broke into applause and loud cheers. Charles flushed and waved them down. "Food," he said. "Let's focus on what matters." He came up to the group and took the glass Karen offered him.

"So was it an enormous hit?" Kent asked.

"Whatever it was, at least it's done," he replied, and drained his glass. "È finito."

"I love it, Charles," Karen said, refilling his glass. "I'm going to do one for the gallery."

"A studiolo?" Charles asked.

"Yes. When you showed it to me a few weeks ago, I started thinking. About what we have and what we don't have. Every home used to have a room like that. I mean, not like that one, of course, but you know what I mean. They called it the library. My grandfather's house, that's what it made me think of, with the wood paneling and the books, how quiet it was. And that's the thing. What happened? TVs and record players, and then VCRs and computers and CDs and play stations. Media centers. And now DVD and broadband and streaming. But the Zen. No Zen. That's what we've lost."

"Zen is key," Alton said, heaping penne onto a paper plate.

"It's key," Karen said. "Think interior space for a new millennium. The studiolo."

"No one could afford anything like that these days, not even a cyber baron," Charles protested. "They might have the money, but who would have the patience? It took ten years to build that room."

"Old thinking, Charles. New millennium. Wood is cute, but is it now? I think not. It's not about the walls, anyway. It is but it isn't. The continuum, yes, but inside the mind. That's what we need to key on."

"We?" Charles asked.

"Alton, tell him what we've come up with."

"Alton, this is Charles," Kent said.

"Hi," Charles said.

Alton lifted his plate in acknowledgment of the greeting. "Pretty simple, really. What you see is what you get. It's inside your head, it's on the walls. Colors, patterns, but also images. From a data bank. Anything you want—old photos, film clips, whatever."

Charles laughed. He looked at Karen and then at Kent. "You're not serious," he said.

"It's going to be huge," Karen replied. "Huge."

"I think it here and it shows up there?" Charles said, gesturing at his head and then the wall with his glass. "That's impossible."

"Technology's all there," Alton said with a shrug.

"So's the software," Kent added. "Alton did this at the New School a year ago. That's how I met him."

Charles gave Alton a more appraising glance. "A year ago."

"Yeah," Alton replied, shaking his head. "Seems like the Stone Age. I used a TV set and electrodes to pick up changes in body temperature and brain wave patterns. Now you can do it all by infrared. And the walls, that's the best. Plasma flat screen. Wall-to-wall, totally."

"The virtual studiolo," Karen said. "What do you think?" she asked Charles.

"I think I could use a martini," Charles replied, and reached up into the cabinet behind him for a glass.

"Didn't I tell you he would hate it?" Kent asked.

"Are you in on this too?" Charles inquired.

"Well, whose idea do you think it was?"

"I should have known." Charles pulled the vodka bottle out of the freezer and poured a solid two inches into the glass. "No, it's a great idea," he said, and laughed, adding a splash of vermouth and an olive. "What are you going to call it?" he asked, stirring the drink with a silver rod he had taken from the drawer behind Kent.

"The Rumor," Karen replied. "The Room, Or—"

"That's good. I like that," Charles said. "The Rumor. What do you think, Matt?"

"I think I'll have mine with a twist," he said.

————

Matt leaned back against the old leather armchair in the calm oasis of Charles's own study, glad to be out of the storm of the party. The initial boost of the martinis had passed like a team of speedboats, leaving him bobbing uneasily in their wake, unsteady on his feet, like a water-skier who has let go of the rope. He was glad to lose himself in one of his favorite paintings, a woodland scene nestled in a faded gilt frame. It was typical of Charles to hang his prize possession in an out-of-the-way corner where it could easily escape notice. He had found it in a gallery in Florence, one that he had happened upon during an afternoon's stroll through the quiet side streets of the Oltrarno, near the Boboli Gardens. He had brought the painting back to the department and cleaned it up, which hadn't required much, for it had been in surprisingly good condition. All the tests indicated it was genuinely old, but as to authorship, that was anybody's guess. "Circle of Paolo Uccello" was the consensus, and in its muted colors and dramatic foreshortening it did show the heavy influence of that Quattrocento artist. Although not a copy, the scene was clearly based on Uccello's *Hunt at Night*, now at the Ashmolean Museum in Oxford, the painting that had been the subject of Matt's master's thesis. "The Perspective of Dreams," he had titled it.

But this was a hunt by day, deep in the woods, and Matt

loved the confusion of the horsemen and the dogs scrambling through the underbrush under the thick green canopy that arched overhead like the roof of a cathedral, supported by the fluted columns of the tree trunks. The prey—a boar, or a wolf—was out of sight, but he had spent hours searching out the figures concealed in the tangle of bushes, always finding some new detail that had previously escaped his eye. Like the flash of color almost out of sight, hidden behind the tree trunks on the gentle rise in the back. What was it? He leaned in for a closer look. Odd, he thought; it looks like an animal. Feathers, bright blue and green, tipped with yellow. A wing, but too large to be a bird. There was more, but it was hard to make out in the gloom and the patterns made by the sun coming through the leaves. Rear haunches like a lion, the muscles bunching as the animal twisted through the underbrush, trying to escape, but covered in scales, not fur. He blinked—had it moved? His eyes must be adjusting to the light. He could see more of it now. The wing was joined to the body, and the tip of another was barely visible just behind.

The noise of the party vanished as Matt concentrated. There was no wind in the forest, the trees were still, and so the yelping of the dogs and the neighing of the horses hung in the air. He listened closely. Yes; the dry scrabble of claws on stone, that's what he had heard. And labored breathing, the beat of wings—it was trying to escape. The tail whipped around, balancing as the animal reared back. Scales coruscated in the dim light, it was a lizard's tail, ending in a broad flattened point. A harsh cry like an eagle cut through the gloom. Matt stared, fascinated and disbelieving—the proud head, lifted on a scaled neck, nostrils flared, black eyes wide, the dragon of his dreams. God, he thought. A manticore.

The dogs, frenzied with excitement, snarled in pursuit, closely followed by the men spurring their horses on. Excited shouts and the sharp repeated calls of trumpets were answered by the shriek of the manticore.

"Come on," Matt whispered, "come on, go."

The manticore found a purchase and leapt up the steep escarpment, its powerful wings at last free of the encumbering underbrush. The dogs, unable to follow, bayed in unison, circling like an earthbound tornado. Matt, aware of a sudden danger, tensed, but not soon enough. A gloved hand slammed his head back into the rough bark of a tree, lifting him as it tightened around his throat. A black helmet, the closed visor with a narrow black slit across it like a sword cut, leaned in as the bronze eagle roosting on its crest, wings raised, nodded down at him. A laugh grew, louder and louder until it hurt Matt's ears, sliding down the scale into the rough growl of the wolf, a tone resonating deep within, chilling him—

He jumped sideways as he felt a hand on his neck.

"Matt!"

It was Sally. Slumping against the chair, Matt closed his eyes and rubbed his face, the skin hot and clammy under his hand. He felt his throat, but it was fine. Nothing.

"You're soaked," Sally said. Her hand, light on his back, moved to his forehead. Cool, like stepping into a patch of shade on a blistering hot day. "You've got a fever."

He opened his eyes. The painting. He stood up, looked. There they were, the men on horseback, the dark trees, the dogs, but in the distance on the hill—nothing. No manticore. He leaned in, closer and closer, hands braced on the wall on each side until his face was only inches from the panel. The trees loomed, fading from sight on each side. The underbrush dissolved into splashes of green and dark brown, but nowhere could he find even a trace of gold. Or yellow or blue, no feathers, no scales shimmering in the refracted light.

"Matt, please."

He felt Sally's hand on his arm, pulling him back. He pushed himself away from the wall. Finding her looking at him, eyes wide with concern, he drew her to him and kissed her as hard as he could.

"Wow," she murmured in his ear, after they broke apart. "Martinis and art, a heady mix. Let's get out of here. You need some fresh air."

"Wait," he said, and looked back at the painting.

"What is it?" she asked.

"A manticore doesn't have wings."

"So?"

"Nothing," he replied. A manticore had a man's head on a lion's body. What he had seen had the body and legs of a lion, but wings and scales, like a griffin, and a dragon's head and tail. But there had not been the slightest hesitation in his mind that what he saw was a manticore. Why?

The party was still well under way, even though midnight had come and gone. Charles gave Matt a pat on the back and then broke the story he was telling for a quick kiss on Sally's cheek. Karen squeezed his arm on the way by.

"Let's be in touch," she said, raising her glass in Sally's direction as though to include her.

"How brazen can you get?" Sally asked, as she and Matt edged their way through the crowd.

"What are you talking about?" Matt asked.

"That bimbo in the too-short skirt, bombed on champagne. I can't believe she made such a pass at you. 'Let's be in touch.' Right. And she had the audacity to act as though she knew me."

"You mean Karen?" Matt asked.

"If that's her name, then yes."

"Sally," Matt said. "We were talking to her earlier. The studiolo, remember? She has a gallery downtown."

"I've never seen that woman before. Look, Matt, a word of advice, just between you and me?" she said, shrugging on her coat. "If you're going to carry on like this, that's your business. But avoid the martinis. You're not good enough at it, and I don't want to know."

"I have no idea what you're talking about."

"Let's just get out of here, shall we?" With a swirl of black she was gone, out the door. The embarrassed looks on the faces of the small group who had overheard the entire exchange lent her accusations credibility, making Matt's confusion complete. Not knowing what to believe, he hurried after her.

chapter 4

In the still room, anchored by the steady tick of the clock, Matt leaned back in his chair, panel in hand. He studied the face he had come to know better than his own, as over the past two months she had emerged from the shadows that had veiled her for centuries. Carefully and painstakingly, a square centimeter at a time, he had loosened and removed layer after layer of overvarnishing and retouching, working slowly inward from the edges like a treasure seeker in suspect terrain. His map had been a tiny chip from the painting that when mounted and photographed from the side revealed every layer, each as distinct and identifiable as the striations in an exposed cliff were to a geologist. Beneath the successive layers of varnish that had been added over time, separated by razor-thin lines of dirt and soot, was the original varnish, the oil now yellow-gold with oxidation. Below that was the painting itself—the wide band of the glazes, glowing with transparent colors, a rainbow frozen in place. The microphotograph was so detailed that he could see the particles of pigment, crushed by hand with a muller on a glass plate. Underneath the colors lay the dull umber of the monochrome painting, and then, last of all, the narrow black stripe of the original drawing, laid down in charcoal on the freshly sized surface of the panel. After patiently traversing the wide empty ocean of the greenery against which she was poised he had at last made landfall: the curl of an earlobe, as delicate as a seashell. Like a castaway wandering a beach, he had traced the line of her jaw, the brushwork so fine that from up close there was nothing but the subtle play of light and shadow. It was only when he held the portrait at arm's length that it coalesced into a lovely curve. He spent more time than necessary on her mouth, gently brushing away the grime to reveal lips drawn as softly as a breeze, and stopped again when he reached her eyes. Deep-set under the stronger shadow of her brow, they appeared almost black, but working closely with a jeweler's loupe he gradually discovered the world inside them, colors as vibrant as a galaxy seen through the most powerful telescope, a deep green glowing with streaks of brilliant red and gold. Pressing on, he found a fine temple, and then finally her hair, fawn-colored, which she had gathered up and pinned in back, a touch both casual and intimate.

Was it chance, he wondered, that had stopped his hand that day in the storage bins, deep under the museum? Like catacombs of art, miles of shelves reached from the floor to the ceiling of the labyrinthine basements of the museum. Crouched on one knee as he flicked through the paintings in one forgotten corner, searching for a panel cataloged as school of Pollaiuolo, he had seen the edge of a small panel way in the back, hidden in the shadows. It was not the right size, and he was running late, but something had stopped him. Like a kitten hiding behind a couch, the square was just beyond the reach of his fingertips, and he had had to stretch out on the cold concrete floor to coax it out.

Serendipity. What else could it be? In that first second of seeing, as the panel emerged into the harsh fluorescent light, he had felt a flash of recognition as certain as looking in the mirror. He saw himself back at the Louvre, five years before, waiting as the curator opened the box and then as reverently as a priest handling a relic of the true cross passed Matt the drawing. Not paper, but vellum, and heavy—it felt like skin, and there in his hands, Matt beheld the face of beauty. He felt as though he had arrived, as though everything he had learned and done had led him to this moment. Leonardo had drawn her in the most difficult of media, silverpoint, as a study for a Madonna. Or so they said, and Matt could see why, for looking at her he understood as he never thought he could what it meant to be a mother. Gazing at her unseen child, the joy and the sadness—all of it was there in her eyes, in the angle of her head, bent in love and acceptance.

Standing in the basement at the Metropolitan Museum, Matt hadn't been able to see anything, just a thickly discolored varnish smeared on a panel. But the vague shadow underneath he knew right away was a head, and the balance of it, the inclination—it was enough. Like seeing someone you thought had gone out of your life, across a crowded street waiting for the light to change; the leap of recognition and hope passed through his hands and the portrait and he knew, without question, that he had found her again.

Who was she? Matt wondered for the thousandth time. A young mother. How young? No more than twenty, he decided. But young in those days was sixteen. Middle-aged was twenty-one, and most were dead by forty. Lorenzo il Magnifico, the greatest of the Medici, died at forty-two, and it was said at the time that he had lived a full term. He gazed at this woman, at the smooth curve of her cheek, the pensive set of her lips, the strong line of her nose, and imagined her smiling; and then what might amuse her, what her voice might sound like, what she would say. A loose wisp of hair fell by her cheek. He thought, looking at the painting now, in the late-afternoon light, that he could reach out and push it back. It would break her concentration, and she would look up, startled, and then smile. Would she? What would be in her eyes then?

"Am I intruding?"

Matt, startled, looked up from the painting. "Not at all," he replied, sitting up straight in his chair. "Can I help you?"

"Johannes Klein," the man said, extending his hand.

"Dr. Klein," Matt replied, surprised. This was not the man whom he had seen Petrocelli escorting into the reception at the opening of the studiolo; he had been young, and fastidious to a fault. Just as well-dressed, Klein had an air of being in motion, as though his edges were not as perfectly defined. Strong features and deep lines like ravines etched in desert hills offset his deep-set eyes, so brown as to be almost black, and he wore his silver hair long, brushed back from his high forehead to descend almost to his shoulders.

"I'm glad to meet you," Matt said, leaning the portrait at the side of his desk, her face angled away. "The studiolo has become one of my favorite places." It was no exaggeration; Matt visited the small room almost every day. As he entered it the world he left behind became muted and quickly vanished, leaving the quiet to wash over him as he drifted along from one panel to the next, his solitude almost never disturbed. He loved the stillness as much as anything else about the room. Karen had hit upon an essential truth in what she had said at Charles's party, he thought. Quiet was what man had lost. Now that nature had been safely vanquished, reduced to an occasional hurricane and the farther reaches of the few wilderness areas left on a shrinking globe, and death confined to hospitals and nursing homes, silence was man's only remaining enemy. Or so it seemed from the relentless and concerted assault made on it. Sometimes, lost in thought in front of one of the panels, Matt would come to and realize that an hour had disappeared, and as hard as he tried, he would not be able to remember what had been passing through his head or where he had been.

"I brought this," Klein said, handing Matt a flat box of stiff paperboard secured by a tape. "Charles said that it might be of some interest to you. You fence," he added with interest, seeing the long white scabbard leaning against the wall.

"Yes," Matt responded.

"You must join us. We meet once a week at the gym at Columbia."

"I'm not very good."

"And why do you assume that we are any better?" Klein looked around the office as Matt untied the ribbon that secured the lid like a courier's dispatch box. Hands clasped behind his back Klein went up to the back wall and looked at the paintings Matt had hung there. "I see what Charles had in mind," he said.

"So you were the one we were bidding against," Matt said, holding the panel he had drawn out of the box. It was a painting of a swallow. Slender wings arched to ride the wind, tail pointed, the small bird soared against a clear blue sky.

"I'm afraid so," Klein replied. "I hope that I didn't upset any plans."

"How could you have known? The whole idea was to keep our interest a secret. That was the only way we could possibly afford it." Matt got up and joined Klein by the wall. "It goes right here," he said, and held the panel up between two of the paintings, covering the enlargement he had taped up of a page from an auction catalog. The swallows rose one by one into a painted sky that changed from the cool blue of morning to the golden haze of afternoon.

"These are beautiful," Klein said.

"Aren't they? They're also unique."

"How so?"

"The fact that they're birds, for one. You don't find paintings of animals until the late fifteen hundreds. As a portrait, I mean, not cut from a larger picture. These were done a century before. Quattrocento, northern Italian."

"That's interesting," Klein said. "It was cataloged as late fifteen hundreds, Flemish school."

"Auction catalogs are a great resource for tracing provenance," Matt said, searching for a polite way to put it, "but I don't know that I would ever turn to them for expertise."

"No?"

"Quite the opposite," Matt said, abandoning circumspection. So what if he had just met the man? Aside from funding the studiolo, and bringing him this painting, Klein was a scientist. And, anyway, he had asked. "Auction houses have a vested interest in limiting their expertise," Matt said. "They handle some very good stuff, but the bulk of their trade is in the gray area. And in the art world, the only place you find black and white is in etchings. The rest is each man for himself and God against all. 'Auction' is a modern English translation of 'caveat emptor.' I don't think they're lying, but I do think perhaps they don't want to know."

"Their experts seem to know what they're talking about."

"Specialists, I would say. Expertise is a different matter entirely. But that's looking at it from the wrong end. It doesn't really matter how much they know. It comes down to time. Everybody buying art wants a name. A Rembrandt is ten million, a 'follower' or 'school of' is under a hundred grand. But that's the last step a true expert will ever take, putting a name to a work. He might have suspicions, be ninety-nine percent sure, but a definite attribution? No. Only after an exhaustive amount of study and research, and that takes time. With the volume that an auction house handles, they simply can't afford to do that."

"So how do you know this is from the fourteen hundreds? And northern Italy?"

"Let's not go overboard. I don't 'know,' in the sense that you know this wall is plaster. There is no 'Envelope, please.' The only way you'd really know is if you had a photograph of the artist holding the picture. That's why paintings of the artist in his studio are so important—all the stuff on the easels and the walls. But in this case the evidence is pretty conclusive."

"Such as?" Klein asked. "I'm sorry," he added. "I don't mean to monopolize your time."

"Not at all," Matt replied. "I'd be more than glad to show you." He took the first painting in the series off the wall. "First of all, this is Lombardy poplar," he said, turning it over and handing it to Klein. "It's like a weed, you find it all over the Piedmont. It grows fast, it's easy to work; best of all, it's cheap as dirt. Like artists. They use the cheapest thing that works, either because they're poor or they're frugal or because even when they're successful they remember what it was like to be poor. It's soft, so you have to leave it thick, and it warps easily and cracks, and worms love it, but still it works well enough. If you see Lombardy poplar in a panel, it came from northern Italy. Nobody else would bother using it. May I?"

Matt took the panel and, still holding it reversed, angled it so the light raked across the surface. Rough and unfinished, it was covered with the marks of a gouge. "You see this?" he asked. "Only in Italy. North of the Alps the backs were as beautifully finished as the frames. Planed, varnished, sometimes even branded with the cabinetmaker's seal. The edges tapered for the frame. Nice work, a real pleasure to see. But this is more often than not what you find in Italy. I guess they just weren't interested. I mean, why bother if no one was going to see it? Of course, that looseness translates into the painting itself, but that's another story," he added, putting the picture back on the wall. He minutely adjusted one corner so that it hung straight.

"And the date?" Klein asked.

"Sometime between 1478 and 1483. I'm almost positive it was 1478, but in this kind of thing, discretion is the better part of valor."

Klein glanced at him with a slight raise of his eyebrows.

"It's the dendro," Matt said. "No big secret. That's how I know. Dendrochronology. Dating wood through growth rings. Some trees grow fast, some hardly at all, but what scientists have found is that year by year they all grow at the same relative rate. Time lines have been assembled that go back to the Bronze Age. You measure the growth rings of any particular piece of wood and move it along the time line until you get a match. The last growth ring for this piece of poplar was 1478."

Klein thought, eyes slightly narrowed. "But it could have been used any year after that, right?"

"True," Matt allowed. "Strictly speaking, all it really tells you is that the painting could not have been done before then. The tree was still in the ground."

"So how do you know it was painted in 1478?"

"As I said, I have no proof positive. It's the weight of the evidence. You have to put the pictures in context. Poplar wasn't a valuable wood, the kind that was carefully stored and dried. It was used for everything and what wasn't used went in the fireplace. So if the last tree ring is 1478, as it is with this picture, the chances are excellent it was used within a year or so. Artists tend to be very consistent in the way they work. This one is 1478. The next one? 1479," he said, pointing as he moved along the wall. Also this one—it's the same piece of wood, actually—and then there's a jump. These last two date from 1483 and 1484. But they're different, as you can see here." He took one of them down and handed it to Klein.

Klein hefted it, glanced at the back. "It isn't panel," he said. "It's canvas."

"That's right," Matt replied.

"How can you date it by dendrochronology, then? Canvas doesn't have tree rings."

Matt smiled.

"Of course," Klein said, and turned the painting around again. "The stretcher."

"Bingo," Matt said. "I almost didn't bother to check. I thought it couldn't possibly be the original. But the wood looked right, and the nails were hand-forged, and there were no other holes in the canvas where it might have been fastened before. It's Alpine spruce, perfectly split on the quarter for maximum strength. Fourteen eighty-four, right on the money. There are other things, too. It's the right kind of canvas—linen, not cotton, since cotton was from the New World, and there wasn't a New World yet. Hand-loomed, too, with a thread count you'd expect to find."

"An airtight case," Klein said.

"But you see it's very important," Matt said. "Because that's the real reason why these paintings are unique."

"How so?" Klein asked.

Matt pointed at the first three paintings, including Klein's.

"Panel, painted in egg tempera. The other two," he said, gesturing to his right, "are canvas and oil. Before and after. In one series, the single greatest transition in the history of painting since man first took charcoal to a cave wall."

"New technology, you're saying. Like the internal combustion engine."

"Sort of. Tempera is like poster paints—really user-friendly. Easy to make and work with, but limited in its expressivity. The surface remains flat. Brunelleschi's rediscovery of perspective allowed the Renaissance artists to break the picture plane, but not entirely. It still doesn't look natural. The colors, the shadows—it's just not malleable enough as a medium. Oil, though, is completely different. It has a very high index of refraction, which means that pigments become transparent."

"The same way that glass disappears in water," Klein said.

"Yes, that's it exactly. You can use glazes, build layers, and the light refracts through the paint to create a truly three-dimensional world. The old way was to draw an outline and fill it in. Botticelli. Leonardo, though, used sfumato—shadow and light—to create his figures. They aren't imposed on the background like cutouts. They emerge, they're an organic part." That was it, Matt thought; that was why he had immediately thought of Titian when he had first seen Klein. There was something of the sfumato about him, the sense of a presence emerging, rather than superimposed. "Leonardo understood how to break through the picture plane. He added another dimension to the world. It was transformational. After seeing his paintings, people saw the world differently. It's only happened a couple of times in the course of history. You're a physicist, right?"

"Essentially, yes. My specialty is acoustics."

"There must have been someone in your field who had the same effect. Newton, or Einstein."

"If I have you right, you mean a discovery that completely altered our perception of the world."

"Yes, that's it," Matt replied, pleased that his question had given the scientist pause.

"Michael Faraday," Klein said after some consideration. "Interesting, I never would have thought of it that way, but, yes, no doubt, I would have to say it was Michael Faraday."

"Sounds vaguely familiar," Matt said. "Who was he?"

Klein laughed. "Sic transit gloria mundi," he said. "The greatest scientist who ever lived, and most people have never even heard his name. He discovered that magnetism, electricity, light, even sound, are all different aspects of the same force: vibration. Which, in a way, is only fitting."

"How so?"

"The birth of science was the discovery by Pythagoras that pitch is related to string length. Vibration. The natural world was ruled by order, and it could be expressed mathematically. They constructed an entire cosmology based on it."

"The music of the spheres."

"Precisely. And once again things come full circle. The latest attempt at a unified theory to explain the way matter operates is string theory. Matter is energy, yes: but the best way to model subatomic particle wave behavior is a vibrating string. From the monochord to string theory. Plus ça change, plus c'est la même chose."

They were interrupted by a knock on the door.

"Matt, I need to get the file—" Charles, walking in, paused as he saw Klein. "Hello, Johannes," he said warmly, extending his hand. "What brings you here? The painting. Of course."

"I stopped by your office, but you were out, so I took the liberty of introducing myself."

"Very nice," Charles said, looking at the wall. "You were right, Matt, it fits right in. We should have bid higher. Well, there's still one to go."

"There's another?" Klein asked.

"Right here," Matt replied, placing his hand on the wall next to Klein's panel. The arc of the swallow's rise took an abrupt jump between the third and fourth painting.

"I won't keep you," Charles said. "I just need that file on the Duccio Diptych."

"It's over there," Matt replied, nodding toward his desk. "Right on top." A manila folder lay on a stack of books in the middle of the desk. "Here, let me," Matt added hastily. The portrait—

"No bother," Charles said. "I see it." He was already at the desk, reaching for the folder. The portrait was right there, her face only inches from the back of his hand. All he had to do was glance over. How could he not see it?

"Quantum birds," Klein said.

"Sorry?" Matt replied, stealing another covert look at Charles. He stood in front of the desk, intently examining something in his hand. Had he picked up the portrait? Was he looking at her right now? The Duccio file was still on the pile of books, untouched.

With a gesture as graceful as a conductor Klein followed the arc of the bird as it ascended from panel to panel. "A bird in flight is motion, a continuous wave against the sky. There are an infinite number of places you might find it at any given time. But then the painter sees and paints and look what happens: the wave disappears, and what we find instead are these. Separate packets of energy. Five little birds. Like a stone skipped across water. What you are left with is not the stone, but the circles where it landed. The stone is gone, so is the bird. We have five birds and none at all."

Matt stared at the swallow, which seemed almost to dart upward in front of his eyes. He saw movement, real movement, out of the corner of his eye. Charles was leaving. Seeing Matt turn his head, he waved the file and was gone.

"Excuse me," Matt mumbled to Klein, aware of how rude he was being but unable to stop himself. He hurried over to his desk. Had the portrait been moved? He couldn't remember. He had set it down when Klein had come in. He thought back, tried to visualize his hand as he had put down the painting, but he had done it so many times he couldn't remember. She didn't look disturbed. A slight movement on the top of the desk caught his attention—a sparkling of light, like dust drifting through a sunbeam. The snow globe. Under a glass dome stood a clown, his arms spread wide to acknowledge the thunderous applause of his unseen audience. A violin in one outstretched hand, the bow in the other, bright red stars on his cheeks to match the green ones on his yellow suit, his face was split in a wide grin. Matt relaxed and smiled. Charles always shook the globe when he stopped by. It was his favorite thing in the museum, he had said once. All around the clown a rainbow of colors swirled gently downward.

Matt picked up the globe, heavy in his hand, the motion stirring the cloud of glitter anew. Surprised, he noticed for the first time that the tiny specks were musical notes. Thousands of notes, sparkling in the light, forming and unforming clouds of music, unplayed, waiting to be heard. Matt set the globe back down on the desk. She hadn't been disturbed. Charles hadn't seen her. Matt leaned forward, picked up the portrait. Every time he saw her he was amazed again at how much of her there was to know, revealed in her eyes, the way she looked at her child, the set of her mouth, just the very tilt of her head. Sometimes it made him smile, other times it almost broke his heart: but each and every time he looked he saw her anew, found something about her he hadn't known.

Klein. Matt had completely forgotten he was there. He spun around, an apology on his lips, but the room was empty. Klein was gone. Matt went to the door, but there was no sight of him. Hell, he thought, and jamming his hands in his pockets went back inside. He sank down into his chair. Oh, well. Klein had left his swallow, at least. Matt picked up the portrait again. Above him the clown grinned, arms outstretched, knee-deep in drifts of gilded notes.

chapter 5

"*Oregano. I know it's here.*" *Matt shifted the bottles on the shelf back* and forth. "Basil, cinnamon, saffron, vanilla bean? Thyme—why do I have two bottles of thyme?"

"Had we but world enough..." Sally said, looking up from the book she was reading, the table before her spread with maps and travel guides to northern Italy. "Do you want that to be that way?" she asked.

Matt grabbed the lid of the pot as bubbles cascaded down the side. "Perfect," he announced, peering in the pot after the cloud of steam, redolent of clams, had subsided.

"Perfetto, signore," Sally said. "Wait." She thumbed through the phrase book. "A che oro mangiamo sta sera?"

"Oro?" Matt asked. "Oro di mare. Gold of the sea," he translated, seeing her puzzled expression.

Sally studied the book. "Ora," she corrected herself. "Che ora."

"Ah, bene," Matt said. "Depende, signora, ha indire voglia di mangiare," he said in a rapid-fire staccato.

"Oui," Sally replied with a blank look. "I mean, sì. Oh, come on!" she complained, and then went back to the notebook, dog-eared and stained, that she had been perusing. "Who's Ginevra?" she asked.

"Who?" Matt asked, intent on pulling a clam from its shell. "Ouch! That's hot."

"Ginevra," she repeated. "In your journal. You don't remember her? She wrote you a poem."

"Ah, Ginevra. A beautiful woman. Married, but not to the man she loved."

"She loved you."

"Me? Not quite."

"She wrote you a poem."

" 'Chieggio merzede e sono alpestre tygre,' " Matt recited. "Lovely, isn't it? 'I am a mountain lion, and I beg for mercy.' Don't you think, sometimes, that it's the capriciousness of fate that's the cruelest thing of all? It's not living or dying but ending up in Hackensack working for the phone company that's so hard to understand. Ginevra was a poet, but of everything she wrote, all that survives is that one line."

"Maybe it was all that was worth remembering. Don't give me that look. I don't mean it in a negative way at all. It's quite an achievement, isn't it? One perfect line that lives in your mind—that's better than most poets can even dream of. Even if they left a shelf of books. Think of how much you have read and forgotten. Things that amazed you, that changed your life. How much do you remember? Go on, tell me a line from Chaucer. Or Wordsworth, or Longfellow. Baudelaire, Pushkin, anyone. Shakespeare."

"Tomorrow and tomorrow and tomorrow . . ."

"All right, not Shakespeare. But anyone else. What is poetry but distillation? She reduced a person, an entire story, a relationship, to just one line. 'I am a mountain lion, and I beg for mercy.' It's beautiful. I think she was in love with you."

"I was out of her league, I'm afraid. She had bigger fish to fry."

"What could be better than a young American art student with a trust fund?"

"Lorenzo de' Medici, for one."

"Lorenzo—" Sally began. "Very funny."

"They were reputed to be lovers."

"Do you need any help?"

"I wouldn't want to put you in harm's way," Matt replied, brandishing the knife that had been keeping up a steady drumbeat against the cutting board as he diced the mounded clams. "Here," he said, finding one that had escaped, and leaned over the counter, just reaching Sally's outstretched fingers with his own.

"What's so funny?" she asked.

"The Sistine Chapel," he replied. "You know, God and Adam, hands almost touching. How postmodern can you get? A clam instead of the spark of life."

"Sorry."

"Hey, don't get me wrong. I'd rather have you and a clam any day."

"*Mmmm,* this is good."

"Do you remember the Leonardo we saw down in D.C.? The only painting of his outside Europe?"

"Yes, I remember. What about it?"

"Ginevra de' Benci. That was her."

"Of course!" Sally exclaimed. "I knew I'd heard the name before Ginevra."

"And I thought you weren't paying attention."

"I was distracted by your ass."

"Yeah, right. I think it was the phone call you were on."

"Look, we covered that ground, Matt," Sally said. "All right? You agreed. Without the phone I never would have been able to be there in the first place. Right?"

"Hey. It was a joke, okay? It's modern life."

"There was something catlike about her," Sally commented, her attention back on the notebook. "But not a lion, more like an Abyssinian. 'The light, as the sun colors the western sky above the roofs across the Arno. I am seduced, overcome by the ineffable,' " she read aloud. "Overcome by the een effa balle," she repeated, puzzled. "What's that Italian for? Car exhaust?"

"I was young," Matt said. "Give me a break. I'd like to see your journal from those carefree college days."

"I didn't write a journal. I wrote memos," she said, turning the pages. She stopped. "Matt, this is beautiful." She quickly glanced at the next page, and then the next. "You did these?

They are superb." She turned the pages back slowly, examining each one.

Matt looked over the counter to see what she had found. "I'd forgotten those," he said. "They're from Gubbio." He had spent a week there. Early June, when the days were long, but the heat had not yet settled into the stones and fields. It was the sun he remembered most of all. It was everywhere, saturating the air. Alone, he woke early in the cool bed, the bright lines that seeped through the heavy wooden shutters warm across his face. From the café he would walk the short distance to the palazzo to spend the morning sketching. Long and blue as he passed through them at that early hour, by midday the shadows would be folded tightly in on themselves, as black as the ink in his pen and razor-thin, hiding in the doorways and under the sills and overhanging eaves.

"You should frame these," Sally said. "Or at least mount them. They're absolutely wonderful. The line, the way you have created that feeling of light."

"I love drawings," Matt said. "They're at the heart of everything. Like you said, distillation—paintings are novels, but drawings are poetry. And making one—you've got a blank page, and in your hand a pen. Two poles of nothingness, black and white. You draw a line, but it's not a line. The black defines the white, they shape each other. It's not what you draw or the places you leave blank. It's not the shadows and the light, but finding that intersection where they meet. That's where the world begins and ends. And if you can find it, if you can allow yourself to see it—there is nothing like that at all. Nothing."

"So why did you stop?"

"Stop what?"

"You know what I mean. This is a major talent."

Matt stirred the clams and added some wine. "Haven't you heard the news? Ask Kent. Or—" He almost said Karen, but caught himself just in time. He had completely forgotten the entire episode at the party; he had been too hung over the next morning to want to deal with it, and Sally seemed to have forgotten, so he allowed himself to just let it go. But she had talked to Karen. He knew she had. He briefly thought of asking again, but dropped the idea. While Sally might not remember talking to Karen—and she hadn't really talked to her, they had only exchanged greetings—he was quite sure that she hadn't forgotten being upset. "Or anyone," he added, covering his change of direction by pretending to adjust the heat under the pasta, just coming to a boil. "Figurative art is dead. The world belongs to Alton."

"Oh, that's bullshit. Yes, it is, Matt, and you know it. What about Hopper? Or Anselm Kiefer? Willem de Kooning made millions. Look at Jeff Koons. He's getting rich."

"Koons has nothing to do with those other guys. Nothing. You've heard of puzzle pictures? They were all the rage in the Mannerist period. Veronese, guys like that. Their paintings were filled with allegories and allusions. The whole idea was to make a select group of viewers feel like insiders, because they knew what it all meant. The fact that the paintings were usually pretty bad didn't matter because that wasn't what they were looking for. Koons is doing exactly the same thing. He makes you feel like you 'get it.' You're one of the cognoscenti. What's truly sick is that the only thing to be gotten is how awful it is. So if you say that is total shit, people just nod and say yeah, with this knowing smile like some kind of secret handshake. Or they say you've lost your sense of humor. Yeah, right. When was the last time a great work of art—a really great work—made you laugh? Profound. Use that word now and people laugh at you.

"This stuff isn't art. It's talk, with art as the prop. It's only an excuse. Like a fund-raiser at the museum. The art is just the backdrop."

"What a whiner! Yes, you are! Listen to yourself. You can't do exactly as you want so you take your ball and go home. It's the real world, Matt. Do you think it was ever different? That Rembrandt lived in some paradise of painting as he pleased? You have to play the game, if what you want to do is paint."

"Okay, so it's a game," Matt said. "But people play games for fun, and for me it's just not fun."

"But it means a lot to you. I think it means everything to you. What makes it sad is that you're really good."

Testing the pasta, Matt just shrugged.

"Are you willing to take a chance?"

"What do you mean?"

"Be an artist."

"Don't be silly. I'm not independently wealthy. I can't afford it."

"I can."

"You must be joking."

"I'm serious. I'll back you. It's a business proposition.

You've got the talent and I'm willing to take a chance that the market is there."

"No."

"Why not?"

"Sally, I know how things work. The critics would slice me up like the sushi chefs at Nobu working on a prime piece of tuna. If they even deigned to acknowledge what I do as art, which I seriously doubt."

"That's what you're afraid of, isn't it? That they won't even see you. All right, fine. It's your life. For what it's worth, the offer's on the table. Think about it."

"Why?"

"You mean, aside from the fact that I love you?" She turned the notebook around and put it down on the counter. "This is why."

The shadows echoed the graceful arch of the loggia, providing some shade from the sun. He had drawn the fountain underneath, embedded in one of the walls of the palazzo. A hot summer afternoon, the still air redolent with the soothing wetness stirred up by the water in the fountain—he felt it again, smelled its fullness, carrying with it the scent of wild rosemary and thyme. Feet crunched across the gravel drive outside, fading away, leaving Matt alone in the silence of the courtyard. It was soon broken by the harsh buzzing of a cicada, joined by another and then others until the air pulsed with a slow cadence, a Gregorian chant stretching unbroken across the length and breadth of Italy. It was the sound made by the radiant blizzard of sunlight that filled the courtyard to overflowing, dazzling him as it pelted against the walls and the tightly shuttered windows and the dusty flagstones, as smooth as a riverbed from centuries of wear.

Matt was content to stand in the cool shelter of the arcade, the plastered groins in the reflected light a creamy yellow overhead. In the palazzo wall next to him was the fountain, the water slipping out of the gargoyle's gaping green marble mouth, his eyes wide in a look of perpetual surprise. Startled out of him, the water ran wet and dark down the glistening wall into the basin, deep and cool, the surface of the water unbroken and smooth. There had been a pool in the river that ran down through the ravine, he remembered, just as still and undisturbed, the stones of the bottom magnified, crystal clear. Which river? He thought back, trying to remember. Was it also Gubbio? He saw the river cascading down the steep defile, pulsing like a vein through the old stone town, the water white and cold against the granite rocks. No; there had been no pool there, no quiet unbroken spot—no sunny afternoon that he now could see so clearly in his mind's eye, the water invisible but for the few patches where the sun gleamed, or where delicate arrows traced the passage of water spiders.

A fig tree, there had been a fig tree—still flowering, it rose by the tall grass to the side of the clearing where they had the picnic. Walking along the path through the hemlocks, catching sight of the gleam of the water under the late morning sun, hearing the voices behind calling back and forth and laughter and the calls of the songbirds—there was grass underfoot, and the sun sparkling through the still leaves, the woods merging into a translucent depth of the steep hillside, echoing with the bright call of birds. The brilliant sun, and the leaves, tossing overhead in the wind, and shadows and then the terrible dissonance he could not forget, the harsh roar of the wolf tone, rising from deep inside—

"Matt!" Sally said. "The pasta—"

Sally reached past him over the counter and turned the heat off under the pot as a mountain of white foam towered up.

Matt, dizzy, leaned his weight on his hands, feeling the marble, smooth and cool, reassuringly solid.

"Matt, are you okay?" Sally asked, holding him by one wrist.

"I'm fine," he said. "It's this dream."

"What is it?"

"I don't know. It's so vivid, and then— I'm in the woods. It's sunny. Beautiful. But then there's this shadow, and this terrible sound—"

"Have you had it before?"

"Yes," Matt said. "I told you—at the party. When I was looking at Charles's painting."

Sally looked at him, as though she were waiting for him to go on.

"The painting of the hunt, in his study—" Matt stopped. It was obvious that she had no idea what he was talking about. "I'd better strain the pasta," he said.

"Let me do it," Sally said. "You sit down. I think you've been working too hard."

"Yes," Matt said, easing onto a stool. "We both have. I don't know if I can wait until June."

"What happens then?" Sally asked, the pasta sliding into the colander in a gush of boiling water.

"We're going to Italy," Matt said.

"We are?" Sally asked. She set down the colander and came around to Matt. "That's such a lovely idea," she said, embracing him. "How long have you been thinking about this? June. I hope I can still get away."

———

"Look, I know I sound like the worst reactionary iconoclast in the world," Matt said, as they began to eat. Perhaps if he returned to the earlier conversation—maybe it was him, after all. It wasn't that things didn't add up, it was what wasn't adding up that was so confusing. It was all equally believable. Had they planned on going to Italy? He knew they had, but now he knew just as well that they hadn't. First Karen, and now the painting, and the trip; yes and no, it could go either way, he remembered it all. So if he went back and tried again, found some connection—

"No, not at all. You're right about Koons."

"But I can't help it," Matt said, relieved to be back on safe ground. "I work surrounded by great art. It's my life. They frame it in terms of then and now, old and new. Great to me means timeless. I mean, take this portrait of Anna. She could be alive right now. I don't look at her and think Quattrocento, to me she is just a beautiful woman caught at a moment anyone can immediately relate to, looking at her child."

"Anna?" Sally asked.

"The name I use," Matt said. "It personalizes her. I've spent a lot of time with her in the past two months."

"No kidding."

Matt looked at her. "You're jealous," he said.

"Not at all."

"Yes, you are. You're jealous of a painting. You think I've fallen in love with her or something?" Matt laughed. "Like the guard at the Louvre. Did I ever tell you about him? He fell in love with the Mona Lisa. Worse than that, though, he was convinced she felt the same way. It got to the point that he would tell people not to stare at her because it made her nervous and she didn't like it. They had to retire him."

"Could we not have this conversation right now?"

Matt stared at her in surprise. "I don't believe this," he said.

"Anna. She sounds wonderful. Why don't you take her to Italy?"

"This is ridiculous," Matt snapped, all his fear and confusion boiling over into anger.

"No, it isn't! What am I supposed to think, Matt? I don't know what's happening with us. You've become so remote, it's like I don't even exist for you anymore. I'm not jealous of a painting because, yes, I frankly don't think she is just a painting to you! I think this idea of yours for us to go to Italy is just because you feel guilty. No, that's not fair. Look, I'm sorry. I didn't mean that." Sally covered her eyes.

She's crying, Matt thought. I don't believe this is happening. What did I do?

"I just don't know what's happening, Matt," Sally said. "I love you. But it doesn't seem to matter."

I know, Matt wanted to say. I know; it doesn't seem to make any difference, and it should.

chapter 6

Matt, waiting for the signal, balanced lightly on the balls of his feet,
legs flexed and body sideways to his opponent. The thin blades
of the foils hung in the air, tips almost touching, a double image
dressed in white with silver ovals where faces should be. At the
harsh buzz the two men dropped slightly, testing their legs, the
tips of their blades circling each other like dragonflies engaged
in a mating dance. Matt let his adversary take the advance,
short step by short step, ready for the lunge. When it came, a
blur of silver, the sharp zinging of the blades as they sliced
against each other raced up his forearm. A quick circle of his
wrist threw the oncoming blade aside and then Matt was
headed in, fast, only to find himself again turned aside just
before touching home. With a quick circle his opponent
disengaged his blade and then retreated. Matt, continuing
the attack, lunged ahead in full extension, but with a deft

movement his blade was deflected into the emptiness between his attacker's torso and arm and Matt was brought to a halt by a dull point resting lightly on his pectoral muscle, a bare inch from his heart. The buzzer sounded.

Twice more the dance was repeated, each time ending as it had the first time, once with Matt's blade being the one to make the touch. The final buzz caught him in the midst of a last desperate attack to try to even the score. He stopped, rose to his full height and saluted. The air felt cool on his drenched head when he took off his mask. Holding the foil and mask under his arm, he shook Klein's extended hand.

"Next time," Klein said.

"You haven't even broken a sweat," Matt protested.

"Economy of motion," Klein replied. He glanced at the clock. "It's still early. If you're free, perhaps you might like to see that drawing I mentioned."

"Sure," Matt replied, his curiosity piqued. Klein hadn't said anything more, just mentioned a drawing that he thought Matt might find of interest, whatever that meant.

The cold air outside the gym was bracing after the humid warmth inside. A light snow drifted from the enveloping black of the night sky, a fine white silt that vanished before it reached the sidewalk. As the two men descended the steep hill to Riverside Drive a breeze off the river ruffled through the tall trees of the park, making the snow dance and eddy through the luminous pools of light held aloft by the old cast-iron streetlamps.

Klein opened the door of his apartment to the sound of a piano. It wasn't until a slight faltering of the tempo that Matt, taking off his coat, realized it wasn't a recording. Like music remembered rather than heard, the notes had a dreamlike timbre, the faint dry echo of hail on a frozen field. The apartment, spare and modern, was almost devoid of furniture. The hallway was bare but for a series of photographs, chrome frames against a white wall, and a narrow carpet on the wood floor, the subtle pattern of blue on blue barely discernible. Matt, as he followed Klein into the living room, caught a quick glimpse of a pool table through a door opposite, the splash of black and white on the wall above it unmistakably a Jackson Pollock. The walls of the living room ended in the night, a curtain of glass that framed the lights of the city and the wide emptiness of the river. The snow transformed the view into a lithograph, a thickly textured abstraction of gray and black.

Seated at the keyboard, a young woman with short black hair, spiked and dyed silver at the ends, played with a delicate grace, barely touching the keys. Bach? Matt thought, knowing that he was probably wrong, that anything Baroque sounded like Bach to him. He realized why the sound had been so distant and ethereal, for the instrument was not a piano at all, but some earlier ancestor—a harpsichord, perhaps. The small oblong case of dark fruitwood had two keyboards, one over the other, the white keys not ivory but the honey yellow of old boxwood. Inside the cover, propped open by a stick carved in the shape of an elongated sylph, was a painted scene of sprites dancing in a sylvan glade.

As they paused for a moment, listening as the young woman played on, unaware of their presence, Matt gradually realized that something was out of place. What was wrong? Not false notes; while no expert, he could still tell that the music had the proper flow to it, that what he was hearing was what he was supposed to hear. It wasn't the distinctive timbre of the sound, for he had quickly gotten used to that. It was out of tune. That was it—he could hear it right there, in a long scale, up the keyboard—the instrument was simply out of tune. Wincing, he glanced at Klein. Unbelievable. Head tilted to one side and a faraway look in his eyes, he was oblivious to the discordant notes.

The doorbell rang, and the music immediately halted, the player's hands poised above the keyboard. She stood and turned, stopping as she caught sight of Matt and Klein.

"Excellent," Klein said.

"I'm glad you liked it," the girl said, and then left to answer the door.

Klein went to the keyboard and sat. He stretched, rubbed his hands together, and then attacked the keys. An explosion of notes poured forth, a cascading series of scales that finally resolved into a series of repeated eighth notes. Matt heard the door open and a familiar voice say, "Ciao, baby. Are you ready? Let's go." He watched Klein's hands as they rhythmically stroked the keys, abruptly shifting to a crashing series of chords that shook the delicate case on its spindly legs in a quick closing cadence.

"Does our friend Charles know?" Klein asked in the ensuing silence, his hands still resting on the keys.

"He doesn't want to know," Matt replied. "He says that Kent is his own man."

"I see." Klein's left hand began to sound a note that on

each third repetition filled out with a chord. "Before I forget," he said, as his right hand added a melody on top of the rhythmical base. "On the wall behind you."

Matt turned around and looked. A frame, but not a painting; a drawing, in brown ink. Patterns, but patterns that he had seen before. He moved up for a closer look, suddenly unaware of the music that had coalesced into a simple fugue. It couldn't be, but he knew it was. He stood, enchanted by the curlicues, the swirling force of the pen strokes, sure and graceful, that created the tension and flow of what could easily have been mistaken for an abstract design. It was nothing of the sort, as he knew, but a precise record of the flow of water from a spout into a basin. But where had Klein gotten it? As far as he knew, none of Leonardo's drawings of fluid dynamics were in private hands.

Without pause, Klein gracefully segued from the fugue to a Beatles song: "What would you think if I sang out of tune..." The familiar melody and chord changes filled the air. The old instrument gave the song a poignant quality, as though it were being played on a wind-up music box. Matt searched Klein's face. It's a joke, he thought, the instrument's so out of tune. If I can hear it, anyone can, and yet he doesn't seem to even notice. Klein lifted his hand and the music stopped, immediately cut off. "Do you have dinner plans?" he asked.

"No," Matt replied. Sally was out of town. Not that it would matter, he thought; she had taken an active dislike to Klein. Sally, as perceptive as anyone he knew, could sense that as polite and attentive as Klein was to her, he found nothing in her to engage his attention.

"I have some friends stopping by. You might enjoy meeting them."

"Thanks, that sounds great."

"I'm going to see what Tante Lisl left us for dinner," Klein said. "I'll be back in a moment."

Matt went to the window and stood looking out at the view. Washed of color, the room reflected back, floating transparently on the other side of the large expanse of glass in the snowy night. The lights of the city twinkled through the shadow that was him, suspended in the night, looking back at himself; I'm a constellation, he thought, an artificial superposition to give some semblance of order to the lights beyond that were the real world. Each one a star, a planet, with a world of its own in its circle of light, for whom he didn't even exist. He was Orion, with the headlights of passing cabs down in the park as his belt, and streetlamps as his arms and legs, and for his crown an airplane, flying up the Hudson. A figure appeared, another constellation drifting through the night sky.

Matt turned around. Klein approached with two glasses of wine.

"I didn't recognize your drawing at first," Matt said, nodding at the Leonardo as he took one of the glasses. "It was the last thing I expected to see. Where did you find it?"

"The result of a genealogical tontine, I'm afraid. I'm the last one standing, so it came to me. I've always been fascinated by it. If you look at water running into a basin, all you see is froth. I know, because I tried. You need a camera to stop the action like this. The eye is quite simply not fast enough. I can't figure out how he did it."

Matt studied the drawing, moving up to the wall for a closer look, getting close enough so that it filled his field of vision. Water gushed from the spigot with a force that was almost palpable, landing and splashing deep in the basin, bubbling back up in foam to a surface choppy with broken waves. Circles and curlicues, lines bending and changing and following around and around, swirling away as his eye followed the motion.

"You know his drawings of a gull in flight," Klein said.

"Yes."

"Same thing. A bird's wing moves too fast to see it. And yet once again he has stopped it perfectly. Here," he said, and led him out to the hallway to one of the chrome frames. "You see? Exactly the same." It was a series of photographs, old and stylized, that traced the movement of a bird as its wings moved up and down through a full cycle. "He drew it to perfection, but it took Eadweard Muybridge and a camera to see it."

The doorbell rang again. "Excuse me," Klein said, and went to answer the door. Curious, Matt looked at the other photographs on the wall. Next to the bird was another of a group of images, twelve in all. A salt print from the early days of photography, it had an almost lithographic texture, with heavy paper and dull black lines that had no semitones. There was an inscription across the bottom, elegant type set in italic. *Faraday: Magnetic Fields of Disturbance,* it said. A variety of strange geometric shapes, two-dimensional, they looked like an architect's floor plans, but of rooms with no doors or windows. What appeared to be hair radiated out from their surfaces, a spiky fringe like cilia surrounding each one. Beginning with a perfect square at the top, the shapes became increasingly complex. Completely asymmetrical, with no true corners, one of them had a small square protruding from the longest of its sides. Where had he seen it before? As he looked, the sense of familiarity grew. He was certain he knew it.

The next photograph was one Matt had seen before. Falling sideways, his arm flung out and the rifle just out of his hand, a Loyalist soldier in the Spanish Civil War had been caught by the camera at the very moment a bullet had found him. The last photograph on the wall was even more familiar, so much so that in different circumstances Matt might not even have seen it, ignoring it the way he would have an advertisement in a magazine. A biplane, listing slightly to one side with white wings delicately feathered, was just rising from a narrow wooden rail laid in the sand at Kitty Hawk. Frozen in the air, with the figure lying at the controls also motionless, all movement was concentrated in the man who stood to the side, black against the gray sand and the featureless sky. Wilbur Wright, leaning forward after he had let go of the wing, willing the fragile plane aloft: watching it rise from one world to land in the next.

chapter 7

Matt listened as the notes rose from one of the pianos arrayed in the
long gallery of the museum's hall of musical instruments. As the
pianist's long fingers carved and molded the music, drawing
some of the notes lightly from the smooth keys, pounding
others into shape, Matt wondered how it could be that in a
building with thousands in it at any given moment, most of
whom were there for the art, there should be only one other
listener, and that a dog? The pianist's hands, long apart, finally
found each other, and the piece came to a graceful conclusion.

"Beautiful," Matt said, after the last note had faded to
silence.

"Thank you," the pianist said.

"Was it Brahms?"

"A good guess. No, it was one of the impromptus by
Sibelius. Ironic, isn't it? He hated the piano. But then Mozart

detested the flute, and two of his best pieces are for flute quartet. Good, this one's done." He put his tools away in the box next to him on the bench and stood up, one hand still on the keyboard. The dog raised his head and cocked his ears. Holding his toolbox, the man guided himself by running his fingers lightly along the side of the ebonized case as he headed for the next instrument in the line, a massive Busendorfer piano.

"I wondered if I might ask you a question," Matt said. "I asked my friend Walter in the department here and he said I was in luck, that you were here today and would be able to give me the best answer to what I want to know."

"I'll try," the pianist replied, lifting the music rack of the piano to expose the heavy brass frame. He took a tool shaped like an oversized key and fitted it onto a peg around which the end of one of the steel strings was wound.

"Why would someone deliberately have a piano out of tune?"

"That's easy enough to answer. All pianos are out of tune."

"That's what Walter said. But when I asked him what he meant, he started in on Pythagoras and the monochord and some mathematics that left me completely confused. He said I should ask you."

The tuner laughed. "Thanks, Walter. I can explain what's going on, but that's different from really understanding it. The problem is that music is mathematical, but the musical scale violates the most basic law of mathematics. The whole doesn't equal the sum of its parts. It's because— Boy." He thought for a second. "Here, let me just show you." He stood and lifted the full lid of the piano, propping it open before sitting back at the keyboard. "Now watch," he said. He played a note, holding the pedal down so it kept vibrating. "Do you see the string?"

"Yes, it's this one here," Matt said.

"A low C. Now this," he said, playing another note. "That's the next C up, an octave. See it?"

"Yes."

"About half as long, isn't it? The fact is, it's exactly half the length of the lower one. That's where Pythagoras comes in. What you see right there is the foundation of modern science, the first discovery that a natural phenomenon, in this case the vibration of a string, has a mathematical basis. A string half as long vibrates twice as fast." He played the two notes together. "An octave."

"They sound perfectly in tune," Matt said, watching the strings vibrate.

"They are."

"So what's the problem?"

"Wait, I'll show you." He played two more notes. "A major third. The most basic interval in music. The two notes are three steps apart, which is why it's called a third. But there are also three of them in the octave, and that's what causes the problem. Three thirds do not make a whole. This is where Walter's math comes in." The man played the two notes again, holding the pedal down so they went on vibrating. "You see them? The higher one is shorter, but not by much. To get it you divide the long string into five and take away one. That's a ratio of five to four. So to get an octave you multiply that three times, which gives you 125/64. But an octave, as we saw at the beginning, is two to one, which is 128/64. You see the problem? Three thirds do not make a whole. There's a missing 3/64th."

"I see," Matt replied, even though he didn't. But since he wasn't going to be building a piano any time soon, the important thing seemed to be that it didn't add up. "But that doesn't sound like much."

"It's enough to make some notes sound completely out of tune with the rest. A note like that is called the wolf tone, because it literally sounds like the howling of a wolf. Over the full range of a keyboard it turns up in the fourths and fifths, too. All sorts of things were done to try to eradicate it. You can just leave the offending notes out, of course, but that seriously limits the music you can write. You can bend a few notes here and there to distribute the inequalities so that the wolf notes aren't so jarring. That's called tempering the scale. You remember Bach and his well-tempered clavier? He wrote those to advocate a tuning system that he thought was the best. Mean tempering was another one used a lot, but there were as many tunings as there are keyboards in this room.

"Equal temperament is what we use now," the tuner said, taking out his tools. "Every note is slightly off so that none stands out. It has its advantages, because every note of every scale can be used. The wolf has been banished. It's extinct. But we do pay a price. We live in a world that's completely out of tune and no one even notices. It only sounds right to you because it's what you know." He struck the key again and, satisfied, moved the tool. "But now you've heard true pitch, you know what music really is. You're like the man in Plato's cave.

You've stumbled outside and seen the sun and now even if you go back, you'll know that what you're seeing are only shadows. But beware of the wolf. The ancients knew its power. It was so strong that to play it or even speak of it was a sin. They called it the diabolus in musica."

"How bad could it be?" Matt asked. "I didn't hear anything that sounded like the howling of a wolf."

The tuner smiled. Holding the handle lightly between his thumb and forefinger, he trailed his others lightly along the pegs to the longest strings at the bottom of the keyboard. Rather than striking the keys he stood up and reached inside. Plucking the string so lightly that Matt couldn't hear the sound, the man made minute adjustments with the tool before moving to the next, and then the next. The dog suddenly raised his head from his paws. His ears cocked forward and he rose to his feet. Head lowered, he growled deeply.

"Quiet, Pablo," the man said. He adjusted a few more strings and then sat at the keyboard, his hands folded in front of him. After a brief moment he raised them and without any ceremony began to play.

Matt, expecting something terrible, relaxed. It did sound strange, but the individual notes were wonderfully sharp and clear, like a polished window, and they resonated with each other in a way that was entirely new. Without sharps or flats, the melody had a modal tonality, like a song from long ago, passed down from generation to generation. Lulled into a feeling of relaxed enjoyment, he was completely unprepared for the modulation when it finally came. The tuner's right hand moved slightly, the arched fingers descended, and the melody stopped as a single terrible note, alien to all the rest, rang in the air. Matt felt the hair rise on the back of his neck. The pianist played the note again, adding others to make it a chord, holding the pedal down so that it continued to resonate, the dissonance boring into Matt. Trumpets, deep in the woods somewhere out of sight, and in the shadows under the trees, the wolf—

———

The urgent blare of the trumpets echoed through the woods, punctuating the muffled tumult of shouts and excited barking, the neighing of a horse as it forced its way through the thick underbrush. Moss underfoot, laurel, submerged in green and dappled in shadow, Matt followed the hunt. Thirsty, he hadn't had a drink since they had entered the forest, high on the ridge past the fields above the villa. Up and then down, rocky defiles and sudden clearings and pools, dark and quiet under the overhanging trees, he was completely lost. He stopped, scanning the steep hillside ahead. A flash of color, of wings, the frenzy of the circling dogs—and then without warning he was on the ground, the moss under his cheek. Struggling to get up, winded, squinting against the sun overhead through the waving crown of leaves, against the branches a shadow and in its hands a sword, held high, descending—

Matt sat bolt upright. Sally, next to him, her face turned away and her hands under her cheek, lay still. Moonlight cast a faint shadow across the blankets, silvering her hair. He rubbed his face, wide awake. He knew there would be no getting back to sleep, so he eased his legs around and got up, careful not to wake the sleeping girl. He slipped into his robe, wondering as he did how she managed to get his pajamas away from him without his noticing. Only the tops, and he didn't mind, really; they felt better on her, next to him.

The apartment was silent, no sound from the deserted street outside. Long rectangles of pale white draped across the furniture, rested on the floor, moonlight mixed with the soulless glare of streetlights. What time was it? Matt had not the slightest idea, and didn't care; too early for coffee, that was all that mattered. He didn't want it to be morning, anyway.

He sat at the desk and switched the computer on, yawning the last vestiges of sleep from the corners of his mind as the machine warmed up. A few clicks and there she was. This was Anna as she must have been, as she had sat for her portrait. Matt had mapped her onto a three-dimensional coaxial model, taking hours of work to get it just right. But it had been worth it. He moved the mouse and her head turned, lifted; she looked at him. She hadn't smiled, yet; that would take time, and he wondered again what her voice would sound like. Buona sera, he thought, and grinned; that, truly, would be stepping over the line. A talking portrait? No. But like this, yes, that was fine.

Matt logged on to check his mail. It was there, the letter he had been dreading as much as waiting for. He opened it.

"Matt?" Sally stood in the door. "What time is it?" she asked, coming over to stand behind him. "Three-thirty," she exclaimed, as she read the time on the screen.

"I couldn't sleep," he replied.

"Well, you should try. You're going to be exhausted. The FBI?" she asked, a hand on his shoulder as she leaned forward, seeing the crest on the document on the screen.

"A test on the portrait." Anna watched from the corner of the screen.

"She's wanted by the FBI, too? So you're not the only one."

"Sally——" His words were cut off as her hand reached up from his shoulder to the side of his face. Her hair, hanging loose, enfolded him as she bent down and kissed him hard. Her other hand slipped down his chest, inside his robe, and Matt leaned back, responding to her kiss and her touch. Her tongue held him, searching, probing, as she moved around and straddled him. He tried to speak but she pressed her mouth harder against his, rising up to guide him into her. Matt surrendered to her insistence, holding her waist as she rose and fell on him. Careless of bruising, her mouth covered his face, sliding over his mouth and eyes, her breath panting and wet as she rode him harder and harder, urging him on until he could hold on no longer and he let go, holding her tight against him. She relaxed, lightness taking form inside the familiar softness of his own pajamas, and dropped her head on his shoulder.

"You're looking at her, aren't you?" Sally asked after a moment, as he stroked her hair.

Matt dropped his eyes from the screen.

Sally lifted her head and looked at him. "You bastard," she said, when he didn't answer. With a quick, fluid motion she rose and was gone, leaving him sprawled in the chair. When she emerged from the bedroom moments later, she was fully dressed, carrying her overnight bag. She left without a word, pausing only long enough to get her coat from the closet.

"So that's that," Matt said aloud, after the click of the door closing behind her had faded into the silence. There would be no June for them, no trip to Gubbio. Fine, if that's the way she felt. If she was so stupid as to be jealous of a woman in a painting, that was her problem, not his. And she was wrong, anyway. He hadn't fallen in love with a woman in a painting. He might have fallen in love with a painting, yes, he was willing to admit that, but why should that be so strange? He had rescued it from oblivion, brought it back to life. He had spent months with it. It was like a child to him. But Anna herself? That was ridiculous. He knew better than that. No one falls in love with a woman in a painting, he thought, unless it could be said that one falls in love with his dreams.

But was Sally so far off the mark after all? She had loved him once, there was no question of that, and he had loved her, too, so the least he owed her was to consider what she had said. As he looked, he made himself think about what it was that he was seeing. Was it just a painting? He looked at Anna, and as he did, he forced himself to look, as impartially as he could, at what he felt. No. As hard as it was for him to admit, Sally was right. It wasn't a painting of a woman he was seeing, it was a woman herself—a person, a real person who had once had a name, a life, a past and a future. A soul. Anna. No one falls in love with a woman in a painting, he reminded himself. So what does that make me? No one.

Matt reread the letter. It was what he had feared. He had

known from the very first moment he had seen the panel, even under the harsh lights of the basement stacks. And then, over the months as he worked, he had ignored the mounting evidence. The hard data of the panel and the analysis of the paint, the intuitive sense of technique and modeling—he had used his professional skepticism as a shield to deflect it all. But this last piece of evidence established the authorship of the panel beyond the shadow of a doubt. There could be no question, even to the most cautious. The painting was genuine. And there could be no avoiding what lay ahead, and just the thought of it filled him with sadness.

chapter 8

Matt stared at the glass of water sitting on the table in front of him,
barely aware of the buzz of excited conversation eddying about
the room like the drone of the cicadas in Gubbio. The glass
shone in the powerful lights of the television cameras, the water
sparkling as though electrified, and he touched it almost
cautiously, half expecting a shock. The water was tasteless. He
put the glass back down and avoided looking around the
crowded gallery.

"Shall we begin?" asked Silvio Petrocelli, head of the
Department of Renaissance Art. Rich and modulated, his voice
was made for a microphone.

Begin? Matt smiled as he slowly turned the glass back and
forth, watching his fingers, distorted by the water, grow and fade
like fish darting around in an aquarium. Begin? It is finished.
He circled the rim of the glass with his finger. Nothing. He

dipped his finger into the cold water, just wetting it, and tried again. A note, faint but clear, rose into the air. Charles, sitting next to him, glanced over, and Matt lightened his touch so that the note faded until it was just barely audible, woven into the steady rise and fall of the measured inflections of Petrocelli's voice. No one else seemed to notice, and Charles went back to listening to Petrocelli. Matt felt the sound as much as heard it, a pure note perfectly in tune. Slowly his finger circled, the note trailing behind like the white ribbon unwinding from the blade of a skater gliding on one leg.

Charles took over. Leaning forward, he looked out at the audience over his glasses. "The correct dating of an object is perhaps our most difficult task," he explained. "There are issues of attribution, of course, but we cannot even begin to consider them until we know if it was in fact possible for an artist to have done the work. However, we can date some materials with a fair precision. The wood of the panel, for example."

The panel, Matt thought. Four pieces of Lombardy poplar, joined and roughly planed. He loved poplars. They rose from the steep slopes of the terraced hills of the Apennines like the souls of the forgotten. Late in the day, when the soft golden light fused the air with the hills into a fresco of burnt umber and raw sienna, and the breeze that had awakened under the heat of the afternoon sun to stir the olive groves had grown still, the poplars stood out against the hillside, punctuating the dream that rose with the mist from the distant hills and valleys. It was not a dream, he thought, and lifted his finger slowly from the glass, wondering how lightly he could touch it before he lost all contact, before it floated away. Not a dream, all the lost afternoons he had spent with Anna. Like the sea in August, the quiet had surrounded them, holding the other world at bay, a distant shore imagined as much as seen. At those moments the arc of the small brass pendulum behind the polished glass became the waves, as unending as the ocean, and what he knew would happen to her was banished far off, out of sight over the horizon.

It had been the Friday before Memorial Day, and although the calendar said it was a month too soon, to the birds and the squirrels and the early morning runners in the park it was already the first day of summer. It would be a short day for Matt, for he planned to be off early, getting a head start on the traffic for the long drive to Watch Hill and the traditional opening of the house. He swung into his office, tossed his jacket onto the chair and then stopped, halfway through rolling up the sleeve of his shirt. Anna was gone.

Matt stared at the desk where he had left the panel the night before. Why put it away? As far as the world was concerned, it was nothing, just an obscure portrait of an unknown woman. The clown gazed at him in blank surprise from under his glass dome, his arms spread as if to say, Who, me? Matt, feeling as though he had fallen out of an airplane, turned to the bench. He had left her there; he must have. Or put her on the bookshelf. He spun one way, then another, searching every possible surface, anyplace he might have laid the small panel, sick the entire time with the certainty that he only ever left her in that one spot, now vacant. Hot suddenly, and short of breath, he stood rooted to the floor, unable to move. Think. He would have to alert Security. No. First he would have to tell Petrocelli. Thinking of what he would say, the enormity of the loss became real, and he almost fell down. He reached for his coat, noticing the pattern of the tweed, the feel of the weave under his hand. He held it for a second and then shrugged it on, aware of every motion of his shoulders and arms, the weight of the coat, the hang of it.

Matt's own voice sounded oddly flat to him as he asked the secretary if Petrocelli was in. She didn't seem to find anything amiss, though, responding with the absentminded cheeriness that was always exactly the same. Petrocelli glanced up when he entered, his eyes as black as cuttlefish ink over his half glasses. Charles slouched comfortably in the chair next to the desk, his long legs crossed at the ankles and his lab coat open. His elbow on the desk and his hand turned palm up as though he had been in the midst of a comment, he looked back over his shoulder.

"Ah, there you are," Petrocelli said, as though he had been expecting him.

Matt stared at him, unable to speak. In Petrocelli's hands was the small panel.

"Have a seat," Petrocelli continued, before turning his attention back to the portrait.

Charles shifted his chair around. Matt, unable to do more than nod to him, dropped numbly into the chair in front of the desk. Silence flowed back into the room, the long seconds running together like cold linseed oil. Petrocelli sat, lost in reverie. "Remarkable," he finally said, and smiled. The rigid lines of his face bent and softened, and Matt saw him for an instant as he never had, a man lost in the simple pleasure of a lovely work of art.

Petrocelli put the painting to one side and picked up a plain file folder. Matt, recognizing it immediately, saw his own handwritten inscription on the tab: *ANNA,* in bold, slanting capital letters. He felt violated. How had Petrocelli known?

Charles reached over and took the panel while Petrocelli began going through the documents Matt had assembled, one by one, over the past six months. He read each page, turning it carefully facedown when he was done. "So," Petrocelli said, taking off his half glasses. He folded them in his hands and regarded Matt. "You visited the National Gallery last week."

Matt, his throat suddenly dry, swallowed. "Yes," he said.

"You took a personal day."

"Yes. I went to visit friends." Petrocelli just stared, waiting, so Matt went on, like a badly tuned car dieseling after the ignition is cut off. "I took the portrait along to compare it to some of the things in their collection. I thought as long as I was there."

"Some things?"

"Ginevra, mainly."

"And what did you discover?"

Matt coughed. "Well," he said. He glanced at Charles, who was engrossed in the picture, seemingly oblivious to the conversation. "There are a number of similarities," he said.

"I gather as much from this." Petrocelli tapped the folder with his glasses. "But you didn't have to take the picture to see that. The results of all the tests are readily obtainable."

"I wanted to see the panel." Matt had stood in the gallery lab, the paintings facedown, his friend Reynolds by his side. Matt had tried to do it while he was out of the room, but he wouldn't budge. With the curator of the department away, Reynolds might have been willing to take it upon himself to remove the painting from exhibit, but there was no way he was going to let the picture out of his sight. His interest had been piqued. When Matt moved the two panels together the grain had joined as seamlessly as a closed door. Two separate pieces of wood suddenly became one.

"Jesus," Reynolds said.

"A studio work," Matt had hastened to say. "Leonardo used part of the panel and then took off for Milan. So someone else in Verrocchio's studio used it. You know, it was lying around, ready to go. Lorenzo di Credi is my bet."

He had moved them side by side and then turned them back face up. First Ginevra, framed by a lushly growing juniper bush, an allusion to her name. With sharp features, and a mouth verging on querulous, she looked like a young girl used to having her way—demanding and capricious, but charming when she needed to be. And then there was Anna; quiet, observant, a generous face, patient. And yet, as different as they were, there was something that united them. It was in their eyes, Matt realized. Ginevra's, as black as obsidian, and Anna's, a deep green, but both with an animation and spirit, a sense of awareness, that showed a shared heritage, if only in the hand that had painted them.

"Wow," Reynolds had breathed.

"Lorenzo di Credi," Matt had repeated.

"You think?" Reynolds asked, gazing at the portrait.

"Stuart, old buddy. Promise me you won't say anything about this just yet, okay?"

"My lips are sealed," his friend had replied.

"You see, Matt," Charles said, looking up from the painting, "it's just that it looks a bit odd. You didn't file the proper notification that you were taking the painting out of the museum—"

Matt looked from him to Petrocelli in disbelief. "You think I was going to steal it?" he asked.

"Well..." Charles looked distinctly uncomfortable.

Petrocelli, his lips as thin as the paper knife on the green leather baize in front of him, didn't answer.

"I want a lawyer." Matt stood.

"That's ridiculous," Charles said. "You're overreacting. Sit down."

"I had to find out from a phone call!" Petrocelli said. " 'Congratulations on your discovery.' A Leonardo, for God's sake! In my own department, a Leonardo, and this is how I find out!"

"It looks a bit odd—" Charles interjected.

"Odd!" Petrocelli spat out.

"It's not a Leonardo," Matt said. "From the studio of Verrocchio, yes, but not Leonardo. Lorenzo di Credi, maybe."

"Lorenzo di Credi? Do you seriously think that Lorenzo could ever have painted something like this? Never. And all the tests match." He tapped the folder. "The style is consistent. The underdrawing, the use of white lead, the craquelure—I don't need to catalog it for you. Everything." He opened the folder and began searching through the documents.

Matt couldn't answer. He had to admit that Petrocelli was right. The underdrawing had the characteristic cross-hatching that descended left to right, an unmistakable indication that the artist had been left-handed. As Leonardo had been. And the strokes matched perfectly. He had also been one of the first to use white lead to block out the figures, something that only could be known through X rays, which had been invented after the panel had already been entered into the museum's collection. Ultraviolet photographs, another recent invention, showed the presence of madder lake, which had fallen out of use by 1830, replaced by modern synthetic aniline dyes. The dull brown of the background foliage, originally a luminous bottle-green, betrayed the use of verdigris—copper acetate— also long abandoned, and a staple of Leonardo's palette.

The craquelure was equally important. The gessoed ground had developed microscopic fissures, in turn fracturing the layers of paint and varnish above, like a slow current pulling a sheet of ice apart. It proved that the painting belonged on the panel, for no forger could have made the painting match the underlying spiderwebbing of the ground.

Petrocelli found what he was looking for. He turned the document around and sailed it across the desk, where it came to rest in front of Matt. It was the FBI report.

"It's brilliant, Matt," Charles said. "A stroke of genius."

———

"Leonardo leaves Florence for Milan in 1482," Petrocelli said. The audience was quiet, intent on his every word. "We know from his own notebooks, confirmed by the diary of a monk who traveled with him part of the way, that in his packs he had two Madonnas. One was finished. That painting is the Benois Madonna, now in the Hermitage. The other, however, was incomplete when the monk saw it. Only the underdrawing had been executed, but he called it as perfect a rendering of the maternal spirit as he had ever had the good fortune to gaze upon. It has always been assumed, based on his description and the fact that it was with another Madonna, that it was to be one also. Instead, we discover that what Leonardo had in mind was a portrait. But to call it a portrait, no matter how beautiful, is to overlook its greater significance. It is truly a landmark in painting, for with this picture the age of humanism truly begins. He has secularized the Madonna. He has found divinity in the features of a mortal."

With that, the easel was suddenly bathed in a circle of light. Matt, glancing back, was not surprised to see that the spotlight had been carefully angled so that there would be no glare for the television cameras when the painting was revealed. Petrocelli nodded to Charles, who got up and walked to the easel as slowly as though he were escorting a bride to the altar. He lifted the cloth covering the panel and then stood aside, his back to the audience, his gaze on the painting. The momentary silence that greeted the unveiling ended in a wave of applause. As it rolled over the stage Petrocelli joined in, and then the men at the table, and at last it reached Charles, who began to applaud as a broad grin spread across his face. Matt felt the sound wash over him, wave after wave, carrying him ever farther away from Anna. She seemed so small, so vulnerable. She couldn't even see him, looking out into the blinding glare, peopled only by the unblinking red eyes of the cameras. What had he done?

The applause died away. Petrocelli faced the audience, one hand on the podium. "As you all know, there are only fourteen paintings in Leonardo's oeuvre. To add another to the canon requires more than just scholarship or intuition, it demands proof beyond the shadow of a doubt. And to give you that, I'd like to introduce the member of our staff who made this remarkable discovery. Matthew O'Brien."

Throw a ball in the air, Matt thought, as hard as you can. Watch it sail up, higher and higher, as high as it can go. There is a moment when it stops, caught between rising and falling. But the world keeps moving. He saw again the white biplane, wings drooping like a hawk at the very moment it became airborne, and in that moment of balance between one world and the next, a man standing to one side. Where will it land, he wondered, and what has happened to the world it has left?

"Matt?" Charles touched his arm.

"Yes?" Matt glanced at him. "Oh," he said. "Leonardo was one of the first artists in Italy to use the new medium of oil," he began.

"Louder," someone called out. Charles moved his microphone in front of Matt.

"Can you hear me now? Oil is great stuff. Tempera dries pretty quickly. There's really not much you can do with it. Oil, though, is a whole new world. It's much more malleable. You can build it up, blend it, push it around. You don't even need a brush. Leonardo sometimes used his fingers. He left some papillary marks. Could we have the projectors, please?" Two images, side by side, flashed onto the screens behind him. "Thank you," Matt said, leaning sideways to see the screens as he spoke into the microphone. "Fingerprints, as you can see. Neither is complete, but I showed them to a lieutenant in the NYPD and he told me that's all they usually get. People don't pick up a glass and put it back down, careful not to smudge the prints. He said what I have here is more than enough for a positive ID. I used a raking light—it lets you see the brushstrokes, which are like a signature. The one on the right is from the painting we have here at the museum."

"Anna," Petrocelli added, breaking in.

"Yes. At first I thought I had left one of my own prints on one of the microphotographs I had taken. But it was on the painting, and under an original layer of glaze, too, so it couldn't be from a restorer or somebody handling it later. The one you're seeing there on the left is from the portrait of Ginevra de' Benci, in the National Gallery."

"The National Gallery of Art, in Washington, D.C.," Petrocelli broke in again. "And we must express our gratitude to our colleagues for the unstinting and irreplaceable generosity and cooperation they extended to us in the laborious and exhaustive analysis and research that was put into this project."

"It's an earlier work," Matt said, "so I wasn't sure if Leonardo would have been comfortable enough with the new medium to have worked it with that freedom, but apparently he was, because I did find that one. I—we—sent them down to the

FBI just to be sure and they said the same thing. Left quadrant of the left index finger. Same angle of impression. Or as the lieutenant put it, 'It's the same MO, you've got him cold. A prosecutor would get a conviction on this alone.'

"Could you?" Matt asked, looking past the audience to the technician manning the projector. "Thanks," he added, as the two images began to move toward each other, collided in a confusion of lines, and then miraculously cleared into a single fingerprint, bold, cleanly etched in black against the white background, like the underdrawing of a painting.

There was another wave of applause. Aides fanned out through the hall, distributing the freshly printed bulletin of the museum. Hundreds of Annas, searching for a new home— sideways, upside down, a glimpse of an eye clasped under an arm, a hand across her cheek, looked at curiously before being tossed in a bag. Stacks of them, and millions to come. Posters and coffee cups and fund drives. Why should Matt feel empty? He had done his job. His future was assured, he would be famous, they were already treating him differently. The airplane soared away, into the cold wind of a March day, flying toward the distant roar of the surf—he had to get away. He stood.

"Where are you going?" Charles asked in a whisper, grabbing his arm.

"Men's room," Matt said, and edged his way past the others sitting at the table. Outside the room, he paused, the metallic cadences of Petrocelli's amplified voice droning on in the background, and tried not to think about the interviews that would come as soon as the news conference finished. The event had been staged in the same room that had been used for the reception for the studiolo, using the majestic sight of the mounted knights of the arms and armor gallery as a backdrop. To Matt's side was the massive doorway to the studiolo. The sight of it was like seeing an old friend in a strange foreign city. He was tired, as worn out as though he had run a marathon that had gone on for days. He couldn't remember the last time he had slept through the night. The studiolo beckoned him, a quiet refuge from a future Matt, as a restorer and art historian, had always dreamed of but, now that it was upon him, dreaded.

Entering the studiolo he felt the familiar breath of air against his cheek, the warm scent of aged wood. When was the last time he had been here? He tried to think of why he had stopped coming, but now that he was back it was hard to imagine ever having been away, much less why. The parrot was still there in his cage, the door open. The armor leaned on the shelves, the instruments were ready to be tuned and played; the books open, waiting to be read. He circled the room, happy to see the familiar images, trying as he did to empty his mind and just let the quiet and the stillness take over, but the amplified voice continued to drone from the distance. He drifted from one panel to another, like a swimmer treading water as the current carries him sideways down the beach. There was something so familiar about the room, the oddly disproportionate shape, where had he seen it? Not here. There was a light high up, in the clerestory window behind him, that he had never noticed before. Perhaps it's new, he thought. What could be new in a room that is five hundred years old? Not me, he decided. I am not new. I am old, the walls are old, and as he moved his shadow followed him, sliding along the cabinets. He watched as the round shadow of his head was drawn closer and closer to the twin circles on the wall, the Garter and its own shadow, the heart and center of the room. He felt the weightless light from the clerestory window on his back, holding him up, moving him to the focal point, and as he drew close he became aware for the first time of the vibration—was it from the light? He felt it settling into him from the air, rising up from the floor beneath him, a pulsing like that of a deep underground generator, as regular as the blood coursing through him.

Matt watched, fascinated, as the two shadows, of his head and the Garter, slowly merged, a double eclipse, and as they did, the slow, steady vibration grew more and more pronounced until he wasn't sure if he was hearing it as well as feeling it. He gazed at the wall, opened up before him, and saw the white bird, double winged, at the moment it became airborne, heard the clear, high chirp of a parrot behind him, felt the warmth of a summer breeze, redolent with rosemary and horses, through an open window, the heat of the sun on his back. The vibration was almost overpowering, hypnotizing. The black ring of the Garter's shadow floated before him, penumbra to an unseen fire, growing and expanding, but as he fell toward it the amplified drone from outside grew ever more insistent, a discordant growl chasing him, and ahead he could see, in the blackness, the red eyes of the wolf, waiting—

chapter 9

Matt, standing in the room, felt the warmth of the midday sun on
the back of his neck. He held his hand up in the shaft of light,
watching how it molded the veins and fingers into a desert
landscape of stark shadows. He turned his hand over, cupping
the weight of the sunlight in his palm.

The clip-clop of hooves on paving stones echoed up
through the high window of the studiolo from the alley below,
punctuated by the high whinny of a horse. "Ercole," a voice
called in the distance.

Matt felt the material of the doublet he was wearing.
Linen. Soft. Under it a silk shirt, and on his legs, hose. Strange,
he thought. This is very strange. Not the clothes, but how
natural they felt. The colors were bright. That's indigo, he
thought, looking at the doublet, I wonder where it's from. He
fingered the silver pin that fastened the coat. I'm standing in a

room, he thought, looking around. I was standing in a room, and I am still standing in a room. He looked down at his feet, standing on the same octagonal terrazzo tiles, but now in leather boots, with soft brown felt uppers that angled up in the back to his midcalf.

The studiolo was just as he had always known it. The same inlaid panels—the weapons, the instruments, the bench with the mazzocchio. And above it, the Garter. A shadow passed at the edge of his mind, an echo of darkness, like low thunder in the night, that grew as he looked at the empty black circle behind the Garter. A memory, something he had once known, but as he tried to bring it forward the feeling passed, and the circle became just a shadow of inlaid wood.

Matt looked farther up, above the Latin inscription that ran like a frieze around the room over the inlaid panels. The studiolo was unchanged, but different. A series of allegorical paintings hung on the high walls above the frieze, a complete cycle representing the liberal arts. Two of them, Music and Rhetoric, he had seen on his last trip to London. And there, over the door, was Astronomy—Ptolemy kneeling as he was handed an astrolabe—although Matt knew it only as a photograph, for the original, in the Kaiser Friedrich Museum, had been destroyed in the war. The studiolo was furnished, too.

Next to Matt was a small table, standing by the side of a barrel chair of heavy carved wood, with arms that curved up in a semicircle from the crossed and intertwined legs. He ran his hand across the surface of the table, smooth and oiled, and then picked up the globe of brass loops in the corner behind a thick book with a tooled leather cover. An astrolabe, like the one in the painting, or in the inlaid scene on the wall just behind him, with the ambits of the sun and the moon marked off. Shining in the sunlight, the astrolabe cast turning circles of black shadow on the terrazzo floor as Matt looked at it. He set the astrolabe down and opened the cover of the book. A miniature of the sun, with beams like curved swords, puckered the thick parchment with its gilding. *Geographia,* the title proclaimed in elegant black lettering, inscribed by hand. Matt let the cover drop.

He looked at the closed door again. He could stay here. He could sit down; he didn't have to go anywhere. Tired, he found the idea appealing, but the door pulled at him. What lay beyond? He found it odd that he felt no urgency, or even sense of danger, but instead only an expectant curiosity, almost as though he already knew what he would find. He walked over to the door, under the lowered ceiling of the entryway, inlaid with the Duke of Urbino's coat of arms, and, pushing it open, stepped through.

The long room of the ducal library stretched in front of him, reaching the entire breadth of the palazzo. Furnished, it looked even larger than when Matt had seen it, stripped bare, on his trip to Gubbio years before. Shelves of books, broken by tapestries and pictures, lined the tall room from floor to ceiling. Two massive tables, laden with thick tomes and bronze sculptures of heroic mythical struggles, sat in the center. Matt walked over to the nearest painting, a forest scene of a woman bathing, while beyond her a man changing into a stag was being attacked by dogs.

Matt, entranced by the painting, became aware that he

was not alone. Someone was standing in the entryway to the library. He looked over to find a man dressed in the long red robes of a scholar but with the broad shoulders and short, stocky legs of a wrestler. He had a face to match, with wideset eyes framing a nose that had long before been flattened and left that way, like a rock wall tumbled by a frost heave and never repaired.

"Actaeon and Diana," Matt said, as the man walked up to him. "Van Eyck. I saw it in Brussels."

"The duke just got it. I'm Rodrigo de Aranjuez, the duke's librarian. And you are?"

"Matt. Matt O'Brien."

"Might I ask where you are from? I can't place your accent. Ireland?" he asked, looking at the ring on Matt's finger. A gift from his parents, passed down from generation to generation, it was a ruby set in a golden coil.

"No," Matt said. "An island west of there."

"Interesting," Rodrigo said. "I didn't know there were any."

"The colors are so fresh and clear," Matt said, looking at the painting again. Even restored, it had not had anything approaching the richness and transparency of what he saw now.

"The secret of Van Eyck, or so they say."

"No. That's what everyone used to think, but it was a myth. It was technique. The oil, and the way he built the glazes."

The man glanced at the painting, and then back at Matt. "You know about oils?"

"Of course. Everyone does."

"Not exactly," Rodrigo said. He thought for a moment.

"I'm leaving today to join the duke. I think you should come along. Would you like to meet him?"

"Federico?"

"That's the only Duke of Urbino I know of. Are you all right?"

Matt, caught by Rodrigo, regained his balance. The clothes, the paintings, speaking Italian—he had studied the period so well and spent enough time in the country that they were like second nature to him. But to meet Federico, the great duke. How or why it had happened, he had no idea; but it undeniably had, and what was strangest of all, he realized, was that it wasn't until Rodrigo had mentioned the duke that it had really hit home where he was. It was as though he had woken from a dream to find himself not at home but in a place he knew just as well.

———

It had taken four days to get to the villa. Matt could see it long before he could see the way up to it, high on the opposite ridge, across the narrow river and beyond the carefully cultivated fields. The hillside folded in on itself, making it much longer to get to the top than he thought it would at first. The fields gave way to olive groves that rose in gnarled profusion to rank upon rank of grapevines, already sagging under their ripening harvest, the wine-dark sea cresting at the very top against a sun-baked brick wall that hid a garden from their sight. All that could be seen of it, as they mounted the rutted track that ran alongside, were the upper branches of fruit trees and the darting songbirds that ignored their passing.

They had arrived late in the afternoon, after the hawking party and the hunters had returned and the horses were being brushed down and led, hooves clattering loudly on the cobbles, to the stable. The simple neoclassical façade that had led them up the hillside had masked the true size of the house. The dirt lane led them around to the side, sweeping up in a final curve lined with poplars to the forecourt that was hidden behind. The stately row of trees was punctuated the last hundred yards by massive marble urns chipped and green with moss, vines tangled around the bases. The hillside leveled, as though taking a breath before its final steep lunge to the summit, leaving the house on a gentle rise. Three tall stories of stucco fronted by a terrace, the villa was flanked behind by a myriad of smaller buildings, stables and storerooms. They had passed the duke's troop, camped in the valley below, but his honor guard was here, their tall pikes stacked against the stable wall, the pennants hanging limp in the still air.

The distant chant of evening services rose and fell from somewhere inside the villa as they stretched and turned, limbering muscles stiff from a full day of riding. The shadows slanted across the forecourt, offering some welcome shade.

"Let's see who's here," Rodrigo said after they had dismounted. He set off for the kitchen, on the right side of the massive villa.

The room was surprisingly large, Matt discovered, as he followed Rodrigo through the open doorway. An open hearth, large enough to stand in and flanked by two earthen ovens, took up the greater part of one wall. The light from the windows opposite was balanced by the glow from a fire that roared high despite the heat. Suspended by hooks, several large brass pots shone like Christmas tree ornaments, while behind them, its skin a dark red, a pig roasted on a spit, the fat hissing as it dripped on the coals. Like a world turned upside down, a meadow of dried herbs hung from the beams overhead: bunches of rosemary and thyme, braids of garlic, garlands of crimson peppers shining with a latent heat like sleeping scorpions. A heavy table took up a good part of the center of the room, the little of the top that could be seen scored and dark from untold years of use. A huge wheel of pecorino, partly excavated like a mountainside in Carrara, towered next to a jumbled stack of bread loaves, like logs that had rolled off the mountain, cut and ready for use. Beside them were bowls of grapes and olives, and brightly colored majolica jars with the name of their contents boldly inscribed, and, in front, a row of birds plucked and trussed. Too small to be chickens, larger than quail, Matt wondered what they might be.

"Antonio, if you let that fire go out I will make you think it is in your hose," a sturdily built woman called out, her attention focused on the wooden paddle she was shifting in one of the ovens. Like a risotto that hasn't been properly stirred, her melodious Italian had a hard crust of Germanic inflection.

Antonio, an overgrown child whose open mouth and vacant expression showed him to be as dull as the bucket of charcoal in his hands, just stared at the librarian. Rodrigo, finger to his lips, took the scuttle and stood just behind the woman.

"Antonio," she called again sharply. "Damn that boy," she muttered, and yanked the paddle out of the oven. Holding it like a mace, she turned to look for the hapless youth, only to find Rodrigo grinning at her elbow. "Ach!" she cried. "Did you remember my cloves?" she demanded, recovering immediately.

Rodrigo laughed and gave her a hug and a kiss on the cheek. "Lisl, mein Kätzchen, please. Why do you think I came all this way?" he asked, and held up a linen bag secured with a double loop of ribbon.

"I know what you came for. A good meal," the cook replied, slapping his hand off her waist. She brushed the thick apron that covered her simple blue dress.

"Ah, Lisl." Rodrigo sighed. "The unrequited passion is a pleasure unto itself. What sets it apart from all other stirrings of the soul is that it is the only one that will ever last. When desire is the fuel, the fire will never burn out. This is Matteo," he added, seeing her sharp glance taking him in. "He has come from the farthest reaches of the globe on a noble quest. Diogenes searched high and low for that rara avis, an honest man. My good friend Matteo has an even higher goal in mind, for he searches not for himself but to satisfy the longings of his people. In the cold and dismal winters of his desolate homeland, lashed by the angry western seas, they huddle in caves of peat around smoking, wind-driven fires—"

"You are Irish?" Lisl asked.

"In spirit," Matt replied.

"—even great Helios," Rodrigo continued, "in his golden chariot of fire forsakes these hardy souls for warmer climes, barely visible on the horizon as he flashes by, dawn coupled with dusk like the frantic mating of dragonflies. The sweet bosom of Mother Earth that nurtures us with her bounty is there a withered teat. They subsist on dried fish and raw eggs, stolen out from under sleeping birds in the dark of night."

"Hah," Lisl exclaimed. "Scottish."

"A little of both," Matt admitted.

"And still they have faith," Rodrigo went on. "They dream. And they whisper in awe of a legend handed down for untold generations from the shrouded mists of bygone times, ever since the returning Crusaders brought word of it to the far shores of this mortal domain. They say it has magical powers to restore youth and vitality, to make the blind see and the dumb sing. Shipwreck, kidnapping, piracy—he has survived them all in his unflagging search."

Antonio, his eyes as big as the wheel of pecorino, looked at Matt with a mixture of fear and respect.

"He will not rest until he finds it," Rodrigo continued. "And what is the object of this glorious quest?" He paused. "Porcini mushrooms. When I found him, he was headed for Siena."

"Oh, please!" Lisl, kneading dough, slammed it hard on the marble slab.

"Exactly!" Rodrigo exclaimed. "In the last siege the Florentines catapulted the putrefying remains of dead mules into Siena to spread pestilence and disease," he explained to Matt. "A common tactic. But the Sienese? What did they do? They ate them! Even today the most highly regarded dish in that town is rat. Stewed with peas and onions," he added as an aside. "Mules and rodents, but not a single decent porcini in the entire place. I told Matteo that true north was the only direction on the porcini compass, and thus rescued our itinerant pilgrim from the terrible fate of a most certain culinary crucifixion."

Antonio, shuddering, crossed himself.

"So many words," Lisl said, her powerful forearms flexing as she kneaded the dough. She stopped just long enough to tuck back an errant lock of hair. "They are like flour for you," she continued, as she lifted the lump of dough and dusted the surface of the table. "But when I am done I have a loaf of bread. What do you have? Cake."

Antonio nodded eagerly, a big smile on his face.

"Porcini would be nice," Matt said. "But what I would give my soul for right now is a strudel."

"Ach, a strudel," Lisl said, pushing the lump of dough with the heel of her hand. "Apples. Mein Gott. Here they have no decent apples."

"We have the best apples in the world," a boy said from the door behind Matt, correcting her with complete self-assurance, as though Lisl had asserted that the earth circled the sun. There was something familiar about him, Matt thought, as the boy came to the table and reached for a wedge of cheese. What could it be? Not his face, although there was in the line of his jaw and his sea green eyes an echo of someone he had once known. He was around ten, Matt guessed, but he had the confident manner of someone who is more often deferred to than deferring.

"Not now, Orlando, you will ruin your appetite," Lisl admonished him.

"But that's exactly what I want to do," Orlando replied.

"I'm hungry now. What's the point in waiting? Why is it that eating at certain times that bear no relation to anything as far as I can tell is satisfying your appetite but any other time is ruining it? The cheese is the same, I'm the same, the only difference is where the sun is in the sky, and I don't think the sun cares." He glanced down at the smaller boy who stood in his shadow, who nodded vigorously in agreement. "Cosimo, may I offer you some cheese?" Orlando asked.

The boy paled, caught between the Scylla of loyalty to his friend and the terrifying Charybdis of Lisl. He looked from one to the other, unable to speak.

"Allow me," Orlando said with exaggerated grace, like a host refilling a wineglass, and handed Cosimo a piece of cheese that he cut off with a quick stroke of the knife before the boy could find his voice. Cosimo took it with a wary half-glance in Lisl's direction. Matt saw Rodrigo struggling to keep a straight face. "The guest in my house is hungry," Orlando announced to Lisl. "It is my duty as a host to see to his needs and wants. Father Bonifacio told me this just yesterday when we read Lucullus. 'It is of primary importance for the proper host to attend to the needs and wants of his guest before all other obligations, for the way we treat those who depend on our beneficence is the truest reflection of our humanity,' " he intoned, mimicking his tutor. He took a piece for himself. "And so it would be equally rude for me not to join him. He is a guest, after all, not some mendicant pilgrim. Let's go," he said to Cosimo, hearing the laughter of a party approaching from outside.

". . . depends on what time everyone gets up," a young

woman said, walking into the kitchen, to the man following her.
Young and vivacious, with fawn-colored hair pulled back and
braided in a French knot, she wore a pale red dress over a white
chemise with a scalloped neckline. Embroidered on the shoulder
of her blue cape was a golden star with curved tongues of fire.
Her only jewelry, aside from the thin gold band encircling her
forehead, was a pin on the bosom of her dress, three irises with
emerald and azurite blossoms set in gold with silver stems.

A villa, Matt thought. That's what Rodrigo had said. We'll
meet the duke on his way to Mantua. But he hadn't said which
villa, or who the owner might be. Matt should have known
when he saw Orlando, for now the resemblance was
unmistakable. It was Anna, but not as he had imagined her at
all. Younger, she had an animation and quickness that was both
entrancing and unsettling, too, since it was so different from the
pensive quiet he had assumed, from the painting, was her
nature. While he had no doubt that was a part of her, he could
tell already it was not her usual disposition.

"Orlando!" she said, as the boys wormed their way by the
two women who had also come in. "Father Bonifacio is looking
for you...." But they were already gone. "That boy!" she said,
and turned to one of the women. Older than Anna by a few
years, and with a quietly observant air, she was wearing a dress
of dark blue, unadorned but for a simple gold braid piping
around the square bodice and at the hem. She was the only one
of the group, Matt had noticed, to have taken in him and
Rodrigo.

"Francesca," Anna said. "I want Father Bonifacio to see me
immediately after dinner. Lisl," she continued, turning to the

cook, "we are going to Virgil's cave Friday. There will be twenty of us. The duke is quite fond of your trout, is there any chance we might have some? We'll be leaving midmorning. Very good," she added, tasting the sauce in one of the pots hanging to the side of the fire. "It needs more honey, don't you think?"

Her voice, too, was not as Matt had imagined—vibrant and laced with humor, but with an underlying foundation of authority.

"At the end," Lisl replied, chopping the dough into half with a huge knife held in both hands, and then into quarters, and then again. "If I put it in now, it makes it mush. I put it at the end and it makes the best flavor but not mush. If you want I add it now."

"Not at all, you know best. Cinnamon, too. I would add more cinnamon. You did well with just one kid," she said, putting down the spoon.

"Three, madam."

"Three?"

"Yes. But there are pies with what was left," she added, pointing with her chin to the row resting on the shelf by the window.

"Well, there are twenty of us," Anna said. "It's like feeding an army."

A laugh rumbled from the man who had accompanied her into the kitchen. "It is an army," he said, his voice like a shovel biting into gravel. He leaned against the table, arms crossed, with the latent power of a strung bow. Powerfully built, and with features as strong as forged metal, he was clothed in black from his short jacket, crossed with belts and a broad dagger hanging at his side, to his tall leather boots. "We're going hunting tomorrow," he said to Lisl. "Would you like boar, or stag?"

The cook shrugged, not looking up from the dough as she shaped it into round loaves. "Either one," she answered. "See where the arrows land. You dress it, I cook it. But save the organs," she ordered, sliding one of the loaves onto the wooden paddle. "This time, please do not give them to the dogs."

"They expect them."

"I expect them."

"Then you shall have them," the man responded with a bow. "We'll be leaving at the crack of dawn," he added.

"That is, if the crack of dawn is loud enough to wake the dead," Anna said. "The sleep of the just is nothing compared to that of the just in bed, and your party has a habit of keeping the stars company."

"We'll be away at daybreak," the man repeated to Lisl.

"Yes, Your Excellence," the cook replied, her precise Germanic inflection masking the tartness of her words.

"Master Rodrigo," Anna said. Matt tensed as she turned in his direction, but her eyes stopped just short of him, coming to rest on his escort. "You don't have much to say. That's not like you."

"Contessa," he replied, with a deep bow. "The mere thought of daybreak has rendered me speechless."

"So you will not be joining the hunt?"

"It would not be a good idea," he replied. "Keeping in mind Saint Augustine's dictum that we are what we eat, I must admit that I am as much quarry as hunter."

Anna shifted her gaze to Matt. This, he thought, was

exactly as he imagined, but even more so; eyes of deep green like sunlight filtering through the stillness of a forest. I am a mountain lion, and I beg for mercy—Ginevra de' Benci would know her, he realized; they weren't that far from Florence. They might be friends.

"Madama la Contessa Amoretti de Cavalcaselle," Rodrigo announced. "Matteo O'Brien," he added, hand on Matt's shoulder. "He made the journey with me from Gubbio."

Returning Anna's steady gaze, Matt felt Rodrigo's hand, still on his shoulder, push him. Remembering himself, he bowed, sweeping his hand before him just as Rodrigo had shown him.

"Leandro Castellano da Montefeltro," Rodrigo said.

The man, still leaning against the table, bowed slightly in response to Matt. "From Ireland?" he asked.

"No," Matt replied. And who are you? he wondered. Da Montefeltro; that meant he was a member of the duke's immediate family. The duke had two sons who had survived to manhood, Matt knew—one legitimate, named Guidobaldo, who would succeed his father as duke but would never achieve the same success as a condottiere. The older son, Antonio, a bastard, died fighting in the service of a neighboring state. But Leandro? The name was new to him.

"We must go," Anna said to Leandro. "If the count's meal is ready, we shall take it with us," she said to Lisl, who deftly ladled soup into a tureen, which she then covered and put on a tray with some bread.

"Antonio," she called out, starting the boy like an ungainly rabbit from the shadows where he had retreated when Anna and her party had come in. He took the tray and followed them out the door.

"Lisl, we must leave you, too," Rodrigo said.

"I am heartbroken."

"Take solace, then, Liebchen—it's only temporary. We're here until the duke moves on, like the invisible finger writing on the wall: 'Mene, mene, tekel, upharsin.' "

"A movable feast," Lisl said.

"Feast or famine, such is the way of the world; and all is famine, my dear, when compared to this oasis of plentitude and succor. Let's go find our room and get settled," he said to Matt. "Dinner is soon enough."

"So that's Anna," Matt said, almost to himself, as they left the kitchen.

"The contessa?" Rodrigo asked. "How did you know her name?"

"You must have told me," Matt replied, flustered to discover that Anna was her real name.

"Did I?" Rodrigo asked. "I don't remember— Not that one!" he yelled to the servants who were starting to unload the last of the horses they had brought with them from Gubbio, a massive gray dray horse with a single large oaken box on his back.

"Give me a hand with this," he said to Matt, as he went to the horse.

"Did Saint Augustine really say that?" Matt asked. "You are what you eat?"

"He most certainly did," Rodrigo replied, working free the tongue of one of the heavy straps securing the box.

"Unfortunately it was lost, or perhaps just never written down. It's a shame, really. So little of what is said survives in recorded history. Even by someone as monumentally important as Saint Augustine."

"Then how do you know he actually said it?"

"It's right there, in everything else he said. Ready?" he asked, and then together they lifted the box free and set it on the cobblestones next to the wall. "There," Rodrigo said with relief. Matt wondered again what could be inside the box to warrant such care. Rodrigo, who had encouraged his questions about everything under the sun, and had kept up a steady commentary about the things Matt hadn't thought to ask about, had cut him off abruptly when he had shown curiosity in the stoutly built box, crossed with leather straps and brass studs. The box might have contained gold for all the care that had been taken with it on the trip. Rodrigo, allowing no one to handle the box without his supervision, had set an armed guard to watch over it every moment they weren't on the road. It couldn't be bullion, though, Matt thought; a box that large filled with gold would have been too heavy to move. He picked up his bag and walked with Rodrigo into the interior courtyard of the villa.

chapter 10

The house was quiet, the morning light just beginning to warm the shadows of the halls, tiled in cool terrazzo. Matt leaned on the windowsill of the stairs down to the second floor, enjoying the morning air. The hunting party was already in the valley below, setting off through one of the fields and leaving a wake of bent wheat like a fleet of tiny ships crossing the yet-to-be discovered Sargasso Sea. Rodrigo was not with them; he was still asleep in the bed Matt had fallen into early the night before. Exhausted by the unaccustomed exercise and fresh air, Matt had slept soundly with only Rodrigo as company, a welcome change from the inns where as many as six might pile in together. The bed, blissfully, was free of the fleas and bedbugs that had so tormented him the first week, leaving him sleepless as well as bone-weary and sore from the unaccustomed exertion of riding a horse day in and day out.

Matt, curious as to the extent and layout of the complex of buildings that surrounded the villa, decided to explore. Rodrigo had told him before he fell asleep that the first meal of the day was after the morning service. The villa was built around an internal courtyard, with the main living areas on the second floor. Their room was on the third floor, with a tiny window that boded sleepless nights if the weather turned sultry. Small as it was, though, at least it was not on the even more cramped top floor, under the roof with the servants.

Matt passed the dining hall, quiet and dark, where the night before he had sat unnoticed at the foot of a table at the end of the long, high-ceilinged room. Anna, whose laugh he could occasionally pick out over the buzz of conversation and the music from the gallery, where two lutenists kept up a lively succession of dances and frottole, had sat at the head table between the duke and Leandro. That there was something going on between Anna and this Leandro, Matt thought, was made more obvious by the transparent way they tried to conceal it. Listening intently to the duke, her back to Leandro, Anna inclined her head very slightly when he leaned over and, not looking at her, made a very brief comment. Did they think that everyone was so oblivious as not to notice?

"He's the duke's natural son," Rodrigo said.

"Who?" Matt asked, nettled that Rodrigo had seen through the air of indifference he had assumed. Until he knew more he thought it only prudent to conceal any interest he might have in Anna.

The sharp lines radiating from the corners of Rodrigo's eyes deepened with amusement. "Leandro. You might try to be a bit more discreet," he added. "I don't know that he would find your attention entirely flattering. He's the kind of man who thinks with his sword, and he doesn't allow himself or others the luxury of a second thought."

"My attention was on the duke," Matt protested. "He's famous."

"Ah," Rodrigo replied, with a noncommittal nod.

"A pretty tune," Matt commented.

"By Tromboncino. One of his charming little barzallettes. You know it?"

"No, this is the first I've heard it."

"It won't be the last," Rodrigo said. "It's all you hear these days. Which raises a most interesting question. How is it that mediocrity is often elevated to the same level of acclaim as a work of true excellence? 'Oh heaven or fortune, treat me well or badly as you choose.' That's a far cry from Dante, but people listen to it over and over. They even quote it with the same heartfelt conviction that they do the great canzoni, and the tears that come to their eyes are every bit as salty and wet. The corrupted scansion, the contrived rhyme—piace, audace, capace—the threadbare metaphors. 'Fleeing the wounds of love.' It's true that he did kill his wife when he discovered she was unfaithful, so one must concede that he knows whereof he speaks, but unfortunately veracity is not an ingredient called for in the recipe of art. It doesn't make the music any better or the poetry any finer. But look at them, they love it. Like love, it's the sentiment aroused and not the thing itself that matters."

"Not everything has to be a work of genius," Matt replied.

"Of course not. I'm not talking about the work but the response it engenders. Let's consider a different emotion, one just as strong as love but more often true: fear. Blind terror. The most beautiful sword or the crudest ax will elicit the same response if wielded with similar force. Or consider a passion more consuming than love, one that banishes fear. Intoxication. No matter how good or bad the wine the effect is the same."

The servants leaned over their shoulders, taking the large squares of bread, dripping with fragrant gravy, that had served as plates for the stew and putting them on platters for the dogs and beggars outside to fight over. They placed a glazed bowl brimming with scented water and rose petals before each of the guests.

"Reduce the cause still further, to the purely physical," Rodrigo continued, rinsing his fingers in the bowl. "Heat. Whether the stimulus is a fire, or the sun, or making love, or just being in love, the effect is the same: we feel warmth. From the basest urge to the most noble sentiments, it makes no difference. The stimulus may vary but the response is the same. Even beauty."

"Not beauty," Matt said, looking away from Anna, who was smiling as she listened to the duke tell her a story. "Exquisite beauty has no equal."

"You are most certainly right," Rodrigo said. "And said exquisitely well. I commend you. No equal indeed. Singular, unique, nonpareil. But I must ask—exquisite beauty by whose designation? Every man awards his own golden apple. Your rapture at a rare Greek statue is identical to that of a farmer beholding his prize pig. Every baby looks up and sees a beautiful mother. Just as every new husband sees the most beautiful woman alive and every weary traveler returns to the sweetest home on earth. We like to think that we grow more refined, increasing our ability to distinguish excellence in all things, but the truth is much more prosaic. We just get bored. The stimulus is most sharp at its inception. It fades with time and repetition. We don't grow more refined, our senses just get dulled. Good or bad, you're sated, and you move on to something else."

Rodrigo took a bunch of grapes from the large platter of fruit in front of them. "The most fortunate man, to my mind, is the least refined. His enjoyment is the most universal. And ecumenical. In fact, one might say he is the most universally refined, for he is open to all experiences equally."

"Or closed."

"Have some," Rodrigo said to Matt, offering him a bowl of what looked like bright yellow gumdrops before taking a handful himself. "The refinement of taste, as we call it, is a narrowing of our perspective, not a widening. The world shrinks as you experience it. While the world of what we know is perhaps enlarged slightly, the wider world of the unknown is vastly reduced. That which you have yet to know is an undiscovered continent, an Africa of the imagination; those things once experienced, no matter how exotic, are taken from the realm of the imagined and become mundane. Wonder is the horizon, not experience; and knowledge is the death of wonder. Not for you?" he added, watching Matt's tentative reaction as he chewed.

"No, I like it," Matt said, crunching the drops, and swallowed. "Interesting flavor. Some kind of nuts?" he guessed.

"Candied locusts," Rodrigo replied, taking another handful. "I love them, and no one ever serves them anymore." He tilted the bowl in Matt's direction.

"Thanks," Matt demurred. "I'm all right for now."

"Suit yourself," Rodrigo replied with a shrug. "Leandro's the heir apparent, unless Federico remarries, which is always possible."

"What about Guidobaldo?" Matt asked, curiosity winning out over his desire to seem disinterested, which didn't seem to be working anyway. He realized that it was silly, in any case; he wanted to know as much as possible, and who better than Rodrigo to guide him through the maze of court intrigue? In this case, what he was saying was basic, and known to anyone. As a natural son—a bastard—any dynastic hopes Leandro had would yield to those of a legitimate heir.

Rodrigo, his face suddenly closed, sat back.

"Guidobaldo's the heir," Matt said.

"Was," Rodrigo said in a fierce undertone, with a quick look around to be sure they weren't overheard. "Have you taken complete leave of your senses?"

"Sorry," Matt replied. What did Rodrigo mean by "Was"? Guidobaldo's life was well known. He would be about Orlando's age. Matt had assumed that was why the duke was going to Mantua—to visit his son at the famous school of Vittorino da Feltre, where the duke had as a child himself been so deeply imbued with the precepts of a nascent humanism. Assuming the dukedom when his father died, Guidobaldo had married and lived to an old age. If the locusts had not been quite so crunchy and sweet, or the beds he and Rodrigo had slept in on their journey here so uncomfortable and flea-ridden, Matt might have thought he was dreaming the whole thing. A woman who stepped out of a painting being courted by a man who never existed, himself supplanting a rightful heir who had vanished before his time. But Matt knew he wasn't dreaming. For one, he never would have dreamed Anna with a husband, much less a suitor, too—particularly one so formidable as the one sitting right now at her left elbow.

"Where is the count, anyway?" Matt asked, exasperated. Orlando, Anna's son, sat in the place his father should have occupied, to the right of the duke Federico. He wore his coat— blue, with floral patterns embroidered in gold on the sleeves— with an authority far beyond his years. He might be a child, but under the soft contours of youth Matt could already see the outlines of the man who would soon emerge to claim his inheritance.

"Bedridden," Rodrigo answered. "The doctors say it's a wasting disease of an Oriental nature that they are helpless to treat. The truth, if you'd care to know, is that he discovered the infinite pleasure of a moving object that has allowed itself to come to rest. Soon—very soon—Lethe will gather the willing lover into her gentle arms and whisk him across the river Sharon to a welcome oblivion."

Leandro glanced over at them. Matt averted his eyes, but it was too late. Pushing back his chair, the powerfully built man rose to his feet.

"Wonderful," Rodrigo said as Leandro edged around the table and headed for them. "Didn't I warn you? But you wouldn't listen."

Matt fought off panic as he felt the looming presence of the knight grow closer. He had not the slightest idea of what to expect or what he might do in response. He flinched, a large hand appearing in the air above and behind him, but it landed on Rodrigo's shoulder, not his.

"Rodrigo," Leandro growled.

Relief, as refreshing as a wave, washed over Matt.

"Your Excellence?" Rodrigo asked.

"Did you bring them?"

"Yes, Your Excellence," Rodrigo replied. "That was the cause of my delay. Finding an effective seal was more difficult than I thought it would be."

Matt jumped, feeling something cold and wet and hard poking into his side like a used knife that hasn't been wiped clean. He looked down to find the broad head of Leandro's mastiff sniffing at his lap.

"But you did," Leandro said.

"Yes. I think we solved the problem with the gas leakage, too."

The dog shook his head and snuffled, leaving a trail of warm spit on Matt's tights as he explored further.

"Good boy," Matt said as he pushed the animal's head aside. Growling, it backed off.

"Excellent," Leandro said. "We'll find out tomorrow, then."

"I have something else that you will find very intriguing."

"Surprise me," Leandro said, and then with a final squeeze of Rodrigo's shoulder was gone, his dog padding after him like a trail of smoke from a smoldering fire.

————

The dinner had ended soon after. Matt continued his exploration of the villa. Around the corner from the dining hall he found another long room, this one also hung with tapestries that gave the space a hushed quality, as though the room itself was still asleep. He walked slowly around, going from scene to scene as Zeus descended on Danaë in a shower of gold, and then as her son Perseus freed Andromeda from her stone and married her. Matt had never studied tapestries as closely as he should have. Were these Belgian? He automatically glanced at the wall by the door, and then grinned, finding no small plaque detailing the date and source of the acquisition. About to leave, he paused, a cassone catching his eye. The painting on the front looked familiar. It couldn't be.

Matt bent down for a closer look. My God, he thought, it is, and dropped to his knees. Dark green, with patches of red and white, it was a confusion of activity under the arching canopy of a forest. With a verdant carpet underfoot, flowers and ferns, two horsemen waited alertly to one side as dozens of lithe greyhounds darted through the dark glade. Bright against the undergrowth, men in red and blue tabards armed with long staffs followed the dogs as other horsemen charged through the distance. How many hours had Matt spent poring over this very painting at the Ashmolean? He knew it, square inch by square inch; the paired dogs in the center, tan and black, the almost cutout appearance of the one hunter, leaning back rigid, as he pulled hard on the reins of his protesting horse; the echoed arches of the other horses' necks, and high above, faintly inscribed through a gap in the canopy, stars and the delicate crescent of a waning moon.

Matt, fully stretched out on his belly, his face propped in his hands, studied the man on the leaping horse to the left. Hand raised, mouth open, he was in pursuit—of what? The deer was almost invisible in the distance. What was he saying? Whom was he talking to? And the colors; Matt marveled at how rich they were, untarnished by time. The night glowed with a dark luminosity.

"Are you all right?"

Torn from his reverie, Matt turned and looked up, his chin still on one hand. He scrambled to his feet, the sudden rise making him dizzy. Anna was standing in the door, regarding him with a mixture of curiosity and concern. She was alone.

"Quite all right," Matt replied, brushing off the front of his doublet. "An interesting scene," he said, nodding at the chest.

"It was my mother's," Anna replied. With her hair pulled back in a French braid, her face was framed by the curls left free at her temples and a thin silver band set with a single pearl encircling her forehead. Her dress, blue silk embroidered in an elaborate floral pattern of gold set with pearls, fell in folds from the gold belt fastened under her bodice. The simple pin of three irises set in gold was on her breast.

"Paolo Uccello," Matt commented.

"Yes," Anna said with interest. "How did you know?"

"His style is unique. He used the same themes in much of his work. The rider there—the one leaning back—is identical to one in the *Rout of San Romano.*"

"Which panel?" Anna asked.

"The one—" Matt stopped himself before saying "at the Louvre." Originally in Lorenzo's chamber of the Medici palace in Florence, the three huge panels now hung separately, at the National Gallery in London, the Louvre, and the Uffizi.

"Is something amusing?"

"I'm sorry," Matt said, realizing he had been smiling. Now? What did that mean? Now, they were hanging in the only place they had ever been. And somewhere, right now, Piero was painting, and so was Leonardo, and Filippino Lippi, and Raphael was in Urbino, just learning to draw; and soon Bellini and Giorgione and Titian—"The panel on the left," he finished.

"I haven't seen Lorenzo since last Eastertime. How is he?"

"He wasn't there," Matt replied.

"He was a strange old man," Anna said, looking at the painting on the chest. "Uccello, I mean. More of an old crow than a little bird."

"You knew him?" Matt asked, remembering that "Uccello" meant "little bird" in the Tuscan dialect.

"I wouldn't say that. I was just a child. He came to paint a fresco in our house, but he never finished it."

"You're lucky to have known him at all. More than anyone else, he was the master of modern perspective."

"Are you an artist?"

"No," Matt replied.

"We have met before," Anna said.

"People often think that," Matt said, not wanting to contradict her. "I always seem to remind them of someone else."

"Perhaps I am mistaken. Orlando!" she called, hearing the sound of feet racing down the steps at the end of the hallway. "You will have to excuse me," she said.

Matt bowed as Anna left.

chapter 11

Hoping it might be time to get something to eat, Matt went back upstairs in search of Rodrigo. He opened the door to the small room, finding Rodrigo with his back to him, busy at one of the packs they had brought.

"Found them!" Rodrigo exclaimed, and stood up. Turning around, he stopped as he saw Matt.

"Aren't you a bit old to be playing with dolls?" Matt asked, and then followed Rodrigo's glance past the open door. He crimsoned in embarrassment.

Francesca, standing by the window, finished adjusting the lover's knot in the silver belt under the bosom of her long green linen dress. She took the two small figures, exquisitely costumed, that Rodrigo was holding. "They're lovely," she said. "I'll take them to her right away. Good morning," she added to Matt, unfazed, as she passed.

He held the door for her and then looked at Rodrigo.

"Don't you knock?" Rodrigo asked, tucking in his shirt.

"You might have warned me," Matt replied.

Rodrigo, reaching for his boots, plopped down on the coarse hempen sheets on the bed. Lifting his foot and pulling a boot on, he said, "We've got to get moving or we'll be late."

"Where are we going?" Matt asked in surprise.

"I don't have time to explain," he said as he tied the belt around the waist of his doublet, a bright carmine red. He reached for his hat and settled the wide pile of red and black on his head like a load of unfolded laundry. It had a rakish effect, when taken with his unruly mop of black curls and broad features, making him look even more like a prizefighter enjoying his newfound wealth. "You'll find out soon enough. Let's go."

"What about something to eat?" Matt protested.

"Lisl will have something. We'll eat on the way. Come on," he commanded, as he pushed Matt out the door in front of him.

As they walked down the grand stairs from the second to the main floor, they saw Anna in the hallway below engaged in conversation with Francesca. Anna, keeping one of the dolls, handed the other back to her lady-in-waiting. "This one," they heard her say in passing. "C'est très charmant." Francesca, glancing up, caught Rodrigo's eye. Matt saw the trace of a smile touch her lips and her eyebrows rise slightly. Rodrigo grinned, and then frowned as he saw Matt's eyes on him.

"A waste of money," Rodrigo said. "All the way from Paris. Fashion is a bitch goddess. Heaven help the poor souls who come under her sway. If you have any doubt about the primacy of base desire over sweet reason," he continued, as they entered the kitchen, "then just consider the sight of an educated, intelligent, otherwise eminently practical woman confronted with the latest designs of the Parisian milliners. Lisl, my heart is yours for eternity," he added to the cook as he gathered up a loaf of bread and a sizable wedge of cheese, adding a fat sausage before he closed the bag.

"But it's unfair to the fairer sex to limit the enticements of fashion to their tender souls," Rodrigo continued as they headed for the stable. "That might be the latest style," he said, glancing at Matt's head, "and I have noticed that it does catch the ladies' attention, but personally I would feel naked, like a puppy fresh from the womb."

Matt ran his hand through his hair, aware of the fact that he was probably the only man in Italy without bangs and with his ears exposed.

"There's a reason why we have hair," Rodrigo continued, checking the straps holding the sealed box to the back of the gray horse before mounting his own. With two soldiers in the rear, the party set off. Matt fell in next to Rodrigo as they rode out of the courtyard, pleased that it felt perfectly natural to be back in the saddle. All the stiffness and aching muscles of the first week's journey were gone. The sweetish smell of the horse, the pull on the reins as she tossed her head, followed by a whuffling snort and jingle of the tack—it had become second nature to him. He patted the mare's shoulder, feeling the rippling muscles under her warm hide.

"The cranium is fundamentally not pleasing to the eye,"

Rodrigo continued, "and nature has developed this way to shield us from its view. Likewise the ears. Or the male ears, to be specific, which are as different from a woman's as a seashell is from that of a snail."

"Then why do we shave?" Matt asked, feeling his own exposed ears grow to the size of his mare's. "Aren't we interfering with nature's plan?"

"That's free will. Male features are designed to attract the female so that we can fulfill the primary injunction of the Lord, which is to go forth and replenish the earth. Some are more attractive than others, so nature has provided us with a way of tempering the effect, if we so desire."

"Women don't shave, and their features are often less than compelling."

"They have other features that are compelling regardless of their form."

"The stimulus may vary considerably but the response is the same."

"Well put," Rodrigo said.

The small party was climbing a steep path up the hillside behind the villa. The house, when Matt chanced to see it in a gap in the thick undergrowth, had grown small and toylike, a geometric paradise perched high on the edge of the valley below. The square of the villa, doubled by its shadow from the sun, still low on the horizon, and then echoed by the low rectangles of the outbuildings, was joined by the precise lines of the dark green hedges of the surrounding garden to the rows of crops that marched away across the surrounding hillside.

Matt had no more time to take it in than it was out of

sight, and they had crested the top of the ridge and were swiftly descending the other side. An hour of riding, up and down, through a clearing and across a stream and then on a narrow dirt path winding between more fields, smaller and less lush in their narrow defile, struggling valiantly to hold back the overhanging forest that was always present, waiting patiently and silently, breathing with the quiet dark rustle of deep woods and unseen beasts.

The sharp stench of human waste assailed them as they rounded the bend of the path and discovered a large, wide clearing, a field that rose at one end to a low building with a large, smoking chimney. The sound of banging, like a giant with a bad cough, came from inside the thick earthen walls, while outside several huge vats of cast iron steamed over dancing red and yellow flames. Matt followed Rodrigo as they angled up the side of the field to stay as far upwind as possible from the drifting smoke, the sour bite of ammonia stinging their eyes and taking away their breath. Matt had gotten used to the smells of the Quattrocento—sweat and waste, exotic spices, the sweet floral scent of perfume doused on everything in sight, even the horses—but this was beyond anything he had imagined. A goatherd watched them pass with a dull glassy stare.

Riding up to the building Matt caught a glimpse of a calf tethered in the shadows, dressed in the armor of a knight's steed. The pieces of armor, much too large and made up of mismatched odds and ends, clanked and swung like a tinker's cart as the calf shook off the flies that swarmed about. One eye peered out through a gap in a helmet that had been secured to the top of its broad, flat head. Several horses were already tethered to the rail by the building. The magnificent black charger of the duke stood next to that of Leandro, distinguished from the other only by a white blaze on its face.

Matt dismounted and followed Rodrigo as he strode off toward the steaming vats. A short, wiry man with curly hair was gesticulating with one hand, as with the other he stirred the pot that was the source of the vile odor, the violent yellow of his short coat giving him the appearance of a parrot with clipped wings trying to get off the ground. A priest, his hands clasped behind him, nodded as the man chattered on.

"Ah, there you are!" the wiry man exclaimed as Rodrigo walked up to him. "You were right about the urine. What a difference! I have improved upon your recipe, however. The results are fantastical. The urine of a wine‑drinker, Rodrigo. But not just any wine!" He stopped. "Can you guess?" he asked.

"How should I know?" Rodrigo replied.

"Guess!"

"Vernaccia."

"Hah!" the man waved his hands in glee. "Not vernaccia, or, if it was, that's not what makes the difference. The padre prevailed upon the bishop, who deo gracias et profundis maximus graciously allowed us a staph of his own urine! It's the wineskin and the wine, so it's twice‑blessed."

"Powerful are the ways of the Lord," the priest said.

"You brought them!" Tommaso said, catching sight of the box on the gray horse. "Careful!" he shouted at the two assistants who had emerged from the shed and, squinting in the bright sun, were working the straps free.

"So we can go now," Matt said.

"You want to leave?" Rodrigo asked, surprised. "Why?"

"We've delivered the box. We can go back."

"To the villa? Is there some reason you need to get back there?"

"No," Matt replied, thinking of Anna, and how she had looked in the hallway, talking to Francesca. "Not at all."

"Where is the duke?" Rodrigo asked Tommaso.

"The duke?" Tommaso replied. "Oh, he's inside."

"I suspect it might be the mercury," Rodrigo said to Matt as Tommaso darted to the horse and checked the box as the men lowered it to the ground, and then raced to meet them at the door. "I told him to be careful. Although they say he was not much different as a boy."

Matt ducked under the low lintel of the doorway. The banging inside was almost deafening, shutting out all other sounds. Four boys stood in front of a machine against the end wall, each one in front of a pillar that rose slowly as they furiously cranked a wheel and then fell like a pile driver with a dull clang. One of the boys reached over to a stack of black bricks and lifted off the top one. As his piston reached the top and was about to fall, he opened a door at the base and quickly shoved the brick in, closing the aperture just as the heavy rod slammed down. He took the bucket from under the machine and dumped it into a bin close by.

Tommaso was yelling at Rodrigo, the words that poured out of him getting lost in the din. Rodrigo, shaking his head, finally grabbed the man by the shoulders and, putting his mouth right to his ear, shouted at the top of his voice. Tommaso jumped, nodded, and then went over to the boys, slamming each one with his fist between the shoulder blades. One by one they stopped spinning the wheels, the noise gradually diminishing as the pistons came to a halt.

"You see?" Tommaso asked, picking up a brick and showing it to Rodrigo, who hefted it, rubbed the surface, sniffed, and then nodded appreciatively. "And look at this!" Tommaso reached into the bin and lifted what appeared to be a handful of tiny pebbles. He then pulled out a small row of trays under the bin, one by one. "Here," he said, reaching in and taking a small handful of black grain.

"Not bad," Rodrigo said, taking the grain and sifting it from one hand to the other. "For the arquebus?"

"Yes."

"Corned powder," Rodrigo explained, seeing Matt's incomprehension.

"Corn?"

"Gunpowder. We used to use it loose, like flour—"

"A total disaster!" Tommaso broke in. "No control. Pack it too tight, the gun doesn't fire. Too loose and it explodes."

"And it separates," Rodrigo said.

"By the time you want to use it." Tommaso said. "Sulfur to the bottom, carbon on top, saltpeter in the middle. What use is that? The last thing you need on the battlefield is to be shaking up a barrel of gunpowder. And the dust—caboom!" he shouted, waving his arms.

"So you take the stuff and wet it," Rodrigo said. "Mix it with some wine—"

"Let it dry into cakes, pulverize it in this machine, and here it is."

"Perfectly safe and usable anytime."

"And twice as powerful. There's the duke," Rodrigo added, looking at the knot of men standing at the far end of the building.

"Rodrigo," the duke said, as they walked up. His short red coat, gathered at the waist with a gold belt, was unadorned, and his tall boots, dark brown with the top turned down, showed the effects of heavy use. "Did you see this?" the duke asked, showing Rodrigo the gun he was holding in both hands. With the heavy barrel and the thick wooden stock that drooped like the heavy tail of a dragon, the weapon was almost as long as the duke was tall. Polished to a high luster, the barrel gleamed in the dim light, the octagonal facets perfectly straight. Leandro stood next to the duke. The priest, who had followed them in, crossed himself as he eyed the gun.

Rodrigo took the gun and hefted it. "So this is it," he said to Tommaso. "Let's see what it can do."

chapter 12

The group, Rodrigo in the lead with the gun in his hands, emerged from the building.

"How's the saltpeter?" the duke asked as they passed the steaming cauldrons, stopping by the one that reeked of the foul odor.

"Better." Tommaso hastened to his side to assure him. "Although still not as pure as the Indian."

"The problem is the purification," Rodrigo said. "We can wash it and boil it, but the crystals are still contaminated. It's the other salts."

"If you want to get rid of other salts, why don't you try potash?" Matt asked. "Wood ash," he added, when they all looked blankly at him. "Like making alizarin crimson from madder root. You boil up the chopped roots with lye and then add potash to precipitate the salts."

"I take it you've had experience with this process," the duke said.

"I've done it a few times," Matt replied, trying not to flinch at the sight of the duke's face head-on. The victim of a lance that had found its way through the visor of his helmet during a jousting match as a young man, the duke's left eye was an empty socket, and his nose, a massive parapet that sprang from a craggy brow and tall cheeks, lined and cavernous, had a huge chunk carved from the bridge. He refused to wear a patch.

"Boil it with potash and then add the urine!" Tommaso said, thinking about Matt's suggestion.

"I don't know if that would help," Matt said. "Urine's mostly salt."

"Tommaso, the urine is for making the bricks, not the saltpeter," Rodrigo said.

"Oh," Tommaso replied, crestfallen. He leaned over the pot, peering in. "But it works!" he protested. "Can't you smell?"

They moved on to the field. Rodrigo handed the gun to one of the soldiers, who expertly loaded it, pouring in some powder and then adding a small wad of linen before the bullet, which he rammed home with vigorous hammering of a mallet on an iron rod.

"He's aiming for that?" Leandro asked Tommaso, pointing to the small white square pinned to a post a hundred yards away. "Impossible. That's twice as far as any gun can shoot."

The soldier primed the pan and inserted the thin rope of slow match, already lit, into the serpentine holder above the trigger, and then lifted the gun. He sighted down the barrel, the silence broken only by the hissing and popping of the match.

The priest, intoning a prayer, crossed himself. The soldier pulled the trigger and the match fell on the pan, sending a tongue of brilliant red leaping out. Two plumes of white smoke erupted simultaneously, a small one straight up from the base of the barrel and a larger from the bore, as the soldier staggered back from the recoil of the heavy weapon.

A young boy darted out from behind a wooden hoarding and snatched down the target. He scurried back and handed it to Tommaso, who slapped the soldier on the shoulder, making him reel almost as much as the gun had, and then brought the paper over and handed it to the duke. A perfectly round hole the size of a walnut was torn through it.

"Luck," Leandro said.

"He's hit the mark nine out of ten times," Tommaso informed them.

"You know how arrows fly farther and straighter if the feathers are angled?" Rodrigo asked. "It makes the arrow spin in flight. I was watching the gunsmith score the grooves inside the barrel for the burned powder one day and I thought, why not spiral them and make the bullet spin like an arrow? Why it works I have no idea, but it does."

"It's the devil," the priest interrupted. "An arrow has feathers, like an angel—an avenging angel, when employed in the name of the Lord, as any weapon must be. The gun, though, is an agent of the devil. The Holy Father has said so. It spouts fire and brimstone and you can hear the devil's voice in the screaming of the cursed bullet. But this gun—" he came forward and ran his hand along the barrel—"it has shaken off the devil. You say the bullet spins. The devil can't ride it! It is on earth as it is in heaven. The stars are pure, for they spin, and the devil can have no purchase; but here on earth, which is stationary, the devil is all around us. We have been witness to a miracle. We have seen the devil dispossessed, cast out. By the grace of the Lord, we shall defeat the enemies of Christ."

"Glory be to God," Leandro said. "Is it difficult, cutting these grooves?"

"No, he just spins the barrel while he's scoring it," Rodrigo replied. "It takes no time."

"We have another idea!" Tommaso exclaimed, reaching into his coat and pulling out a sheaf of papers covered in drawings. "Wait until you see this." The group clustered around him. The soldier, bored, leaned against the gun, staring off in the distance. "It's to replace the matchlock for firing the gun. We call it the 'wheel lock,' " he said, enunciating the words as though his audience were a bit slow and hard of hearing. "It's brilliant! A simple idea, really. What you do is wind up this spring with a key. When you pull the trigger here, this arm comes down and pops this one up, which releases this catch holding the spring, and so the wheel here spins, and these teeth strike the iron pyrites here, throwing off sparks here to ignite the powder in the pan!" he finished in a tumble of words. "Simple!"

"Simple?" Leandro asked.

"No more match," Rodrigo said. "Think of what that means. The soldier won't have to carry a burning match around. He will no longer be at the mercy of rain, or run the risk of an accidental explosion. And in the dark, no one will know he is there until he fires."

"How much?" Leandro asked.

Tommaso exchanged glances with Rodrigo. "A bit more than the matchlock. We don't know, these are just drawings. We have to build one before we know."

"Are these from Leonardo?" Matt asked, hazarding a guess.

Rodrigo looked at him in surprise. "You know him?" he asked.

"A friend of a friend," Matt replied. It would have been more accurate to say he knew the drawings, which were copied almost exactly from the ones he had seen in the Codex Atlanticus.

"He's a good friend of mine," Rodrigo said.

"Forget it," Leandro said. "It's too complicated. Look at that mechanism. It would take a skilled gunsmith weeks to make one of those. And if it broke, which you can be sure it would, then who would fix it? We would have to buy these things at a huge cost for each one and then bring gunsmiths along to fix them. And you know how much they get paid. Go ahead and build one if you want, but there is no future to this."

"It's a clever idea," the duke said.

"The cost is too great," Leandro replied. "It doesn't pay. Multiply it by several thousand. So we lose more men with the old way. Men are cheap, and easy to replace. There are better ways to gain an advantage. We're wasting time. Let's get on with it."

Tommaso ran off back to the building as Leandro walked off, talking with the duke.

"That was fascinating," Matt said to Rodrigo. "But I'm famished. Aren't we going to be late for lunch?"

"What lunch?" Rodrigo asked.

"Back at the villa," Matt said.

"The villa?" Rodrigo asked. "Why are you so concerned with the villa?"

"I don't want to appear rude. Aren't they expecting us?"

"No. We brought food with us, remember?"

A team of horses appeared, dragging a heavy wheeled carriage with a long brass cannon barrel mounted on it. The party walked up to the gun as the driver unhooked the team and drove them away. The barrel, cast bronze, was about eight feet long. Squat and thick, among the floral carvings at the end could be seen the crest of Louis XI, the king of France.

"Where did you get this?" the duke asked.

"It wasn't easy," Leandro replied. "And it cost. They're being made by the wagonload for Louis."

"This thing's too small to even dent a wall," the duke said, unimpressed. "The balls would just bounce off."

"It's a field cannon. And you can see how maneuverable it is—light enough that we can use horses instead of oxen, so it can travel with the army. And look at this. . . . " He pointed to the rear of the barrel, which rested on a wedge. "Knock it in or out, you can raise or lower it. Fire it anywhere you want, close or far."

Two men brought up the sealed box that Rodrigo had so jealously guarded.

"Aha!" exclaimed Tommaso. He pried the lid off and tossed it aside. As he threw out handfuls of straw, the rounded domes of six bronze balls came into view. He lifted one out gently, a look of reverence on his face as though he were holding a golden chalice. "The seal is perfect," he said, tracing the iron band that bisected the polished orb. "And this is the fuse," he added, touching the cord that extended like a tiny vestigial tail out of a small iron pipe on one side. "Gracias, deo gracias!" he exclaimed, and set the ball carefully back into the box.

Matt, at the sound of mooing, glanced up to see the calf being led, armor clanking, to the far end of the field, where she was left to stand amidst the flock of goats. Tommaso loaded the powder and wadding into the barrel, following with the ball, which he carefully rammed home with a special rod that had a cup-shaped end. He ran to the back of the gun and began hammering the wedge with hard swings of a large mallet, stopping now and then to sight down the barrel. He whacked it hard a few more times and then threw the mallet aside. "All ready," he announced, and took the slow match from an assistant, the long rope sputtering and hissing in his hand like one of Medusa's locks.

Matt followed Rodrigo and the others as they retired to a safe distance. They looked down the field, where the goats peacefully cropped the grass, one chasing another around the armored calf which stood rooted, legs splayed.

Tommaso touched the match to the breech of the gun. It leapt back with a loud report, sending out a jet of white smoke that looked oddly peaceful, like a cloud from a child's dream. Matt followed the round ball as it sailed up in a lazy trajectory across the field to land short of the grazing livestock. Like an errant soccer ball it bounced, skipped, and rolled up to the animals, finally coming to rest. The cow ducked its head, giving an uncertain moo. Silence returned, as the geyser of smoke from the cannon drifted sideways in the slight breeze, stretching and pulling apart.

"Well—" the duke began to say, when he was suddenly cut off by a bang and a brilliant flash of red and yellow. The animals all fell over as if on cue, leaving only a single goat on its feet, staggering in circles and bleating pitifully as it stumbled over a dead companion.

"Exultate, jubilate!" Tommaso shouted, jumping up and down.

"Behold the granata," Rodrigo said to the duke. "A hollow shell filled with gunpowder and bullets. Like a pomegranate."

"And armor is no defense," Leandro said. "What kind of a range can we get with this?" he asked.

"I'll show you," replied Tommaso, who had joined them. He ran back to the gun and, opening a different box, began to measure out powder.

"Just think of twenty of these lined up on the battlefield," Leandro was saying to the duke. "Like having an extra five thousand men. And the effect on the enemy—they'll run like scared rabbits."

"That would cost a fortune," the duke replied.

"In this case we can't afford not to. If Louis has them and we don't, we're finished."

Matt watched Rodrigo, who had gone off to help Tommaso load the gun. They seemed to be having some disagreement, for Tommaso's yellow coat was even more agitated.

"He's in France," the duke said.

"You think he'll stay there?" Leandro asked.

Rodrigo rejoined them. "He's ready. Over here," he said, hurrying them behind the stone wall of a small shed.

"We can't see," the duke protested, and tried to move back past Rodrigo.

"We'll see well enough," Rodrigo replied, standing his ground.

"Ready!" Tommaso shouted from a distance.

There was a pause, followed by the bang of the gun discharging, and then a huge report like a thunderclap in the empty sky. The group exchanged startled glances as another volley of explosions sounded in rapid-fire succession, like a string of firecrackers going off.

"Damnation," Rodrigo said, peering around the side of the shed.

"What happened?" the duke asked.

"I told him not to use corned powder," Rodrigo replied. The rest followed him around the edge of the shed, pausing when they had a clear view of what was left of the cannon—a few chunks of blackened bronze and the smoldering remains of the wooden carriage. The box of shells was gone. Tommaso was nowhere in sight. "It's too powerful, but he wouldn't listen," Rodrigo added.

"Rodrigo!" Leandro yelled, the hard angles of his face sharpened with anger. "Do you have any idea what that thing cost?"

"What could I do? He's the armorer, not me," Rodrigo replied. "Was, I mean."

The priest crossed himself repeatedly as the assistants,

who had run from the shed at the explosion, began combing the area, littered with smoking debris.

"We should rejoin the hunt," Leandro said to the duke, ignoring the wreckage of the gun as they walked past it. One of the soldiers sat on the grass, glassy-eyed, as his head was being bandaged, blood drying in a thick gout down his neck. Rodrigo stopped and picked up an arm, still in a yellow sleeve, and wrapped it in his cloak.

———————

"We're back in Florentine territory," Rodrigo announced as their horses forded the narrow stream and clambered up the other bank.

"I didn't know we had left," Matt replied, close behind.

"We were in the duke's territory, the Duchy of Urbino. His powder mill is right on the border. It's one reason he likes to visit his old friend the count. That's also why Leandro is so interested in the contessa; her lands would give the Montefeltro a foothold in Florentine territory. The money doesn't hurt, either. With the count's bank he could buy more cannon than he could ever use."

"That's pretty cold and calculating. You think she knows that?"

"What makes you think she doesn't have aims of her own?" Rodrigo asked. "Being the Duchess of Urbino would mark a huge advancement for her family. And I doubt Leandro will stop there. He's nothing if not ambitious. Do you know what he sleeps with as a pillow?" Rodrigo asked.

"The *Iliad*," Matt replied as a wild guess. It was a part of

the myth of Alexander the Great that he had slept on his copy
of Homer.

"Yes. How did you know?"

"I didn't. I was just joking. Are you serious?"

"Alexander is his idol. The young warrior who swept out
of the black hills and conquered the world. I am always
suspicious of the obvious parallel. More often than not it's an
attempt to make anything new fit in the Procrustean bed of
experience. A philosopher's stone in reverse, you might say,
transmuting the gold of the strange and new into the dross of
the familiar. But Leandro makes me think of Alexander, and
Constantinople."

"Constantinople?" Matt asked. "I wasn't aware that
Alexander had ever been there."

"How could he have been?" Rodrigo asked, giving Matt a
strange look. "There was no Constantinople in those days."

"I know," Matt said, relieved that history, at least in the
main, was as he remembered it.

"I was thinking of the fall of the city."

"How so?" Matt asked. Holiest of holies, center of the
empire since time immemorial, he remembered that the city
had fallen to the Turks only decades before.

"The city was thought to be impregnable, but the sultan's
cannon reduced it in only a month. The days of the fortified
city ended right there. Wars are won on the battlefield. Taking
the city is now just forcing open the strongbox to get the
treasure. Everybody knows it. Federico does—he was thirty-one
that year. But Leandro was born a year after the city fell. And
that's the difference. For him, it's the way it's always been. Did

you hear them today? The duke saw the cannon and immediately thought about whether it would be effective against fortifications. You see, he can't help thinking that way. But it didn't even occur to Leandro. He saw the cannon and thought of how it would affect a battle. How did Alexander succeed? Mobility. It was on the field at Issus and Gaugamela that he defeated Darius, long before he reached the walls of Susa and Persepolis. Leandro understands this innately. It's not something he's had to learn, it's the way his world is."

"There's another similarity that I can see. Alexander had a worldview that extended far beyond the confines of Greece. It was interesting to me that Leandro sees Louis as the primary threat. Not Milan, or Venice."

"That's true," Rodrigo said. "What is it?" he asked after a few moments of silence.

"Nothing," Matt replied.

"Something's on your mind."

"Alexander conquered the world, but at what price?" Matt asked. "Great cities leveled, civilizations destroyed, and nothing left in their place. And if I remember correctly, the first thing Mohammed did after overrunning Constantinople was to drown his younger brother and marry his mother to a slave. He's still sultan, isn't he?"

"Yes," Rodrigo replied. The two men halted for a brief rest as the villa came back into view far below. Rodrigo drank from a leather bag and then passed it over. The wine, greatly diluted and mixed with honey, had a sweetly pungent tang that Matt found refreshing in spite of its warmth. The sun was directly overhead, washing all color from the deserted buildings and fields, blanketing them in a white haze of dry heat.

"It was always rumored that Federico had a hand in the death of his brother," Matt remarked.

Rodrigo glanced back at their escort, but the soldiers were well out of earshot. "His brother was an animal," he replied. "Raping and stealing from his own people. The citizens of Urbino killed him after six months. Federico had nothing to do with it. They wouldn't open the gates of the city when he arrived until he promised that no one involved would come to any harm."

"The count's estate devolves on Orlando, doesn't it?"

"That is indeed correct. The count has no family or other children."

"But if something were to happen to Orlando, the fortune would go to Anna."

"It would take papal intervention, but that could be had at a price."

"And then to Anna's children. And Leandro's. Not a stepson."

"What are you saying?"

"Like father like son? Do you have that expression in these parts?"

"Careful, my friend," Rodrigo said. "Speculation such as this will lead you nowhere but trouble."

Matt leaned forward, his attention suddenly diverted by a bright flash of color below. "That was the contessa," he exclaimed.

"Where?"

"Down there."

"I don't see anything," Rodrigo said.

"She's gone now. You didn't see them? Francesca was with her." Blue and green—the dresses he had seen them in this morning. Where could they be going? It was siesta, no one would be about. That was just the point, he thought, his heart filling with a sudden unreasoning rush of jealousy as he remembered Leandro, in such a hurry to rejoin the hunt.

"They didn't have an escort," Matt said. "What about bandits?"

"No one would even contemplate interfering with them on the count's own lands," Rodrigo said.

"It's not safe," Matt protested. "Where are they going at this hour?"

"Are you a complete fool?" Rodrigo snapped. "Leave it alone!" With a slap of his reins he spurred his horse on.

chapter 13

"A perfect day," Leandro announced. Perched on his glove was a large falcon with the distinctive gray and white banding of a peregrine. He carried the twenty-pound weight of the mature bird as lightly as Matt might have worn a watch.

I can't argue with that, Matt thought; it is a perfect day. Nothing is lacking. And what a glorious country. It had seeped into him like the summer heat, dry and penetrating, becoming a part of him. These were his clouds, his fields of grain, rippling green and silver under the sun; his horse, sweaty, shaking its head and tugging the reins as it reached for the long grass. These are my hands, he thought, and this light that molds them, mine, too. It was a land of infinite possibility, and there was nowhere else in this world or any other that he would rather be than right here, sitting astride this horse, in this field, under this sun.

"She's magnificent," Matt said, looking at the hawk.

"The best hunter I've ever had," Leandro replied, lightly stroking the falcon's ruffled chest with the side of his forefinger. "Athena is her name."

"A haggard," Matt ventured. Although he had never been hawking, his studies over the years had left him well versed in the most popular sport of the time. The haggard, a fully grown falcon trapped in the wild, had a style and ferocity that a bird hatched from an egg or taken from the nest could never equal. Training one took infinitely more skill and patience, and the bird often disappeared when at last set free, but Matt had seen enough of Leandro to know that he would never have flown anything else but a haggard.

"Yes. It took me three weeks to break her, but it was worth every minute. Last week she brought down a heron all by herself." The tufted plume of feathers on the falcon's hood tossed as she cocked her head this way and that. "What do you hunt?" Leandro asked Matt.

"I don't," Matt replied.

"You don't hawk?" Leandro asked in astonishment.

"In my country it's just not done."

"Then what do you do?"

"For sport?"

"Yes."

"We golf."

"Golf?" Anna asked, shifting her gaze to Matt from the thicket where the servants had disappeared with their guns to flush the game. She sat next to Leandro on a mare as pale as milk with a small gray hawk, a rare kestrel, resting lightly on the thick yellow glove that protected her arm. Her cape, a shade of blue verging on violet that made Matt think of Mantegna and the frescoes in Mantua, was thrown back on her shoulders. With no belt under the bodice, her dark red dress fell in open folds from the square neck, the sleeves slashed and tied to show the white chemise underneath. "I've never heard of golf. What is the quarry?"

"There isn't any. You use a club to hit a ball around a course of holes. Each person has their own ball and set of clubs. The one who uses the least number of strokes to get his ball in the holes wins."

"That's a sport?" Leandro asked.

"How far apart are the holes?" Anna asked.

"About the width of this field, sometimes more. There are eighteen of them."

"Why eighteen?"

"I don't know," Matt replied. "Tradition."

"Which is saying the same thing twice," Anna said. "Like a caterpillar turning into a butterfly—when does the humble 'I don't know' metamorphose into the much grander and infinitely more respectable 'tradition'? Do women play?"

"It's a game that requires patience, concentration, finesse, and extraordinary physical poise and control. Women excel at it."

"I'd like to try," Anna said.

"It sounds like a pleasant diversion, well suited to women," Leandro said.

Their horses stood in a large field that had been left fallow, the grass long and patched with wildflowers. The duke, on the other side of Anna, listened to the man on the horse next to him, who gestured with one hand as he spoke. Hair falling straight and black to his shoulders, the man also had a pointed beard, which accentuated his narrow aquiline features. His hat was a coiled satin snake, bands of brilliant red and blue topped by a gold tassel. Dressed in the flowing long white robes of an Arab prince, Kamal al-Rashidiyah, as Rodrigo had explained to Matt, was an emissary from the king of Persia to the pope. He had stopped in Urbino to confer with the duke before continuing on his journey to Rome. Behind the duke sat his honor guard, pennons stirring fitfully from the points of their silver lances in the light breeze.

As a series of bangs erupted from the nearby wood a bright bundle of feathers burst from the copse. The thrumming of a pheasant's wings could be heard from where they sat as it began to rise into the air. The duke quickly swept the hood from the massive bird resting on his glove and unhooked the leash. A gyrfalcon, largest of the species, the hawk blinked its huge eyes, a bottomless yellow, as it arched its wings. With a powerful stroke it was airborne, pushing away from the duke's extended arm. Leather jesses dangling from its feet, it rose slowly at first and then with increasing speed circled higher and higher, in seconds a mere speck against the sky.

The pheasant was halfway across the field, heading away from the group that sat still upon their mounts, watching the sky intently, their hands shielding their eyes. Just as Matt found the gyrfalcon, pivoting in a tight circle around one feathered wingtip, the bird folded its wings and began its stoop. Faster and faster, growing larger as they watched, it plummeted like an avenging angel toward the pheasant winging desperately for the safety of the far wood. The hawk hit with a slam that they could hear from where they sat, streaking past in a flash of white and then pulling immediately up. Its strong wings pulled it skyward as the pheasant tumbled out of control toward the green field, a few loose feathers drifting behind. And then, before they could even blink, the gyrfalcon hit it again, a death blow that caused the pheasant to drop like a stone, its bright feathers vanishing into the wildflowers. One of the servants ran to retrieve the fallen bird.

"Rodrigo tells me you are an artist," Federico said to Matt.

"No, Your Excellence," Matt replied. "I have a love of art, but that's a far cry from being an artist."

"Have you traveled in the Low Countries?" the duke asked.

"Some."

"Are you familiar with the paintings of Van Eyck?"

"Very much so," Matt said. "The one you have in your library in Gubbio is the finest I have seen."

"Look," one of the ladies next to Anna exclaimed, pointing up at the sky. "There it is again."

"It's that damned kite," Leandro growled, looking up as a low murmur spread through the group.

Matt searched the sky. The gyrfalcon had circled higher and higher until it was once again a tiny crescent far overhead. But a second bird, even higher, was circling above the hawk. Huge and black, with long, drooping wings, it rode the updraft with a lazy menace.

"I am fascinated by the amazing depth of his colors," the

duke said, watching the sky. The gyrfalcon was climbing, trying to gain height on the other bird.

"A gorgeous bird," Leandro agreed.

"I meant Van Eyck," the duke said. "His pigments. I would love to know where he got them, but I am afraid the secret died with him."

"There's no secret," Matt replied. "He used only the finest quality, but it's the same ultramarine or vermilion you can find here."

The two tiny shapes far overhead merged, only to spring apart immediately, one of them wobbling slightly. Feet extended, wings widely arched, they fell through the sky, together and apart. Steep short dives, not at all like the headlong, unbroken plummet into the pheasant, were followed by a quick beating of powerful wings as each bird clawed its way to the higher ground.

"I find that impossible to believe," the duke said.

"Piero uses them liberally," Matt said, referring to the duke's court painter, Piero della Francesca. "But Your Excellence would know that, since after all you were the one that paid for his materials."

"True enough," the duke replied with a deep laugh. "The bill for ultramarine was outrageous. More than gold leaf, ounce for ounce. I refused to pay it. But Piero's blue has nowhere near the clarity or glow of Van Eyck's. None of his colors do, in fact. How did he achieve that?"

"It was in application," Matt said.

"How so?" Anna asked. "What did he do?"

"It wasn't just one thing. It was everything. The oil, the glazes, the ground—every step."

The larger bird rose more and more frequently, striking the other with a growing audacity. Quiet now reigned, the group engrossed in the struggle far overhead. The kite hit the gyrfalcon a quick series of strikes. The last was enough; the white bird rolled over, wings spread wide, and cartwheeled toward the distant meadow. It grew and grew as they watched, picking up speed as it fell, pushed along by one last violent slam from the other bird. The gyrfalcon crashed to the earth, a crumpled heap of white feathers that lay motionless in the bright green grass. The kite sailed overhead, tilting almost contemptuously on one wing before lazily pumping itself back skyward.

"Please go on," the duke said, to all appearances unperturbed by the loss of his bird.

Hearing the jingle of hawk bells, Matt looked over just in time to see Athena lift away from Leandro's arm. The graceful wings drew, lifting her higher and higher toward the distant comma of the kite, circling idly far overhead.

"You have to think of how the light strikes the painting," Matt said. "Tempera is opaque. The light illuminates the color and bounces off. What you see is what you get. Oil, though, is like a glass prism. Light passes through the oil and then refracts back, breaking into a rainbow of colors. It's like the difference between a single note and a chord."

"But Piero uses oil," the duke said, "and his paintings look nothing like Van Eyck."

By now the peregrine had reached the other bird. Wasting no time, the falcon engaged the much larger kite immediately, a first strike and then a quick dive. The kite recovered and followed, and the two danced through the sky, trading the lead back and forth. The peregrine exploited her greater agility, hitting the larger bird and darting away, staying close inside as the kite tried to find her. The crowd cheered, anticipating a kill.

"That's because he's a tempera painter. Like Botticelli, or Lippi, or Ghirlandaio. All of them use oil, but they're tempera painters at heart. They model a figure and then use color to fill in the outlines. Van Eyck models with his glazes. With his ground. You know how bright Piero's figures are? Or Botticelli? They leave the ground bone white and pile on the color. Van Eyck, though, colors the ground. He then layers the glazes, builds them, makes a figure out of shadow and light."

The kite had broken off and sailed free, the peregrine following at a close distance. Suddenly the black bird thrust its wings, stalling, and wheeled on one wingtip. The peregrine, taken unawares, was on top of him, unable to stop, and the kite fell on her with all his fury. A second later the kite was circling, alone in the sky, as the tiny bundle that had been the peregrine spun earthward.

Matt glanced at Leandro. Expressionless, he watched the bird fall until it hit the ground, disappearing in the long grass on the other side of the field.

"A shame," Anna said. "She put up a good fight."

"Indeed," Leandro replied, acknowledging her remark with a slight bow.

Al-Rashidiyah leaned forward and spoke to the duke, who nodded. Turning to his assistant, the Arab snapped his fingers.

The man ran to the covered cadge and fetched a bird, bringing it back and handing it up. The falcon settled on the man's arm, and he spoke to it soothingly as he drew off its hood. Almost as large as the gyrfalcon, it was a speckled dark brown, banded with black, with piercing eyes that glared around the assembled company, searching for prey.

"A sacre," Orlando exclaimed. Matt turned to the boy, seated with his friend Cosimo on their smaller mounts behind the main group. Both boys were wide-eyed, their faces shining with excitement. Orlando held a small goshawk, hooded and quiet on his wrist. "The great desert falcon," he explained to Matt, proud to display his knowledge.

"I've always wanted to see one," Matt replied, careful not to let on that he had already known what a sacre was. Turning back, he saw Leandro's gaze also on the boy. Leandro, sensing Matt's eyes on him, shifted his gaze to meet his, smiling at the boy's naïve enthusiasm, but not before Matt had had a glimpse of what had been in his face. He had looked just like the sacre, sizing up his prey.

The large hawk shifted its feet, flexing the long, curved talons as it arched its wings. Opening its cruelly hooked beak, it uttered a harsh cry, and Kamal unhooked the leash from the braided black jesses. With a quick spring the bird was gone, racing skyward.

"You seem to know an awful lot about painting," Anna said. "For someone who is not an artist."

"Thank you, Contessa," Matt replied with a bow. "But knowing and doing are worlds apart. I also know how birds fly, but I can't do it myself."

"There's no mystery there," Leandro said. "We have legs, they have wings. Anyone knows that."

"I've always wondered how they soar," Anna said. "Look at the kite—it's not moving its wings, and yet it stays aloft. It can even rise higher, without any effort at all. How is that possible?"

"It glides," Leandro replied. "Like a leaf blown by the wind."

"The kite, I think, is a bit heavier than a leaf," Anna said.

"No, he's right," Matt said. "A bird rises on updrafts. Columns of air heated by the sun. But that's not how it stays aloft, like the kite is doing."

"And how is it able to do that?" Anna asked.

"It's the shape of the wing and how the air flows over it," Matt said.

"How do you mean?" the duke asked, looking down from the birds to rest his good eye on Matt.

"The wing is curved," Matt said. "Like this." He cupped his hand. "The air flows around it. It takes longer for the air to travel over the top. This creates a vacuum here, underneath; more air rushes in, like water under a boat, and it lifts it up." Matt wasn't sure if he had it exactly right—it had been a long time since high school physics. But it was close enough, and he doubted there would be an aerodynamic engineer anywhere within earshot to contradict him on the fine points.

"A vacuum," Leandro said. "Sounds like another name for witchcraft."

"Not at all," the duke replied. "A vacuum is an absence of a material. An imbalance which nature tries to correct. I have a text of Archimedes from Alexandria, translated from the Arabic"—he nodded to the prince, who bowed in return— "which explains the phenomenon. It's the basic principle upon which hydraulics is founded."

The sacre had reached the kite. It rose higher, circling toward the sun, the kite describing larger arcs as it kept pace. Without pausing, the sacre wheeled into the kite, striking it point-blank. It stayed close, using its wings to pivot into the larger bird again and again, breaking off to swing underneath and appear again out of nowhere. The kite struck back, hard, vicious blows that even from that great distance jarred the watching crowd, but the sacre was relentless, always attacking. Struck, it would fall away, only to wheel and come back to rake the other bird and then fall again, the two following each other lower and lower. The sacre suddenly broke away and began circling higher with quick strokes of its tapered wings. The kite rose, too, but slower, the sacre slowly outstripping it, the kite working to keep up. Higher and higher they rose, the sacre leading the way, farther and farther in the lead, and then with one last powerful stroke the falcon folded into a stoop and dropped on the kite, hitting it with full force and knocking it sideways as it rocketed past. The kite struggled to regain its balance, but before it could, the sacre hit it again, even harder, and it was done for. The long wings slumped, the neck went limp, and the black bird, now a shadow on the sky, spiraled downward.

The sacre swooped low overhead, circled, and then landed

on the branch of a nearby tree. It waited, shifting its feet and arching its wings, as the party clustered around the prince, congratulating him. Looking past the group Matt saw Leandro galloping away across the meadow. He watched, curious where the knight was going. Reaching the far end of the field, Leandro wheeled his horse around and then, quickly dismounting, disappeared from sight momentarily. He appeared again, on foot, carrying something in his hand as he led the horse by its reins to a towering maple on the edge of the wood. There was a quick glint of steel, and then the prince remounted and spurred his horse back toward the group.

Matt stared at the tree, trying to make out across the distance the pale form that Leandro had left pinned to the dark bole. White, speckled with brown, as limp as old clothes hanging to dry—the carcass of the peregrine, he realized, and looked back to the group, searching out the knight. Startled, he found Leandro staring straight at him. The knight gave a quick glance back at the tree and smiled.

chapter 14

"You need something to occupy your time," Rodrigo said to Matt's back as he stood at the window. A breeze tossed the trees and roamed through the field of grain below the villa. Just past midday, not a soul was in sight.

"Like what?" Matt asked.

"That's for you to decide," Rodrigo replied, intent on his tools. "It's your time, not mine." The knife, razor-sharp, sliced deep through the flap of skin. He used a pair of forceps to pull it back. The skin resisted, stretching, slowly baring the tangle of muscles and veins that lay just underneath, as though reluctant to share its secrets. "Could you move to the side a bit? You're blocking the light."

Matt, stepping aside, turned to watch Rodrigo work.

"A book?" Rodrigo asked.

"I've read *The Decameron* twice. And there's only so much *Paradiso* I can take in a day."

With a series of swift strokes Rodrigo began to untangle the web of smaller muscles. Using the forceps, he lifted them free one by one and stretched them aside, pinning them to the table through the remnants of the yellow sleeve. "Tommaso, old friend, you always were a slippery devil," he muttered absently under his breath as he exchanged the forceps for a slender pair of tweezers and began probing the mass of muscle and bone. "There. Got you." He lifted a long, thin red string as fine as a strand of cappelletti from the spongy red mass and carefully pulled it to one side, letting it droop loosely, like the unfastened ribbon of a chemise. "Something wrong?" he asked, glancing up to find Matt's eyes fixed on him.

"No," Matt said. "Not at all." He looked away, and paced back to the window. "Yes, there is. I need money."

"Is there something you want to buy?"

"I mean an income," Matt said. "A fortune."

"I can think of three reasons why a man needs a fortune," Rodrigo said, cutting away what was left of the deltoid to find the ends of the biceps and the triceps, nestled underneath. "One, to get a red hat." He slowly worked the biceps free, lifting it by the rubbery end of the tendon like a sleeping salamander from its bed. The muscle stretched slowly, the striations showing, as he pulled it aside and drove a pin through the tendon to secure it. "Two, to mount an expedition to find the Western Passage. And three—" Rodrigo put down the knife and reached for the long feather lying to the side—"to make a good match," he said, trimming the point of the quill.

"I want to make my place in the world," Matt said. "And that's reason enough for me."

"Any ideas spring to mind?"

"Nothing," Matt said. "Let me do that," he added and sat down next to Rodrigo. He took up a piece of colored chalk and began sketching in the dimensions of the flayed arm. That done, he dipped the quill Rodrigo had sharpened and began drawing. The two worked together side by side in a companionable silence.

"Very good," Rodrigo said, looking over at Matt's half-completed drawing. He stretched and yawned, working his broad shoulders. "That process you mentioned. The one for the madder root."

"Yes?" Matt asked, taking a closer look at the exposed bones of the wrist.

"Do you know how to get the true orange?"

"Sure. Have you ever heard of chromium?" He dipped the pen and began drawing in the delicate structure. "No? Well, tin salts, then. It's easier with chrome, but tin's better anyway. The chrome runoff is pretty serious poison. You need lots of water for making a dye like this."

"You could do it?"

"It's easy," Matt replied. "Anyone could. Are you saying—"

"I'm saying that you're wrong. Not anyone could, as you put it. Do you know how to make other colors as well?"

"Yes," Matt replied. "I mean, I'd have to think about it, and see how much I could remember—"

"The duke mentioned it again to me just yesterday. He was curious to know how much you knew."

"You think he'd be interested in buying some, if I made it?"

Rodrigo shook his head. "Selling alizarin to the duke is not going to make your fortune. He wants to make it. Like the powder mill, but for colors. He at first mentioned hiring you, like Tommaso here, but I told him that you would be offended by the very idea. A company, however; a joint venture—he didn't say anything, but I could tell he found the idea intriguing. We could make a lot of money."

"We?" Matt asked.

"It's a treasure hunt, isn't it? You've got the map, I've got the compass. And the duke has the money to set us on our way."

"You don't strike me as the cardinal type, so I doubt you want a red hat," Matt said. "And you told me yourself that the voyage from Spain was the last time you ever wanted to be on the water. So that leaves number three, a good match."

"I, too, want to make my way in the world."

"We'll need a source of water. Lots of it."

"Water is something we have in abundance."

"It's feasible," Matt mused, bouncing the feather against the back of his left hand. "We don't have to worry about the madder root, it grows like a weed around here. Are you sure there's a market for it?"

"It's all imported now. Costs a fortune. And the quality is as undependable as a Venetian."

"It has possibilities," Matt said, laying the pen down. He got up and went over to the window. He liked the idea of supplying the weavers and artists with their materials, helping to create the great masterpieces he loved instead of rescuing them after ages of mistreatment. He walked back and forth, mulling the idea over. "How do I know you won't cut me out as soon as we get the operation up and running?" he asked.

Rodrigo laughed so hard he had to lift the knife away from the forearm. "Less than a month in Italy and you already think like a Tuscan. And how do I know you won't cut me out and go straight to the duke?"

"Because you're my friend."

"You are going to be a master," Rodrigo said with admiration. "That's very good."

"Well, I'm right, aren't I?" Matt said.

"Yes, of course. That's what makes it so good."

Suddenly, the idea of Anna was no longer a dream. Just as she had become real, Matt realized, so had now the possibility of his being able to win her. It would take time. Would she wait? The count, according to Rodrigo and what Matt had been able to glean from the conversation he overheard, was on his deathbed. Matt felt an impatience to get going; there was no time to waste. Winning Anna, he thought, gazing out the window again at the rich fields and the valley and the range of hills beyond, blue in the midday sun. And then as though his thoughts had called her forth, she appeared on the path by the upper field, Francesca mounted by her side. "I can't believe it!" Matt exclaimed.

"She's a bit late today," Rodrigo remarked.

"What on earth can she be thinking? In broad daylight like this? She's a married woman!"

"And you're not her husband. So what concern is it of yours where she's gone off to?"

"It's just not right." Matt could tell, even from this distance, that she was wearing the pale red dress that he had taken a particular liking to, for it was the one she had been wearing the first time he had seen her in the kitchen. Could it be just two weeks ago? It seemed like a lifetime. "Call me old-fashioned, but what happened to the idea of fidelity? The Ten Commandments?"

"You have a particular one in mind?"

"How about 'Thou shalt not take another man's wife'?"

"I doubt she's doing that."

"Very funny."

"If adultery weren't such a widespread activity, then I doubt anyone would have felt it necessary to engrave a prohibition against it in stone. And even if this were adultery, then it would be just barely so. Her husband is teetering on the edge of the grave. He never much liked women anyway." Rodrigo, finished with the dissection, cleaned his knife with an old cloth. Like a dead tree reaching blindly to the sky, the flayed hand rose from the table, fingers outstretched.

"Yes, well, I'm not surprised at your casual attitude."

"How so?"

"Your inamorata is right there with her."

"You want to be more careful," Rodrigo said. "Such a casual use of language could easily be taken amiss."

"What? Oh, forget it," Matt replied. "I'm sorry, I didn't mean to offend you. I'm being a fool. You were right. An ax or a sword, love or lust, it doesn't matter."

"I never said anything like that."

"Yes, you did. At dinner, just the other night."

"We were talking about a song!"

"Love is an art, just like song. And just like any art its only purpose is to produce an effect. And if it's not the proper time or place, it's no more than a nuisance."

"To make a literal application of something that was put forth in a purely philosophical vein—that goes against all reason."

" 'Miracolo d'amore,' " Matt said. "What is the miracle of love? I'll tell you." He reached across the table and began counting off on the splayed fingers of the dead hand. "One, to act contrary to one's best interests. Two, to abandon the path of reason. Three, to sacrifice everything in the pursuit of the unattainable. And, four, to surrender oneself to the rule of arbitrary emotion." He pushed the hand dismissively. "Another word for that is madness. No. If there is any miracle of love, it's the persistence of man's belief that it even exists."

"It doesn't sound to me as though belief is in question here. Disappointment is not another word for disbelief. In fact, disappointment is, if anything, a proof of belief," Rodrigo said. "You've been inside too much. I think you need to get some fresh air."

"No, I don't," Matt snapped. He stood up and stalked across the room.

"There's an old church you should go take a look at."

"I don't want to go see an old church. I've seen enough old churches."

"It has some frescoes."

"Well, that's unique. That really makes it different from every other church in Italy."

"These are supposed to be by somebody important."

"Giotto, I bet." For Giotto to have painted every work ascribed to him he would have had to work night and day without interruption his entire life.

"No, a longer name. *M* something. You mentioned him to me when we were talking about Florence."

"Masaccio?" Matt asked. That would be impossible. Masaccio had died young, after producing a mere handful of works. The chances of there being a fresco series of his in an obscure countryside church were nil.

"That's it."

"No. Are you sure?" Matt turned and looked at Rodrigo. "Masaccio?"

"Yes. Isn't he the one whose work you liked so much?"

"Where is this church?"

Matt reached the edge of the wood. Weathered and unadorned, the old Romanesque church rose from the opposite side of the meadow like an outcropping of rock after the land around it has been washed away by uncounted seasons of torrential downpours. All that was left of the porch, if there had even been one, were the worn steps, leading up to a plain wooden door. The solitary niche on the façade was empty, as was the bell tower, giving it the air of a place half-remembered but never visited, with three gnarled fig trees left to one side to stand a lonely vigil. It didn't look promising, but he knew better than to give up hope; the most humble church might house the greatest treasures. As he walked closer, he stopped at the quiet whicker of a horse, on the other side of the church. Someone was here. Mindful of bandits, he hugged the weathered stone and peered around the corner. Anna's white mare cropped the grass, Francesca's roan tethered to the tree next to it. No one was in sight; they must be inside. But where was Leandro's mount? He must have left it somewhere close by and arrived by foot. What should he do? Matt paused, irresolute, torn between withdrawing silently and wanting to wait and explore the church. Explore the church, he thought to himself; who am I kidding? Retracing his steps, he halted as he heard the door to the church creak open. He leaped behind one of the old fig trees.

"...any longer and we'll be late." It was Anna. The response, low, was lost as she and her companion turned the corner and vanished. Moments later they reappeared, mounted, Anna leading with Francesca close behind. They set off at a brisk pace.

Matt, conscious that the tree was no bigger than he, concentrated his attention on making himself as thinly inconspicuous as he could. The women rode off without noticing him. Which way would Leandro go? If he turned right, the way they had, Matt would have a chance of remaining undetected. But if he went left, he would pass right by these trees, and Matt would be as exposed and vulnerable as the pheasant at the hunt had been to the duke's falcon. He restrained the impulse to break and run, knowing his footfalls on the packed dirt would be too loud and the inviting cover of the cool woods too far away. How long would he have to wait? It already seemed like forever. The breeze tugged at him, soughing in the dry, rustling limbs of the fig trees. The door creaked, and he went rigid, holding the rough bark until his fingers ached. No one appeared. There was no sound of heavy boots.

The door creaked again, slowly, the high-pitched rasp drawn out, ending fitfully, and then starting again. Still no one appeared. Minutes passed, the breeze played in the trees, the sunlight danced and sparkled in the leaves, making waves across the grass, until even Anna's presence began to seem as though it had been a dream. Tired of standing behind the tree, Matt began to feel impatient, and then ridiculous. Leandro couldn't be inside. He wouldn't be able to spend even five minutes in a deserted church. He would have left first, anyway. Matt let go of the tree and leaned against it, wondering what Anna had been doing if Leandro hadn't been there after all. Leandro had missed the rendezvous. That was it—they would have no way of communicating, no way for him to let her know if something had come up to interfere with their regular meeting.

Cautiously, Matt approached the church. He mounted the few steps and pushed open the door, already half ajar. The old latch, rusted almost through, hadn't caught, and the door creaked. It had been the wind. He stepped across the threshold and paused, holding his breath as he waited in the hushed silence for his eyes to adjust to the shadows. The narrow windows, barely wider than slits, let in thin shafts of sunlight that banded the stone floor and solid columns lining the nave. The air, cool after the heat of the afternoon, was redolent of ancient brick and cedar laced with a faint trace of incense. There was no one there.

It wasn't much of a place for a lover's tryst, Matt thought. The nave was empty but for one dusty old bench, angled near a pillar as though someone had started dragging it out and then thought better of it. The altar was bare, the rough granite stripped of any adornment. Behind the altar, around the curved back of the nave, Matt found a gap in the stonework, a low opening with narrow steps leading down into the blackness. The crypt, he thought, or the old original sacristy, but his curiosity ended there, outweighed by a childhood fear of dark, close spaces that had never gone away. And why should it? He was suspicious of adults who claimed to have vanquished all their early terrors.

Where were the frescoes Rodrigo had told him about? They were nowhere in the nave. Matt leaned in a doorway, expecting it to lead to a chapel but finding that it was the short passage to a small cloister. The overgrown garden, choked with flowers and tall grasses, buzzed with cicadas and grasshoppers. Swallows had nested in the corbels of the graceful arches, supported by slender pillars of flaked and worn granite, and they flitted in and out, ignoring Matt as he wandered along the arcade. He turned the corner and came to a dead halt, astonished at the sight of a small room, separated from the arcade by a low wall and pillars and hidden from view by the overgrown garden. Two pillars in the center supported fan vaults, crisscrossed with narrow stone groins, and along the back wall a row of high windows, open to the sky, let in enough sunlight to give the space a bright warmth. Unlike the church, the chamber was fully furnished. So this is where she goes every day, Matt thought, still stunned at the sight of what lay before him. This was Anna's secret, her hidden tryst, the place she vanished to when everyone else retired for the afternoon siesta, only her closest servant to keep her company.

The furniture was plain, not at all as rich as Matt would have expected for a woman of Anna's refinement and position. A stool, a long table under the windows, a broad shelf to the side over a row of drawers, and a chair. On the shelf there was a rainbow of colors in squat glass jars, next to tall decanters of oil, clear and dusky yellow, and small flasks. He took one holding a colorless liquid and pulled the cork, finding the sweet peppermint smell of oil of lavender. Under the shelf, leaning against the wall, were gleaming white panels of different sizes, blank, their surfaces as smooth and unblemished as the finest polished Carrara marble. Matt looked at the panel lying flat on the bench, blocked so that it was tilted slightly up in the back. Only a part was still bone-white, the rest filled with blue sky, and the darker whiteness of a cloud, and in the center, wings arched in midstroke, the slender form of a swallow.

On the table sat a row of small bowls, each filled with the bright colors of tempera paint, and a handful of brushes, the hair still wet from use. Matt set down the panel and picked up the sketch that leaned against the wall. Silverpoint on heavy paper, a series of birds flew, the sheet crowded with quick studies and finished details. Anna was no amateur, dabbling in stilted renderings of pleasant bucolic scenes; this was the work of a serious artist. Matt remembered her insistence that he elaborate when the duke had asked about oil paint, her vivid memories as a very young child of a man painting a fresco at her parents' house.

Searching the room, Matt discovered a stack of finished panels leaning between the drawers and the wall. He went through them quickly, a glance at each one—angels, allegories, forest scenes, a portrait left unfinished—before he found the two he was looking for. He pulled them out and stood them side by side against the wall on the shelf. Yes. He took the panel from the bench and set it to the right of the others. There, he thought, looking at the three pictures with satisfaction. From left to right, panel to panel, just as it had in his office at the museum, a swallow rose into a clear blue sky.

chapter 15

I have come at last to the short day, Matt thought as he walked along the path, his shoes crunching on the gravel. And the long shadow when the hills turn white and the grass fades. Still longing—what? He vainly searched his memory. Casts its spell—no. Still longing—it was no use, empty. Frustrated, he stopped and opened the slim volume in his hand. Still longing stays green. Of course. Long shadow, white hills, fading grass, still longing—stays green. Easy enough to remember. He tried again, reciting it under his breath as he resumed walking, only to halt again as he turned the corner of the topiary hedge, trimmed to represent the animals leaving the ark, two by two. There she was.

Anna was herself reading, sitting on a stone bench in the shade of the tall poplars that lined the walk. Botticelli might have painted her, dressed in white in the morning light, still golden with the early sun. The soft air was tempered with the rich scent of rosemary and lavender, of peach and lemon from the espaliered trees on the tall brick wall that bordered the garden to the north. Her silk dress, edged at the scalloped neck by a thin gold braid threaded with black and silver, had wide sleeves that were slashed and tied to show the white chemise underneath.

Matt began walking again, pretending to be engrossed in the book.

"What are you reading?" Anna asked as he approached. Francesca, sitting on a nearby bench, her needle winking in the sun as she embroidered a square of satin, glanced up.

"Contessa," Matt said with a deep bow. "Dante," he replied, "the great canzoni." He began reading aloud. " 'I have come at last to the short day and the shadows when the hills turn white and the grass fades—' "

"Sad thoughts for a fine summer day," Anna protested.

"But such a wonderful poem," he countered. " 'Still longing stays green,' " he went on, " 'stuck in this hard stone that speaks and hears as if it was a woman....' " His voice trailed off. It had seemed like such a good idea; it was the way things were done. Into the fertile soil of a fine summer morning, watered by the mist of the fountain, accompanied by its sweet music, nourished by the warm rays of a benevolent sun, the seed of poetry should take root and germinate, yielding the tender, vulnerable shoots of a nascent love. And what could be better than the canzoni? The complexity, that was the problem. It definitely sent a mixed message, which was fine for a poem but merely clouded the issue at hand. I should have chosen "Miracolo d'Amore," he thought, even if I can't sing. There, at least, the message was clear.

"You are right, it is a superb work," Anna agreed. "So much better than that inane song about the miracle of love we've been subjected to lately. But being a woman, I always found that line you just read a bit strange," she added. "Hard stone. Who wants to be compared to hard stone?"

"A good point," Matt said. "But I don't know that he really means a woman. I think he's talking about winter."

"That's a northern perspective. Does everything make you think of ice and snow? Does my dress remind you of a snowstorm?"

Matt was tempted to tell her that now that she mentioned it, her thigh, outlined by the sheer silk, did call to mind a gentle slope under fresh snow. "It makes me think of Fra Angelico," he said instead.

"I remind you of a monk?"

"A painting of his," he said, realizing as he did that that might make matters worse. But Anna did not seem to take the comment amiss.

"Which one?" she asked.

"The angel, in one of the cells at San Marco."

"I haven't seen it."

"Why don't you ask Lorenzo? He should be able to get you in. He has a cell there of his own."

"I did ask him. But they're Dominicans. They mean it when they say no women are allowed."

"So if it isn't winter, then how do you understand Dante's meaning?"

"I think he's describing the human heart."

"I hadn't thought of that," Matt said.

"You're not made of hard stone."

"You know, I like that. It makes sense," Matt said, perusing the poem. "This part here—'Now when the shadow of the hills is blackest, under beautiful green, this young woman makes it vanish away at last, as if she hid a stone in the grass.' "

"Would you like to sit?" Anna asked.

"Thank you," Matt replied, and took a seat on the bench next to her. The scent she was wearing, familiar and not overly sweet, like wild roses or honeysuckle at the edge of a stream, blended with the flowers and the musty scent of the box hedge. He could see the fineness of her hair, could feel how close her leg was to his, could not avoid her eye but was afraid to meet it.

"What are you reading?" he asked, looking at the thin volume in her hand, bound in marbleized calfskin. "Something more seasonable?"

Anna opened the book. " 'I am a young maiden, and I willingly rejoice and sing in the new season,' " she recited.

" 'Thanks to love and my sweet thoughts,' " Matt finished the line. "Is that how it goes?"

"Yes. You know it," she said.

" 'The Ninth Day,' " he replied. "It's one of my favorite parts. *The Decameron* was how I learned Tuscan. I just reread it myself. But now I've forgotten how the rest of it goes."

" 'I wander through green meadows gazing at the white and yellow and vermilion flowers, at the roses above their thorns and the white lilies—' "

"What about blue?" he interrupted.

"Too sad."

"Look at them," Matt said, pointing to the bed of irises across from them. "They're blue. Do they look sad? They seem pretty happy to me."

"That's the yellow in them."

"I yield to a greater authority," Matt said. "You know irises better than I."

"Why would you say that?"

"Your compresa." Matt nodded to the pin that she, like many young men and women, wore on the bosom of her dress as a personal symbol. Anna's, which he had noticed on the first day he had seen her, was three irises, emerald and azurite blossoms set in gold with silver stems.

"Three blossoms, each with three petals," Matt said. "Symbolizing the Holy Trinity. But also the three meanings of the iris: valor, wisdom, and faith."

"You know much about it. Are you a gardener?"

"No. I have neither the time nor the patience. A well-made garden is a work of art." Matt winced inwardly; had he really said that? It was why he never talked about art with anyone. His ideas, which seemed so natural to him—more a way of seeing things than ideas—inevitably sounded banal and pretentious when given a voice. Anna, who hadn't replied, evidently thought so, too. He tried to think of something to say to temper the remark.

"You're right," Anna said before he could speak again. "One of the highest forms of art, you might even say, because it combines elements of all the rest."

"That's true," Matt replied, with a quick glance at her face.

Was she teasing him, or did she really mean it? "Like painting, it draws on color and composition."

"And like sculpture, volume and space."

"And music."

"Music?" Anna laughed. "Well, then, why not dance, too? Or poetry? There is sound, I'll grant you that. The fountain. And the birds, and the breeze. I suppose you could call them musical."

"No, I mean it quite literally. Musical ideas, expressed visually. Theme and harmony."

"Harmony?"

Matt thought quickly. Had harmony not been invented yet? He tried to remember, but musical history was one area where his knowledge was hazy at best. Polyphony. Pergolesi. He knew how it happened, sort of, but not when. "Several voices working independently but together at the same time. Most of all, though, what I'm thinking of is the added element of time. Painting is two-dimensional, sculpture, three, and music, four. But in a garden the time unfolds so slowly that you can't see it as it happens. Only the cumulative effects, afterward."

"But painting and sculpture have that element of time in them, too. The ones that work, at any rate. It's the sense of a before and after, of a moment seized out of time. Of time suspended. It's so elusive, the hardest thing to capture. And I haven't described it well at all, I'm afraid."

"No, you've caught it perfectly." He wanted to say that she had achieved it, too, in the painting of the swallow that he had seen in her secret studio. "Paintings are why I know flowers," Matt said. "Their symbolism, I mean. If you don't know that, you lose so much of what there is to find in paintings—" He almost said paintings of the period, but caught himself in time. "Why is it that of all things they have come to have so much meaning invested in them?"

"Pure beauty must have some meaning. Otherwise it's as frightening as pure evil."

Pure beauty, Matt thought, aware of Anna sitting so close to him, is a prism, refracting what lies within. It's that sense of time suspended of which she spoke—of what came before and what lies ahead and everything she is now. "They're not entirely of this world, that's true," Matt said. "They stand somewhere in between—a link, a connection to a larger world. Like the moment between sleeping and waking."

The youthful voice of Orlando was heard, echoing from the lower garden. He appeared, hair tousled and cheeks red, and ran over behind Anna, where he wedged himself into the hedge, his green coat blending in with the thick foliage. Cosimo burst through the hedge and slowed to a walk, coming up to Anna and Matt.

"Good morning, Contessa," he said.

"Good morning, Cosimo."

"Have you seen—" he began, but stopped as he heard Orlando, laughing, take off on the other side of the hedge. Cosimo followed like a flash, gravel spraying from his feet as he disappeared around the turn.

"An interesting man, this Matteo O'Brien, who is made up of all the things he is not," Anna said. "You know a haggard, and yet you don't hawk. You know the secrets of the Netherlandish painters well enough to say they aren't secrets, and yet you are not a painter. You know flowers better than my own gardener, and yet you are not yourself a gardener. Is there anything else you are not?"

"A husband," Matt replied.

"And you are not home. Do you have a home?"

"Who doesn't have a home?"

"And where is yours?"

"An island, far away. It would take a long time to get there."

"Tell me what it's like."

Matt considered where to begin. "Well, first of all—"

"Wait," Anna cut him off.

"Yes?"

"I have a better idea."

"And what might that be?"

"You're a master of poetry," Anna said, laying her hand on the book that he had forgotten was still in his hand. "Let me have one of your own poems. That's the best way to learn about a foreign land, wouldn't you agree?"

"But I'm not—"

"A poet, I know. Then if not one of your own, one from your own land."

Caught unprepared, Matt searched his mind for a poem. Ironic, he thought, that the only ones he had studied she would know also—Dante, Petrarch, Boccaccio, or the sonnets of Lorenzo Il Magnifico. But from his own land? Only one came to mind, from so long ago that he couldn't even remember memorizing it.

" ' 'Twas brillig,' " Matt said.

Anna waited for him to continue.

" ' 'Twas brillig,' " he said, " 'and the slithy toves/Did gyre and gimble in the wabe:/All mimsy were the borogoves...' " he continued, surprised as he reached the last line that he had remembered it all.

"What does it mean?" Anna asked.

"It means...It's kind of hard to find the words. Some things just can't be translated."

"I like it," she said. "It's amusing, in a funny way. Just the sound of it, regardless of what it means. You don't have a compresa."

"I do, I'm just not wearing it," Matt replied.

"And what is yours? A...borogove? Was that it?"

"It's a swallow."

"And what does that symbolize? Are you an authority on birds as well as flowers?"

"I only know what mine stands for. Love and friendship."

"I thought they stood for freedom," Anna said. "Have you ever—" She paused at the sound of boots crunching on the gravel path.

Leandro came up to them and bowed to Anna, followed by the slightest nod in Matt's direction.

"Leandro," Anna greeted him. "Any luck?"

"Luck?" he replied. "It was a hunt, not a game of cards. A fine stag. A clean shot. The dogs finished him off."

"Poor Actaeon," Matt said.

Anna laughed. Leandro gave Matt a penetrating stare.

"Have I ever...you were about to ask?" Matt asked.

"It's slipped my mind," Anna replied. "Is it time?" she

asked Leandro. "You will excuse us," she said to Matt, who bowed in response.

"'When she goes, all wreathed in herbs,'" Matt said aloud to himself, watching the two turn the corner and disappear behind the topiary giraffes. "'As if she hid a stone in the grass.'"

chapter 16

Painted over crushed azurite, the smallest amount of ultramarine
could be made to go a long way. The trick, Matt knew, was to
use it in glue size, even when the rest of the painting was done
in tempera or oil. That brought out the blue most vividly. The
irises would glow; Matt could see them already, in a majolica
vase. Copper resinate would work for the green, if he used it
right. It wasn't a stable color, fading over time to a deep reddish-
brown, but with green earth under it, the effect was wonderful.
Over black, as most of the Italian painters had done, it was a
disaster. But who cared about the effects of time? What
mattered was now, now when Anna would see it, when the color
was fresh and vibrant and as clear as a woodland pool.

What he really needed was the ultramarine. Anna wouldn't
miss it, he thought, the tiny amount that he had balanced on
the thin knife; and, he reminded himself as he carefully

dropped it into the tiny bottle, he wasn't taking it from her at all. He would be bringing it back in a finished painting. He stoppered the vial and slipped it into his pocket. Anything else as long as he was there? No. The panels were tempting; they took a week of arduous work to prepare—but he was going to paint on copper anyway. He had thought of using canvas, but what he intended was small, almost a miniature. It was for her only. And the depth of color, the luminosity of oil on copper— he could see it in his mind's eye, the flowers in the pot on the shelf against a white wall, by an unseen window. Chardin. But not Chardin; what he saw was not a painting, but three slender stalks, crossed, one blossom arched toward the window—which one? valor, wisdom, or faith?—the other two partly in shadow. He couldn't wait to take up the brushes, thick with paint, to feel them spread on the ground, a rainbow dissolved and reshaped into irises, a bouquet of molten color fixed in oil, lambent in the afternoon sun.

He paused for a quick glance at the swallow. It was closer to completion, the underbelly rounded, the fine feathers just suggested with the minute brushstrokes of tempera slowly built up coat after coat. The bird was coming alive, soaring against the sky. The clouds were still unfinished, more like puffs of whipped cream, with no sense yet of their weightless solidity. Not an easy thing to do, but Anna had gotten it in the earlier paintings; more so in the second than in the first.

Matt set the painting back down on the bench, tilted just as it had been left, and looked around to make sure he had left no trace of his visit. Aware of how late after midday it was getting, he hurried along the arcaded passage and into the church, anxious to be away before Anna might appear for her daily visit. Halfway up the nave he stopped, hearing the telltale creak of the door. The knife edge of sunlight widened into a whitened chasm that began to be slowly eroded by the eclipse of a shadow, a person still unseen. Without stopping to think, Matt dashed to the back of the nave, dodging around the side of the altar and into the welcoming black of the low doorway that led down to the basement of the old church. Struggling to hold his breath and slow the pounding of his heart, he strained to listen. He reached out to the wall to balance himself on the narrow steps that curved down into the dark, finding instead of a rough stone wall an oddly curved surface, smooth and round and cool under his fingers. Another was next to it, and another; a row of them, like newels on a banister, the size of melons. His hand strayed farther, finding a serrated edge. Teeth. And then next to it, the barest brush of warmth and fur that slipped away from his hand with an angry squeal and scrabble of tiny claws. A skull fell from the shelf, detonating on the steps like a ghostly grenade, but by the time it landed, Matt was already gone.

He tore back up into the nave, slipping on the slick stone floor and crashing into the wall. He braced himself with both hands, face against the cool stone, eyes closed. Rats; God, how he hated rats. That one had climbed up his arm, he had felt its claws. It might have bitten him. Rats. Huge medieval black ones, with coarse hair and yellow teeth and hatred in their beady red malevolent eyes. Who knew what kinds of terrible diseases they carried? He looked at his arm, examining it in the light. He was all right. It hadn't broken the skin. He would live. Heaving a sigh of relief, he stood away from the wall and turned around. Smothering another exclamation, he jumped back. Anna, with Francesca behind her, stood by the doorway to the cloister, her face wide with surprise.

"Rats," he said. "Nothing else down there, really. A catacomb. Skulls. Nothing of any interest."

The two women continued staring at him as though he had fallen out of a clear blue sky.

"I was told there were some frescoes by Masaccio here," he said.

"Down there?" Anna asked, looking at the narrow steps vanishing into the black.

"I took a wrong turn. I should probably be on my way," he added, and with a bow started to edge his way by the women. As he did, the vial of ultramarine, jostled free by his pell-mell rush into the wall, slipped from his pocket. Lightly, it fell to the stone, fracturing almost soundlessly into a tiny constellation of glittering shards and brilliant blue. The three of them looked at it, Francesca angling to see past Anna's wide skirt. Matt and Anna both looked up at the same time, their gazes meeting.

"It works best in a glue size," he said.

"It doesn't work at all there," she replied. "Come along," she added with a sigh. Matt followed, Francesca behind him, back through the arcaded cloister to her workshop. Anna took the small bottle of ultramarine and the thin spatula and handed them to Matt.

"Your questions about painting," he said, when he

returned with the bottle and put it down on the bench next to her. She was stirring one of the small bowls of tempera, the green liquid shining in the white ceramic dish. "They started me thinking. I haven't used a brush in a long time, and I thought I might give it a try."

"I thought you weren't an artist," she said.

"I had forgotten I was," he replied.

"Who told you about these supposed frescoes?" she asked. "I see," she added, seeing the quick glance he darted at Francesca. "Where were you intending to do your painting?" she asked.

"My room," Matt answered. "It's a very small picture. No one would notice."

"No," Anna said. "That won't do." She thought for a moment, stirring the paint. She wiped the stick and moved to the next dish, a paler green. "If you're going to paint, you had better do it here," she announced.

"But——" Francesca began.

"Thank you, Francesca," Anna said. "That will be all."

————

"Do you need something?" Anna asked the next day, looking up from the panel as she reached over to recharge her brush with a blue as pale as a robin's egg.

"Paper," Matt replied, looking around. "I wanted to do some drawings."

"Over there," Anna instructed him, pointing with the end of the brush to a chest against the wall.

"Second drawer," she said, her attention back on the panel as she quickly and deftly drew in highlights on the swallow's wings.

Matt, the upper drawer half open, was about to shut it when part of a drawing caught his eye. He pulled the drawer open all the way to see the rest of it, a series of quick sketches surrounding a finished study of an angel. Not just any angel, though, but the most famous of the Renaissance: Masaccio's guardian of Paradise from the Brancacci chapel in the Church of the Carmines in Florence. Sword in hand, he presided over the expulsion of Adam and Eve from the Garden, impassive as he watched the two grief-stricken figures leave.

"Did you find it?" Anna asked, glancing up again. "Next drawer," she said, and then, when Matt didn't answer, got up and went over to see what had so captured his attention.

"I'm sorry," he said, realizing she was standing by his side. "You did this? It's superb. I could have sworn that Masaccio had done it himself."

"He did. You flatter me, to think I could draw anything like that."

"But that's impossible," Matt replied. "None of his drawings have survived."

"These are his."

"I can't believe it," Matt said.

"I couldn't, either. It was only by the purest stroke of luck that I even heard about them. And then a lot of effort to track them down. It was the grandson of Masaccio's brother—"

"Lo Scheggio," Matt said. The Splinter, he was called; also

an artist, he had specialized in cassone and deschi da parto, the ceremonial plates commissioned to celebrate a birth.

"Yes. The grandson was an old drunk, a lawyer living in the most squalid circumstances. But he drove a hard bargain. I was not very good at disguising how much I wanted them."

Them. She had definitely used the plural. Matt, hardly daring to hope, held his breath as he lifted the drawing out of the drawer. He could scarcely believe his eyes. "The tribute money," he said.

"Have you seen it?" Anna asked.

"I've spent hours there," Matt said. "I wouldn't even be able to begin to count how many." Looking at the frescoes, drawing them himself—as had generations of artists who had made the pilgrimage to the chapel to see the amazing work that this young man was creating. Like nothing ever seen before; Masaccio had taken up where Giotto had left off. On the walls of that small chapel the Renaissance had been born.

"The Church of the Carmines was our parish church," Anna said. "I saw these paintings every day. The Brancacci were friends of my family's. Until Felice was banished, of course."

"The evangelists must still be there," Matt said. "On the ceiling. And the lunettes, of Christ walking on the water and the calling of Saint Peter, too."

"Well, of course," Anna said, slightly puzzled. "Why wouldn't they be? When were you last there?"

"Ten years ago, at least," Matt replied.

"I might have seen you," she said.

"Possibly," Matt said, thinking that ten years ago for him was five hundred years in the future for her. He lifted the drawing reverently, placing it on top of the cabinet. "Excellent," he said, seeing the one underneath.

"That one's mine."

"Yes, I know," he said. "You've really caught the feel of it." And she had—the neophyte, waiting his turn to be baptized, looking genuinely cold.

Anna shrugged, and hurried the drawing from view.

"No, I mean it. It's a way of seeing, and you have it, too. Why does that upset you?"

"He was a great artist."

"And that means you could never be one, too. I see. Oh, my God," he breathed, looking at the drawing that had been under hers. It was the expulsion itself. Adam, hands covering his face in remorse. And Eve. You could hear her anguished cry. Was it possible? He still couldn't believe it, but there was no doubt in his mind. Looking at the drawing, he knew that it was Masaccio's own study for the single most celebrated painting of the early Renaissance. Matt touched the paper. It was real enough.

"Those walls," Anna said, "is where I first saw the face of God. Did you know that Filippino is finishing them?" she added, as though embarrassed by her moment of unguarded candor.

"Someone once asked me where I would go if I knew I only had twenty-four hours to live," Matt replied. "There was no question in my mind. The Brancacci chapel, I replied right away, without any hesitation."

"Would you really?"

"I left the next day, anyway. Just to go see them. I know what you mean, about seeing the face of God." Matt glanced at her. "You know Filippino?" Fifty years after Masaccio's death, Filippino Lippi had begun work on completing the walls of the chapel.

"He did a Madonna for the chapel of our house," she replied. "It's very nice."

But not like this, Matt thought, looking at the drawing again.

"Nothing like this, of course," Anna said.

———————

A week later, Anna's painting was almost complete, and Matt's flowers were taking form on the small copper plate.

"What are you doing?" Anna asked.

"Darkening it," Matt replied, brushing over one of the stems of the flowers.

"But that's red, not black," she protested, leaning her hand on the bench as she stood next to him. The fine silk of her dress, a saffron yellow verging on orange, shimmered in the light from the high windows.

"Black will muddy it. It ends up looking dirty. Here, try it yourself," he said, and handing Anna the brush moved aside. She dipped it in the jar, freshening the paint and working it into the hair, shaping the point against the lip. The red glaze, transparent and shining, ran back into the jar. With a steady hand she began lightly dodging in the color, tiny strokes one after another.

"Not like that," Matt said. "May I?" He took the brush and leaned over in front of her. Anna stayed where she was, close enough that the loose folds of her dress brushed the side of his leg. He braced his weight on his left hand and lifted the brush, ready to lay it on the panel, and then paused, aware suddenly of her hand resting on his shoulder as she leaned forward to watch what he was doing. He thought of another day, a plane ascending into a gray sky to the sound of distant surf and a man standing just like that, leaning forward, his hand extended, balanced between two worlds. Matt, holding the brush, knew it was his to choose, that Anna's hand on his shoulder was a fulcrum between them, between one world and another. He could just ignore it, or he could look at her.

He barely had to move his head. Absorbed in the brush and the painting and what was about to happen, Anna was unaware of his glance. And there it was, that look of contemplation, as he had first seen her, when all he knew of her was the painting. How could it have seemed so complete? Within every world is another, he thought, all waiting to be discovered.

"Ready?" he asked.

Anna looked at him. A deep green, her eyes were like jade brushed with the finest vermilion lake. But so much more than that, he thought; no painter could ever capture what he saw, a world beyond naming. She nodded, and looked back at the painting. Her hand stayed on his shoulder.

The brush descended and with one long, fluid stroke he was done. "You see?" he said. "Oil is different. Long strokes."

"I can't wait to try it," Anna said, as they both stood up from the table. "I think I'll start the next one now." The panel that Matt had prepared of four pieces of Lombardy poplar carefully joined, with a knot filled and the surface primed with white lead, leaned against the wall at the edge of the table. Drawn in silverpoint, the composition was already laid out, the bird poised in midstroke against the clouds.

"But you have to finish the one you're working on," Matt said.

"I have to?" she asked. "Is that an order?"

"A request," Matt said. "But one heartfelt enough to carry the weight of an order."

"Why would you care if I finish it or not?"

"Thirty years from now when you look at it you'll wish you had."

"That?" Anna asked with a laugh, looking at her painting. "I sincerely doubt that thirty years from now I'll be looking at that."

"I will be."

"You? And how will you come to have it?"

"You'll give it to me."

"You expect me to give it to you? Isn't that being a bit forward?"

"You just said you didn't want it. I do."

"All right, then. I'll finish it." Anna picked up her own brush and added a drop of green to the white, stirring it in. "Why did you leave home?" she asked, as she began shading the underside of the clouds.

"There was no reason to stay," Matt replied, cleaning his brush of the red glaze. "Where did you get this yellow?" he asked, picking up one of the dishes arranged in front of her.

"It's just lead-tin," she said.

"This vivid? I don't believe it. Look at that," he said, tilting the dish so the color ran back and forth. "That's gorgeous."

"It's from a glassmaker in Murano."

"For glazing ceramics," Matt said.

"No. I stopped using that a while ago. The color's too weak and insipid. This is the one used in making glass."

"I wonder if it would work in oil."

"Why not try?"

"It would look great next to the ultramarine—"

"Do you mean the specially floor-cured ultramarine?" she asked, handing him a jar from the shelf.

"A secret I learned from Van Eyck," Matt said. He tapped some of the yellow powder onto the large glass plate used for grinding colors.

"How do you mean, there was nothing to keep you there?"

"My parents are dead, my sister has a family of her own."

"But it's your home. Don't you miss it?"

"No, not really." Saying it, Matt realized that he didn't miss it at all. The world he had left behind seemed completely unreal to him now, like a dream that some chance occurrence had brought to mind days later—it was now a world veiled in a mist that obscured everything but an occasional vivid detail, detached and curiously disproportionate.

"So you are rootless."

"I'm not a plant, so why would I have roots? I know, I know—another not," he said, hand raised before she could speak. "But human beings are equipped with feet, not roots. We were designed to be nomads. This idea of staying in one place is a recent invention." He began to add linseed oil to the color, the thick viscous liquid running from the slender bottle like cold honey. The straw-colored oil fell like the first big drops of rain from a coming storm, each one slightly flattening the mound of yellow powder before rolling down the side to melt slowly into the others. "There's too much of the world for me to feel attached to any one particular spot," he added, using the knife with a swift, casual back-and-forth stroke, as though he were buttering toast, to blend the two into an oily, lumpy paste.

Lifting the tip of the brush from the panel, Anna paused. "I want to see the Parthenon," she said. "I've been to Venice. A long time ago, when I was just a girl. I saw the doge toss his ring into the sea from the Bucentaur on Ascension Day. The Parthenon—someday. I can see it, almost as though I have already been there."

"I hope that you do. It's one of the few things you'll ever see that's more real than the way you imagine it. People talk about the music of the spheres. I don't know much about that, but I do know that seeing the moon rise over the Parthenon is the closest you will ever come to hearing it."

"And Alexandria, and the great pyramids, and the Nile. It would be so amazing! But at the same time I don't think I would ever be able to leave this behind. It's home. Funny, isn't it? Here, I long to see all those places I have heard about. Travelers come through, or traders from Florence or Venice, or someone like Kamal, and I can't get enough of the stories they tell. The wonders there are to be seen! I have heard of deserts wider than oceans and mountains so high no one has ever seen the top. But I know if I were there, I would dream of here. And

I'd miss it terribly. I can imagine all those places, and more, but the one thing I can't imagine is not having a home. Even the widest-roaming eagle has a nest somewhere."

"Then someday I'll find mine," Matt said. He picked up the muller, a heavy mushroom of glass with a flat bottom. Leaning over the tabletop, he moved it in slow, regular circles to grind the pigment finer and finer until it looked as though he were stirring a plate of liquid sunflowers. As he worked, he added the powdered glass he had pulverized in a mortar from the shards of a goblet from Murano. Lisl had shaken her head in exasperation at his insistence, but not just any glass would do; it was the leading in the crystal that he needed as a drier for the oil. Matt used the knife to gather up the thick paste, carefully scraping it into a jar that he then put next to the others.

"What led you to this?" Matt asked. He stretched, rolling his shoulders, trying to relax the bunched muscles. He had forgotten how physically taxing painting was; how much concentration and control it took to have the brush become an extension of his hand and eye, how much pure muscular exertion was involved in standing still, hour after hour. He picked up a piece of paper he had used to make a rough sketch of the flowers and idly began to fold it.

"The church hasn't been used in years, and I wanted the privacy."

"I meant painting," he said, creasing the paper in half. He made another fold, this one on the diagonal, and then a longer one, first one side and then the other. "It's not really—"

"Something ladies do?" Anna asked, finishing the sentence for him.

"Well, is it?"

"No, it isn't."

Matt shrugged, his attention on the paper. He made another fold and then looked up when it was apparent that she wasn't going to continue. "It's fine with me," he said, opening his hands. "I think it's wonderful."

"You're terribly open-minded," Anna said.

"Travel is broadening. Where I'm from, lots of women paint. I was just curious as to what led you to it." He looked at her, a sudden thought dawning on him. "You know, I don't think you realize how good you are."

"You think I'm good?"

"Are you serious?" Matt asked. He reached over and took the panel of the swallow and handed it to her. "This speaks for itself. You created it, but now it exists all on its own. What you think or I think makes no difference at all. Like the Parthenon. Does it matter what anyone thinks of it?"

"This isn't the Parthenon."

"It doesn't have to be. It's beautiful, Contessa. Madame. Your Excellence. It's a beautiful painting. And, like it or not, it no longer has anything to do with you. But I don't have to tell you that, you know it as full well as I do."

Matt picked up the folded paper and turned it inside out, made one last crease, and there: it was done. Holding up the paper airplane, he sighted along the wings and then launched it. With a smile of satisfaction he watched as the tiny aircraft, only inches long, turned its nose up and rose into a graceful loop before gliding to a rest on the worn flagstones, tilted over onto one narrow wing.

Anna put down her brush. She went over and picked up the airplane as gently as though it were a butterfly. Balancing it on the palm of her hand she looked at it, turning it this way and that. "It's wonderful," she said. "What do you call it?"

"The swallow," Matt said, looking at her painting.

"This is your swallow? Show me how to make it fly," she said.

Matt took the plane and, holding it gently between his thumb and forefinger, launched it into the air. Once again it lifted and rose before sailing back to the floor.

Anna picked it up. "Like this?" she asked.

"Almost. You have to balance it," Matt said. "Here, I'll show you." He took her hand and moved the plane slightly back. "There," he said. "Try it now."

With a quick movement Anna sent the plane aloft. They both watched as it looped, up and over and around, before finally curving to one side to land on the bench.

Matt picked up the plane and handed it to her. "Here," he said. "It's yours."

"Mine?" Anna asked. "Are you sure?"

"I made it for you," Matt said.

Anna placed it on the shelf, next to the paints. "Let me see your hand," she said, and then carefully unhooked the compresa from her dress. Without a word she placed it in Matt's open palm.

"I can't take this," Matt said.

"You gave me yours."

"Yes, but—"

Anna reached for the pin, but Matt stopped her, their

fingers barely touching, as weightless as the pin resting in the palm of his hand.

Francesca, out of sight, coughed.

"Yes, Francesca," Anna called out. "We have to go," she said to Matt.

"Anna," he said.

"Yes?"

"Just that."

Anna, smiling slightly, closed his hand around the pin. "You'll know when to wear it," she said, and in a swirl of yellow was gone.

Outside the door of the church, Matt paused, enjoying the heat of the sun, the weight of it on his face and shoulders, amazed to see that nothing had outwardly changed, that the church and the field and the three lone fig trees looked exactly the same.

chapter 17

Rodrigo held a sword in both hands, the point raised. Dressed in chain mail over a leather jerkin, helmet on, he faced his double across the open slate floor.

"Go," he commanded, and the two swords raised and then fell, the zing of the blades echoing off the suits that stood ranked against the wall in dumb witness to the match. The blades stopped as quickly as they had begun, and the two resumed their stance. "Again," Rodrigo ordered, and the quick pas de deux was repeated.

"Isn't it time for a break?" Matt asked, his voice slightly muffled and metallic behind the slitted visor of his helmet. "Aren't you thirsty? I'm sweating like a pig in here."

"Go!" Rodrigo snapped, and the blades again sang against each other. "You're still doing that thing with your wrist," he said. He dropped his sword and went over to stand next to him.

"Watch me," Rodrigo said. "No wrist." He went through the motion again, with Matt watching.

"We've been at it since dawn," Matt grumbled.

"You think I'm doing this for my own enjoyment?" Rodrigo asked with some exasperation. He unsnapped his visor and lifted the heavy helmet free of his head. His hair hung in wet locks around his forehead, a red line showing where the felt padding had supported the heavy steel. "Love comes with a heavy price," he said. "And the way you've been going about it, the bill is going to come due any day now."

"Who said anything about love?" Matt asked, taking off his own helmet. The air was almost deliciously cool after the suffocating closeness of the helmet.

Rodrigo snorted. "That's all you haven't done. Talk about it, thank God. Your demeanor has said enough. Luckily everyone thinks you're Irish, so this air of fatuous good cheer seems perfectly normal. The only other reason a person acts so benighted is if he fell off a horse and landed on his helmet."

"It's a good thing it won't ever happen to you," Matt said. "I can't even imagine what it would be like, a profound cynic in the throes of passion."

"Cynicism and profundity can't go together. It's an impossibility of nature, like a virgin in Rome."

Orlando, running by, came to a halt as he saw the two men dressed in armor, swords in their hands. He entered the room, followed by Cosimo, and went over to the racks of armor. "Let me try," he said, taking down his cuirass.

"Me, too," Cosimo piped up.

"You're too small," Orlando told him, cinching the buckles.

"That doesn't sound like a good host to me," Matt said. "What would Lucullus have to say?"

"We don't have any suits his size," Orlando said, taking down a sword as tall as he was.

"Wait a minute," Rodrigo said, laughing. "That's way too big for you."

A shadow filled the doorway. "Now this is the way to start the day," Leandro said, coming into the armory. He took the sword from Orlando, who surrendered it with reluctance. Leandro hefted the heavy steel in his hand, turning it from side to side to feel its balance, and then raised it up in both hands, as if readying an attack. He brought the blade down, the sharp edge slicing toward the exposed skin where Orlando's neck joined his collarbone. Matt, leaning forward to protest, stopped as Leandro slowed the blade inches from the boy's flesh, turning the blade sideways. Tapping him lightly with the blade, Leandro intoned, "I hereby make thee Sir Orlando." He looked up at Matt with a smile as bright and chilling as the winter sun reflecting off snow. "Shall we?" he asked.

"But you're not wearing any armor—" Matt protested.

"It's just practice," Leandro said.

Matt lifted his helmet to put it on.

"Don't worry about that," Leandro said. "We'll be careful. Just something to loosen up."

Matt put the helmet down. He raised his sword, holding it at the ready as Rodrigo had shown him. Leandro dropped his waist and flexed his legs, his thighs bunching under his black hose. He rose onto the balls of his feet. Matt, letting his opponent set the pace, braced himself for the first blow. It came like a gyrfalcon out of the sky, fierce and blindingly fast, leaving Matt's sword resonating in his hands like a bell hit by cannonshot. He fell back a step, warily watching the circling blade, flashing like lightning against a lowering black thunderhead. It struck again, a blur of silver that slammed his blade so hard his hands numbed from the vibration, making him use all his strength just to hold the sword up.

Eyes black and unblinking, Leandro moved with a sinuous ease, not even breathing hard, twitching the tip of his blade. Matt's followed sluggishly, like a fat bumblebee trying to chase a dragonfly. Leandro attacked again, slashing his sword hard against Matt's and then circling his blade in one quick, fluid motion. Matt's sword sprang from his numbed hands as though it had taken flight. It fell to the ground, the hilt banging and the blade bouncing with a dull, hollow echo. Unarmed, Matt stood helpless as the tip of Leandro's blade, blunt and flat and razor sharp, hovered in the air inches from his throat.

Leandro relaxed, standing up and dropping the blade. "That was fun," he said. "You should take a sword when you go out exploring in the afternoons. Or at least a crossbow. It can be dangerous to be in these woods unarmed. The wild boar can be ferocious." He hung the sword back up on the wall and left, ignoring the others as though they had ceased to exist.

"Your wrists," Rodrigo said with a weary patience. "Do you see why you have to keep them straight?"

———————

It was only after entering the coolness of the pine forest that Matt realized how strong the sun had gotten in the brief half hour it had taken them to climb the ridge behind the villa. The voices of the party rose and mingled under the hushed canopy, linking the small groups into a loosely strung necklace as they descended the path that wound down the gentle slope on the other side. The murmur of conversation and laughter was accompanied by the music of the band of sackbuts and trumpets that brought up the rear of the procession.

"A sylvan glade of Arcadian beauty, such as might have been frequented by Demeter," Tristano, the duke's poet, remarked, looking about with the proprietary air of a true artist in the midst of nature.

"Indeed," Matt replied.

"Laurel!" Tristano announced, leaning over to pluck a white blossom from a low branch as they passed. "Mortal victim of an immortal's desire!" he declaimed. "Perhaps even this very tree the one which encases her gentle heart. Ah, chaste virgin of an idyllic paradise, she would rather live as a tree than suffer herself to be profaned by even such a one as Apollo."

"Although one might ask if it is any better to spend the next hundred years or so having bits of you plucked off by the random admirer," Rodrigo said. "Or to have one's role in love reduced to providing shade for another's dalliance."

"What about Actaeon?" Matt interjected. "Talk about being in the wrong place at the wrong time. You go out hunting in the woods and you happen to see a woman bathing in a pool, and what happens? You get turned into a stag and eaten by your own dogs."

The splashing of a river, at first a distant murmur indistinguishable from the breeze soughing through the tops of the trees far overhead, had grown as they descended the hill. Loud enough now that Tristano had to raise his voice to declaim, the rushing water could at last be seen, sparkling and dancing under the sun as it coursed over the rocks. Ahead, a woman laughed; not Anna, Matt thought, but perhaps at something she had said.

The ground leveled, the path becoming springy under the soft soles of Matt's shoes. He ducked his head to avoid the low branches of a fig tree, white with blossoms, as they emerged from the wood into a meadow, bordered on the other side by a wide pool. Overhung by the drooping branches of hemlocks that rose up the steep bank on the other side, it was only partly in the sun, the surface unbroken but for the occasional tracks of water bugs. The river could be heard, out of sight in both directions, but in the small clearing it barely moved. The long grass, a bright green where it could be seen, was almost completely covered by carpets on which stools and tables had been set, with servants holding umbrellas over the ladies' heads to shield them from the sun. A pavilion of gaily striped linen had been erected by the deep pool where the wood ended, while on the other side of a clearing the band played a lively frotolla near a long trestle table on which platters heaped with food had been set out, framed by tall cornucopias of fresh fruit. Guests were gathered around, loading their brightly glazed majolica plates with bread and pale yellow cheese, joints of chicken and olives. Handed a goblet, Matt drank deeply, relishing the cool sparkling white wine, so fresh that it was like cider just beginning to turn hard.

The duke, standing with the emissary of the sultan, held

up his hand, and the music and animated buzz of conversation came to a halt. The group bowed their heads as Bonifacio, the rotund priest, intoned a brief prayer in Latin.

"Where is Virgil's cave?" Matt asked Rodrigo, looking around the meadow.

"Up there," Rodrigo replied, pointing halfway up the opposite ridge.

Matt craned his neck to look up. "Up there?"

"It offers a spectacular vista," Rodrigo said. "Or so I have been told. I have seen enough of Virgil's caves to know that they invariably offer a spectacular vista. Perhaps Calliope won't descend unless she finds a setting worthy of her presence. Or else, as with refining ore into metal, it requires a certain expenditure of physical energy to provide the heat for the creative process to occur. Considering how much Virgil had to write, it's no wonder he spent half his life scrambling up precipices. We might consider the converse as proof of this; indolence, and the concomitant lack of inspiration . . ." he said thoughtfully, his gaze resting on Tristano, who was regaling a small group backed so close to the bank of the pool they teetered as they nodded, their eyes vainly searching for some escape. "If you want to see for yourself, find Orlando," Rodrigo added. "He loves the climb."

"Let's eat," Matt said, spying Anna momentarily alone by the long table. Here, in a crowd, would be the perfect time to exchange a few words. With Rodrigo following he eased his way through the knots of people busily eating and talking. Anna appeared and disappeared from sight, her red damascene silk dress and yellow cape standing out like a rare flower in the lush tropical jungle of the other brilliantly resplendent costumes. She seemed to be aware of his approach, even though she never looked directly at him, for now that he was almost upon her she was turning in his direction as though some unspoken communication had passed between them to make their meeting seem casual and accidental. As he came up next to her he saw that she was talking to the priest, who had joined her. Francesca stood by, watchful and quiet, her eyes following the conversation. Bonifacio listened, his face working with the words he was rehearsing in his head like a troop of tumblers chafing to take the stage.

Matt bowed as he joined the group. "Contessa," he said.

"We were discussing angels," Anna said to him with a welcoming smile. "I was saying that sometimes during Father Bonifacio's services my mind wanders. I have noticed this to be true of everyone else at one time or another. It is not your words," she said to the priest, "which are of inestimable value and spoken with true poetry and clarity of insight. Rather, it is that the angels that surround us on the walls of the chapel are of such beauty that is beyond my power to ignore them."

"Gabriel," Matt suggested.

"Yes," Anna agreed. "Such an exquisite form, such an expression of beauty in his features. I find myself distracted from the word of God by the irresistible power of his beauty. How can these divine angels, messengers of God, lure us into the same transgression that the snake did in the Garden, to trade the contemplation of the divine for the profane gratifications of sensual beauty, no matter how elevated or refined?"

"The word of God is expressed in many ways," Bonifacio

replied, "and paintings are most certainly one. I myself have spent many hours in profound contemplation of the expulsion from the Garden."

Considering that the artist of the chapel had painted an Eve well worth sacrificing Paradise for, Matt wasn't surprised at the priest's devotion. Tristano, who had joined the group, cleared his throat and leaned forward. "Plato, as we know, spoke at great length about this very subject."

"Angels?" Rodrigo asked. "Plato spoke about angels?"

"The *Republic,*" Tristano said.

"I don't remember anything about angels in the *Republic.* He does talk about the cave, though. Are you sure it wasn't bats you had in mind?"

"He doesn't refer to them by name, of course."

"That's easy to understand, since there was no word for 'angel' in ancient Greek. Where does he mention them?"

"It's implicit in everything else he said," Tristano explained. "Ideal forms. The essence of fire. The shadows, when man steps out of the cave, are revealed to be cast by the sun. Sun is equivalent to God, and therefore we can see that the shadows, ipso facto, as a reflection of God, in their ideal form, are meant to be angels."

"Aristotle is much the better authority," Bonifacio interrupted, "if you wish to consult the ancients."

"Aristotle?" Rodrigo asked. "Are you saying that he saw angels?"

"Not angels per se. However, his reasoning succeeds where that of Plato falls sadly short. Thus: God—or Nature, to use his exact word, but God is what he meant by it."

"Whether he knew it or not," Rodrigo said.

"Precisely. God is perfect. Man, made by God, is perfect, even in his imperfections. Our sensory organs—to wit, our eyes and ears—were created by God to allow us to perceive the world in all its perfection. Behold, God said. And that is indeed the first cause of man, to behold the glory of God. Angels are an essential part of creation. Thus: we perceive them and they exist."

"They exist because we perceive them?"

"No. We exist because we perceive them."

"And as for you?" Anna asked Matt. "Are you an Aristotelian or a Platonist?"

"Must one choose?"

"Choose? No. Declare oneself? Definitely."

"Declare yourself, then."

"By all means, declare yourself," Leandro said, appearing at Anna's side from the crowd. Matt, startled at his sudden appearance, maintained his outward calm. So what if he was talking to Anna? It was up to her to decide with whom she conversed. Or upon whom she bestowed her affections, for that matter. Matt had every right to be there, as long as Anna wanted him to be.

"I'm neither one nor the other," Anna replied, inclining her head in return to Leandro's bow. "There is much truth in what each had to say. Plato, for example, believed that in the beginning all humans were complete. The gods, being gods, were so jealous of this perfection that they cleaved each one in half. And since then—ever since then—each of us has been left to search for our other half. And every now and again, in spite of the gods, you find this person."

"And how is that a truth, rather than a belief?" Leandro asked.

"Because it is so regardless of whether you believe in it or not. Like the Parthenon," Matt said.

"Indubitably," Tristano agreed, with an appreciative nod.

"How wonderful is philosophy," Leandro said, "to show us how a building is like true love. They are what they are, and therefore they are like each other. You must excuse us," he said, and before Anna could speak ushered her away, his hand on her arm.

"And I must eat," Rodrigo said, and excused himself.

Matt, joining him at the table, filled a plate.

"The Parthenon," Rodrigo said, as they went to stand in the shade of a tree at the edge of the clearing. "Are you crazy? When he's done with you they won't need a boat to take you across the river Styx. There'll be so little left a basket will do. Being in love is one thing, but being an idiot in love is something entirely different."

"Is it? What would you know about it?"

"As hard as it might be for you to believe, I am not a stranger to the sensation."

"I'm not talking about sensations. Love is more than lifting a dress on a summer morning."

"And what exactly do you mean by that?"

"I mean, being in love is many things, including being an idiot, but having fun is one thing and one thing only," Matt replied, watching Anna and Leandro move away through the crowd, followed by Francesca at a respectful distance.

"Take care, my friend."

"You take care of your affairs, and I'll take care of mine. At least I don't skulk about in the shadows, slinking from one assignation to the next. Jesus Christ!" Matt exclaimed as Rodrigo drove the tip of his knife deep into the bole of the tree next to Matt's head.

Bonifacio, hearing Matt cry out, looked around from the table where he was refilling his plate. Matt crossed himself, holding his own plate up as he did. Bonifacio bowed and went back to working a leg free from a roasted chicken.

"You're speaking about my wife," Rodrigo said.

"Your wife?"

"Of more than a year now."

"But..." Matt paused, at a loss for words. "Rodrigo, I had no idea. I'm sorry... I never..."

"Forget it."

"I'm sorry."

"Don't be so damned quick to jump to conclusions."

"No, of course not," Matt agreed. He worked the blade free from the tree and handed it back to Rodrigo. "Why the secrecy?"

Rodrigo, sheathing the knife at his belt, just shrugged.

"I mean if you're married—"

"Drop it."

"Wouldn't you want to be with her?"

"I have a wife."

"Yes, you just said—" Matt stopped. "Oh."

"She's in Spain. A harridan, worse than the Furies that drove Odysseus's men insane. There's nothing I can do about it. I left Spain, went to Naples, I've traveled halfway around the world. And then I met Francesca. The duke said he would exercise his influence to get me a divorce, but it's still going to cost a fortune, dealing with those damned bloodsuckers in Rome."

"The dye business," Matt said. "That's why you're so interested in it."

"You're not the only one with expensive plans. And speaking of which, the duke wants to talk to you."

The two men wove their way through the crowd toward Federico, who was standing near the bank of the pool engaged in conversation with Anna while Leandro stood nearby, listening to Kamal. Leandro, glancing at Rodrigo and Matt as they approached, made a brief comment to the Arab prince, who paused and gave them a quick look before resuming his conversation. As they drew closer the duke bowed, Anna taking her leave.

"Your Excellence," Matt greeted the duke, who fixed him with the penetrating stare of his one good eye.

"Have you had the opportunity to consider my proposal?" Federico asked.

"I would be honored, Your Excellence, to join you in this enterprise."

"What enterprise?" Leandro asked, turning to join the conversation.

"A dye manufacture," Rodrigo replied, and explained briefly what it entailed.

"Fascinating," Kamal interjected. "Where did you learn the process?" he said, addressing Matt.

"In the Netherlands," Matt replied.

"You have traveled widely, I gather." He paused, as though inviting Matt to respond. "You are a trader?" he continued, when Matt remained silent.

"I have a variety of interests," Matt said. "Some of which concern trade."

"What, in particular?"

"We are exploring the possibilities."

"We?"

"An association of firms interested in expanding trade and markets."

"Which bank is this?" the duke asked.

"Morgan."

"I haven't heard of it," Leandro said.

"It's out of London."

"And in Florence, their representative—"

The sharp crack of a breaking branch interrupted his words, followed immediately by a loud splash in the pool behind them.

"What was that?" someone asked in the shocked silence. They all turned to look at the river. There was nothing to be seen other than a large circle of waves, halfway to the bank, the center already still again. Something, though, was plowing down the hillside in a headlong rush, screened from their sight by the trees. A bear? A meteor shower of small rocks and branches that had been knocked loose pelted the surface of the pond. Leaves followed, settling gently on the water and then spinning like rudderless boats. Feet shot into view and then stopped as a pair of arms clung to an overhanging branch. Cosimo hung, terror in his face, staring at the water below him. "Orlando!" he cried.

Anna screamed. Like a kaleidoscope given a vicious twist the crowd collapsed, some rushing toward the pool, others shouting, most looking at each other as though not sure what to think. Matt dropped his goblet and raced to the bank. He stared across, shielding his eyes, but there was nothing to be seen. Hiding under the dark green branches of the hemlocks, the water was perfectly still, the leaves on the surface no longer spinning.

Matt stripped off his coat and tore his shirt free. He kicked off his boots and plowed headlong into the pool, gasping at the shock of the ice-cold water. After just two steps the bottom fell away from under his feet and he charged across with powerful strokes until he reached the point where Cosimo stood on the other bank, hanging onto a branch as he looked into the water. Matt took a deep breath and dove. Down and under, into the sudden silence as the light thinned, down in the aching cold to the bottom, to the sodden lump of cloth crumpled in the dead leaves. He seized the small body and tried to lift, but it resisted, the head flopping back, eyes closed. Matt grasped the shirt but the dead weight pulled him down like an anchor. Letting it take him down, he planted his feet on the bottom and jumped with all his strength. The limp body pulled at his arms, but at last it tore free and he held it against him as he fought upward to the growing light, his legs scissoring and his free arm pulling ahead. At last his head broke through the surface, water streaming away from his hair, running into his eyes and nose and mouth. Holding the boy, he took a huge gulp of air, and kicked for the bank.

His feet slipping on the mud and grass, Matt scrambled up the bank, dragging the lifeless body with him, the water staining the carpet. He shoved away the hands that tried to take the boy, fighting them off without thinking or even looking up. He laid Orlando on his side and probed his mouth for any obstructions before rolling him onto his back. Matt seized his coat, lying where he had dropped it on the carpet next to him, and shoved it under Orlando's shoulders. With one hand on the boy's chin and the other on his forehead, kneeling by his side, Matt tried to force air into the boy's lungs. Two deep breaths, and then he moved down by the boy's chest and, rising up to get as much leverage as he could, put one hand over the other on the unmoving chest and began to pump hard, hard enough to crack the tiny sternum, as though he could force the pulse back into him. Again and again, but the boy's face stayed slack, the skin blue, the gash on his forehead where he had struck the branch a dull red line. Matt stopped pumping, leaned down and blew two more deep breaths into Orlando's mouth, and then began pumping again. Hard, the small chest flexing under his hands, again and again, and then, in the deathly quiet, Orlando's eyelids fluttered. He coughed, as Matt kept pumping, and then coughed again, spluttering, and the whites of his eyes showed as his head rolled to the side. Matt stopped pumping and held the boy's face as he coughed, water running down his cheek, and then lifted him up against him, wrapping the coat around his cold body, massaging warmth and life back into him.

Matt yielded to Anna's hands, letting her take her son, still unconscious but breathing. He sat next to her, head in his hands, cross-legged, eyes closed, as Bonifacio knelt by them, his hand on the boy's head. The priest intoned a prayer as the hushed whispering of the crowd grew louder, now that they could see that Orlando was truly back among the living. Anxious suddenly to get away from the close crush into the open air where he could breathe again, Matt stumbled to his feet. The crowd parted around him, letting him pass, the people watching him in silent awe. The circle flowed back together as he collapsed again on the carpet, unnoticed. It had all happened so fast, and now it was over, and everything was back to the way it had been. The shadow of the hawk had come close, but it had missed, the great unseen bird of death swooping down on them out of nowhere and then vanishing as fast as it had appeared.

He didn't know how much time had passed when he felt a hand on his arm, warm and dry. He opened his eyes to find Anna kneeling by his side, her silk cape draped around the two of them like the wings of one of Fra Angelico's angels. "How are you?" she asked.

"I'm fine. How's Orlando?"

"He'll be all right," she answered, and then with a squeeze of his arm she was gone, easing back through the circle of onlookers. Matt, watching her go, saw that at the other side of the crowd Leandro was looking not at the boy or Anna but directly at him, unblinking, his eyes an empty black void.

chapter 18

Darkness held at bay by ranks of candles, the dining hall was a world apart, bounded by embroidered scenes of lost and requited love. In the soft play of shadow and light gold beckoned and jewels glowed, their fire unleashed, and laughter became the music of the night. This, Matt thought as he watched the lutenist launch the consort into a lilting galliard, is the golden voyage, and there is no other shore. There is no beginning and no end, there is only here and now.

Seated at the head table, Anna listened to the duke. Her cape, dark blue with stars and comets embroidered in gold, was turned back to reveal a gray dress, gathered at the bodice with silver braids. Leandro, on her other side, was also listening, his face carved into a smile. He leaned over, interrupting Anna with a question.

"No, it's past the ridge," Matt heard her reply as the music ended. "You've never been up there? The Belvedere Wood, we call it."

"Is it rocky?" Leandro asked.

"Yes," Anna replied.

"And is there underbrush?"

"It has never been cleared."

"A good place to look for boar."

"That's where Orlando saw the manticore," Cosimo announced.

"A manticore, boy?" the duke asked. Anna smiled, glancing at her son, as the rest of the company laughed.

Orlando shrugged and nodded.

"A stag, no doubt," Leandro said with an indulgent chuckle. "It's happened to me, too. You see movement in the distance. Quick, just like that," he said, snapping his fingers, "it's there and gone. I thought I'd cornered a lion once, in the hills near Ancona. I was young, too, Orlando, not much older than you. Too young for hunting lions, but what did I know then? The folly of youth. I know just how you feel, you can do anything. We have to get you a decent bow. There had been reports, some lambs missing, a large track found. I was deep in the forest, and I saw something move. I knew it was the lion. I tracked it all morning and into the afternoon. I don't mind admitting that I was scared, only a fool wouldn't have been, but that didn't stop me. I finally worked it into a defile, and thought to myself, I've got you now. I could hear it in the underbrush. It was huge. I closed in on it, slowly, very cautious"—he laughed—"you don't want to mess around with a lion, for God's sake—sorry, Father—and then finally got a clear sight of brown hide. Front shoulder, just for a second, but there was my chance. *Pfffft*, I let the arrow go—and I don't know who was more surprised. Pure luck, I'm the first to admit it, but I got him right through the heart. I knew I had. He dropped like a stone—but still I took my time. No hurry, it wasn't going anywhere. Finally I got a good look at what I'd been tracking all day, this lion of mine. And there it was. The biggest mountain goat I ever saw!" He barked out a laugh and drank from his cup, shaking his head.

The company also laughed. Orlando played with his eating knife.

"What about the lion?" Matt asked as the laughter died away.

"What lion?" Leandro replied, still chuckling.

"You got the goat, but the lion got away. I just wondered what happened to it. Did anyone ever catch it?"

"There was no lion."

"I must have misunderstood you. I thought you said there were reports of one, and missing lambs, and even a track."

"You heard right. Wolves, most likely."

"But you saw it yourself."

"It was a goat!"

"A goat doesn't look anything like a lion."

"That's right. We might make a hunter out of you yet."

"What did you see, Orlando?" Matt asked.

Orlando shrugged and didn't look up.

"You described it to me," Anna said. "Don't you remember?"

"Of course I remember," Orlando replied, and then fell silent again.

"I'd like to hear what it was you saw," Matt said.

"What he thought he saw," Leandro said.

"Orlando?" Matt asked.

"It was about the size of a horse. It had a body with fur like a lion, and green wings, and a scaly neck and long tail that ended in a point, like a pike. It had a dragon's head. It made this sound I'll never forget, just like a peacock. And it had claws. I could hear them on the rock."

"That's not a manticore," Tristano said. "A manticore has a human head on a lion's body and a tail tipped by a furry ball filled with darts. They don't have scales, and they most certainly don't have wings. What you saw was a griffin."

"A hippogriff, more likely," Bonifacio interjected. "They're more common to these parts."

"You see a lot of them around here?" Rodrigo asked.

"Me? No. I've never seen one. But Virgil mentions them several times."

"I see. Well, that makes sense. His cave would make an excellent vantage point for seeing anything in flight. Pheasants, doves, eagles. Hippogriffs."

"The race of griffins originated in your part of the world, I believe," Federico said to Kamal, seated next to Leandro at the head table.

"Yes, indeed. They were found in Scythia, where they guarded the gold mines against the depredations of the Arimaspians. But these were enormous animals, much larger than a horse. A griffin was quite capable of carrying off a team of oxen. I have seen the claw of one made into a drinking horn—it was easily as long as my arm. What you saw was more like the Simurg. Or the Senmurv, as some call it. That beast was half dog and half bird. It made its nest in the Tree of Life, and its seeds, which it scattered over the entire world, were a cure for evil."

"Orlando," Federico said. The boy looked up at him. "Your description sounds like the dragon that was slain on the island of Rhodes a century ago. That was also the size of a horse. And it had a dragon's head and wings."

"A serpent's head, I believe it was," Tristano said.

"Not a dragon's head?"

"No, a serpent's. But it did have wings. And claws, and scales, and a crocodile tail. But it had a mule's ears. Did your beast have mule's ears?"

"I don't think so," Orlando said. "No. I don't remember seeing any ears."

"It was not a dragon, then."

"It was a manticore," Orlando insisted. "It had a lion's body but the head and tail of a dragon, and green wings, and it made a sound like a peacock."

"That's not a manticore," Leandro said.

"It is where I come from," Matt said.

"And where might that be?" Kamal asked, as Leandro, expressionless, stared at Matt.

"You've seen one?" Federico asked.

"No."

"Has anyone else here seen a manticore?" Federico asked. The gathered company looked at each other, but no one responded. "Or a dragon? A griffin? What about a hippogriff, or a simurg? No? Well, then. Since Orlando's the only one who has ever actually laid eyes on a manticore, I would say he is the authority on the subject."

"On what he saw, perhaps, but not on what it was," Tristano objected. "I cannot call a giraffe a parrot because I have seen one and no one else has. Is not the name of something an inseparable part of the thing itself?"

"Are you saying that it does not exist until we name it?" Federico asked. "What would happen if we choose the wrong name? Does it then have a false existence?"

"But a manticore is well known," Leandro said.

"By whom?" Federico asked.

"History has innumerable accounts," Bonifacio said.

"People see many things," Anna said. "All very real. But some, I think, are more real than others."

Federico laughed. "If Orlando says that what he saw was a manticore, I believe him. How can we say he is wrong, if no one else has ever seen one?"

"I think we should find this creature and see for ourselves what it is like," Leandro said. "The Belvedere Wood, you say. You will come with us," he added, speaking to Matt.

"I'm not a hunter."

"But the chance to see a manticore? I don't know how a man with your varied interests could pass it up. It's settled, then. Tomorrow."

"Tomorrow, perhaps, but now it's late," Anna said, standing. The dinner over, the rest of the company rose as she left, soon to follow.

––––––––––

Luna da cacciatore, Matt thought, watching the huge orange moon descend westward, toward the horizon and somewhere far beyond the sleeping sea: the hunter's moon. How could something so huge pass so silently? he wondered, walking across the patio, the fountain throwing arcs of fractured silver into the dark. He was wide awake, even though the first slight paleness of dawn would before long begin to drain the color from the night.

"Do you hear it?" Anna's voice surprised him from the shadows. Sitting on a bench, she seemed to float on the soft night air, her cape merged with the dark.

"The music of the spheres?" he answered. "No. Do you?"

"Sometimes I think I do," she replied. "When it's late, and no one else is awake and the stars are brightest and it seems so close. But I think it's just my wishing that makes it so."

"I couldn't sleep," Matt said.

"I know," she said, the remoteness and formality in her voice saying more to him than words ever could. It couldn't be, Matt thought, and yet it was. Did he hear sadness, too? He wanted to think so. Anna stood up and walked past him to the marble balustrade that edged the patio. She looked out over the garden lying below, dark patterns sleeping in the moonlight. "I have enjoyed the time we spent together," she said.

"So have I," Matt said.

"You saved my son's life." She paused, as though she wanted to say more. "It's late. I must get to bed," she said, and turned to go.

"Anna," Matt said.

She stopped. "You have to understand," she said, her back to him. "I have obligations I cannot ignore."

Matt walked over to the balustrade and stood there long after she was gone. It hardly seemed possible. The gravel underfoot, the quiet splash of the fountain, the poplars, ghostly in the moonlight—it all seemed so real, as real as Anna, and yet she was gone. And there was nothing he could do or say; it was her world, not his. He began to walk, aimlessly, wherever his feet took him, across the patio and around the palazzo and then out of the courtyard, the moon following along with him on the other side of the sleeping fields of grain, slipping lower and lower, rushing to the horizon as though it had lost all interest in anything remaining behind in this world.

The woods, dark, led him forward, the trees emerging like forgotten memories in the watery light of the early dawn. Reaching the clearing, he could see the gray bulk of the old church rising out of the dull earth. It was still almost pitch-black inside, and he felt as much as saw his way along the nave to the cloister.

There were only a few details on the irises left to take care of; the highlights on the edge of the shelf, a touch of white on the blue petals. But he wanted to finish it. Matt worked quickly, with a few deft strokes of the brush, and then it was done, as it always happened, before he expected it. Ready to continue, he held the brush poised above the surface, only to realize that there was nothing left for him to say. The painting was complete. Like the silence heard when a piece of music ends, as full and rich as the notes themselves, it was a moment of repose, existing entirely within itself but encompassing the entire world, one that would last forever. Anna knows it, too, he thought; this is the world we share.

Matt stood up, stretching, and then laid the brush next to the painting, jewel-like in the richness of the copper and the lustrous paint. Yes, it was done. The painting was no longer his. He picked up Anna's painting of the swallow. This really is as good as anything I have ever seen, he thought. From any angle, the bird was alive, soaring, the clouds moving and changing. The colors, the texture, the fluidity of the brushwork—it was hard not to keep looking. He set the painting down on the shelf and went to the stack in the corner. Flipping through, he found the other two paintings and set them on the shelf. Lined up, the swallow took flight, swiftly ascending against the clouds from panel to panel. She'll paint another, he thought, and then another; and where will I be?

Matt reached up and took the small folded airplane from the shelf where she had placed it. He began to feel the weight of the hours pulling at him, the unbroken day settling like a heavy velvet cloak on his shoulders. It was time to go, past time to be gone. He put the airplane back and then, reaching inside his tunic, found the compresa Anna had given him. He took it out. Holding it in his hand, it seemed so small and insubstantial, so easily lost. He laid the irises mounted in gold on the table next to his painted ones and then, with a last look around, left.

Matt was halfway along the arched passage of the cloister when Anna turned the corner ahead of him. She was still in the gray dress she had been wearing at dinner the night before, with the cape folded back on her shoulders. Her hair was pulled back in a French knot, with curls on each side of her face, and she stood poised like a dancer in midturn, her hand lightly on the wall next to her.

"I couldn't leave it unfinished," Matt said, and stood aside as she passed, the two avoiding each other's gaze.

"Matteo."

About to turn the corner, he paused and looked back.

"Tell me again the three meanings of the iris," Anna said, from the archway into the studio.

"Valor, wisdom, and faith."

"And of those, which is the most important?" Anna walked up to him. She had the compresa in her hand. "I said you'd know when to put this on. How can you if you don't have it?"

Matt slipped the pin back in the inner pocket of his tunic and then took her by the arms, just above the elbows, feeling her pulse under his fingers, feeling how alive and light she was. As he bent to kiss her she rose up to meet him.

"I'll be late for the hunt," Matt said. Her hair, scented with lavender, was soft under his cheek as he held her close.

"Keep an eye on Orlando for me. This is his first real hunt. He'll be trying to impress everybody."

"Orlando's going?" Matt asked. "Was that Leandro's idea?"

"Yes," Anna replied. "Why? Is something wrong?"

"No, not at all. I'll have to hurry to catch them." He looked into her face, holding her by the arms. "There's something I want you to remember, no matter what happens. It's from the *Aeneid*."

"Are you going to start reciting poetry again?"

"No, it's just a phrase. 'Amor omnia vincit.' "

"Love conquers all."

"Yes. You'd remember that, wouldn't you? Amor omnia vincit."

"Yes, of course I would, but why?" she asked. "What might happen?"

"It's a hunt."

"Well, be careful then. And hurry back," she said, with a light kiss. "I want to start painting with the oils."

"You'll do fine," Matt said, and then he turned the corner and was gone.

The hunting party had already left by the time Matt got back to the villa. His horse saddled, he mounted, and with a sharp dig of his spurs was off, climbing up to the ridge above the house. Down the path, past Virgil's cave; Matt urged his mount on, galloping through the clearing where they had only the previous day had the picnic. The horse splashed through the rapids downstream, hooves striking hard on the rocks. Matt leaned forward as the powerful mare scrambled up the far bank and then pumped up the steep hill to the plateau high above. Far in the distance he heard the baying of hounds, the excited cries of men closing in on a kill. Left, right, leaning one way and then another he navigated the narrow path through the dense

laurel, white blooms like starfish in the cool green light filtering
down through the tall trees. Figures appeared in the
underbrush, glimpses of servants and beaters, dogs straining at
the leash.

Bursting into a clearing Matt's horse bucked and reared,
frightened by the flash of light on the flat blade of a sword
rising close to one side. He had the barest glimpse of a small
figure in a white coat laced with gold embroidery on the ground
holding his leg, bare flesh visible beneath the torn red hose.
"Orlando!" he cried out, fighting to control his horse, but the
reins twisted out of his grip and he was falling, motionless as
the black boles of the trees spun around him until he slammed
into the hard ground, unyielding beneath its thin layer of dead
leaves. Scrabbling to hold on to the earth that eluded his grasp,
he fought for breath. He braced himself up on his hands and
then staggered to his feet, the ground angling away from him.

The manticore, Matt thought, hearing a harsh cry like
a peacock above the frantic yelping of the dogs. Sensing
movement, he swung around and stopped, his eyes fixed on the
polished steel of a short sword, the blade angled up, the point
aimed at his sternum. Reaching for his own sword a flash of pain
lanced through his arm, dangling uselessly at his side. The point
of steel closed on him, at last gently coming to rest on his
doublet. Digging like a talon through his shirt it tested the soft
flesh, driving him back step by step until his back came to rest
against the broad, smooth trunk of a tree. The point stopped,
changed direction, lifted slowly up. Matt rose with it, breath
held.

Leandro came closer, head cocked, the point unyielding. With a swift swing of his free hand there was another point, cold and broad, the steel against Matt's cheek, an inch from his eye. Impaled on the exquisite needle of white pain in the center of his chest, breathing without moving, Matt felt the cool steel on his cheek.

"You don't belong here," Leandro whispered, holding Matt between twin points of steel. He stood the blade of the knife on end, poised, ready to thrust. "Do you?" Leandro murmured, leaning against Matt, the muscles of his thighs trapping him. Matt searched for Leandro's eyes in the black slit of the visor, but found only emptiness. "Do you?" Leandro shouted. He lifted the knife from Matt's face. Holding it straight out, he opened his hand, letting the weapon fall, and then jammed his hand under Matt's jaw, slamming his head into the trunk, gloved fingers digging in, choking, his other hand out of sight, still holding Matt pinioned on the sharp point of the sword.

Matt's scalp ground across the rough bark like a glacier creeping over stone as Leandro lifted him higher. Breath hissing through his clenched teeth Matt brought his leg up and jammed his knee as hard as he could into the unyielding leather. His fist glanced off the side of the helmet as his toes left the ground.

"I could put my hand right through you," Leandro said. "You're nothing but air." The light began to turn red and then darken to purple and then blue as Matt gasped for any breath at all. "Time to go back where you belong," he heard through the thickening air, the words followed by a laugh. As the blue turned to an oily black, closing in on him, sparkling with brilliant pinwheels of color, the laugh grew louder and louder, a raw chord that collapsed into the single note of the wolf tone. The terrible note sang through him, filling him with its harsh resonance, crowding out everything else but the endless vibration, suffocating him—

chapter 19

A woman in white. Matt, waking, was content to lie still and watch as she rearranged the flowers in a vase on the stainless steel table by the wall, humming a pretty tune under her breath. He drifted back to sleep, lulled by the steady movement of her hands while she shaped the rest of the blossoms into a pastel burst, purple and blue heads blossoming like languid fireworks from their long green arcs. Irises, he thought—

When he awoke again, it was to rainbows shimmering around a glowing blue star on the bare white wall. Matt turned his head on the starched pillowcase, finding the window. Framed in silver and hanging by an invisible cord, a glass sun glowed with the warm yellow rays of late afternoon. Blue in the center, its rays, curved like tongues of fire, were made of a prismatic glass that fractured the strong light into multicolored comets on the white wall. Tongues of fire. Where had he seen them before? Matt tried to think but was too tired, just the effort making him drift off to sleep again.

———————

"Well, look who's awake," the nurse said as she bustled into the room the next day.

"What happened?" Matt asked, his voice sounding strange to his own ears.

The nurse's laugh was as melodious as the tune she had been singing when Matt had first seen her. "Well, now, that seems to be the question of the day," she said, sorting the flowers in the vase again, pulling out the ones that had wilted overnight, their petals crumpled and brown as though scorched by fire. "You remember anything?"

Matt shook his head. The last thing he remembered was telling Charles he would be right back. At the press conference. But how had he ended up here?

"Nothing?"

Matt looked out the window. The sky, an empty blue, glowed like melting ice.

"I'm not surprised. You arrived here seriously concussed," the nurse said. "And with a dislocated shoulder. They said you fell, when they brought you over from the museum. Nervous exhaustion is what it says on your chart, and I believe it. You were dehydrated something awful, the next best thing to a pillar of salt. This water has got to go," she decided, holding the vase up to the light. "You've been working too hard, I'm willing to bet," she went on, going over to the sink in the corner. "Not taking care of yourself. Nobody does anymore. They're always worrying. And about what? Usually about working too hard, that's what. And look at you, so young. Makes no sense to me. But I have to wonder— What on earth!" she exclaimed. There had been a loud clink as the water had poured out. She put the vase down and searched the basin. "Now if that doesn't beat all," she said, holding up a glass rod the size of a breadstick. "Some people have a strange idea of a joke," she added, laying the rod down on the table next to the basin, and then filling the vase back up with water. "There," she said, standing back to admire her work, after she had replaced the flowers and arranged them to her liking. "They'll last another day or so. Now let me take a look at you."

Matt tilted his head this way and that as the nurse gently felt the bruises on his neck. Esperanza, her name tag said. Her hand felt cool and smooth.

"My, oh my," Esperanza said. "That must have been some fall. Looks like the floor tried to throttle you, too."

"I had a dream," Matt said. Cicadas, a stream, woods; drawings and a brush, loaded with paint, poised over a copper panel. Chardin—in his mind he saw a bowl with oranges. No, they were flowers, and not in a bowl but a majolica jug, a bright yellow and green under a glaze that shone where it caught the light from the window. Irises. Or was that because of the ones he had wakened to, here in the room? No, these were others. Blue, he saw blue—a tiny bit mounded on the end of a knife, so vivid and intense, like instant sky. Just add water. He glanced over at the vase.

"You had a dream, huh? You and everybody else," Esperanza said with a laugh. "Oh my," she exclaimed under her breath, as she opened his gown. "These ribs of yours. What'd you fall on, the New York Giants?"

"How long have I been here?" Matt asked.

"A week."

"A week?" It didn't seem possible. A week, gone from his life, and he had no memory of it. A complete blank, like the copper panel, primed and ready—primed, he thought. White. He could see it—covered in white lead, smooth and pristine, waiting for the underdrawing. How did he know it was copper? "Did anyone come to see me?" he asked, pulling himself away from his dream.

"Your boss has been in a few times. He calls every day. Such a nice man! And a girl called. All the way from Japan." Esperanza picked up the pad on the table next to the bed. "Sally Thorpe," she read aloud. "She left a message. 'Bill and I are thinking of you, glad to hear you'll be okay.' And she'll see you as soon as she gets back."

Bill? Matt, still too tired to think, had no idea what it meant, but he was glad to hear that Sally was all right. He turned his head sideways on the pillow. There was a postcard on the table, an old black-and-white photograph, that he could just see. Reaching for it, he gave an involuntary groan.

"Let me," Esperanza said, and handed him the card. A biplane rose from the sand, white wings against a gray sky.

Matt turned the card over. It was blank.

"That came with the flowers," Esperanza said. "The man who brought them didn't leave his name. He said he was an old friend. Is he a musician?"

"No."

"I thought maybe he was a rock star. He had that long hair. They're all getting so old. But then, who isn't?"

"Not you," Matt replied.

"Aren't you sweet. He also brought you that," she added, pointing to the prism hanging in the window.

"May I see it?" Matt asked, conscious again of the faint pull of recognition as she unhooked the ornament and handed it to him. A sun with curved tongues of fire, no bigger than his palm, it was made of leaded glass, like a pane from a stained glass window. The chain was silver, double links finely woven. Tongues of fire, silently burning. He had seen this sun before. The memory of where came to him—it had been in the studiolo, inlaid in the decorative borders of the panels. Federico, as a student in Venice, had joined a fraternity of young men who had taken the flame as their compresa, to represent the way they burned with love. A compresa. Light as it was, the prism grew too heavy for him to hold and he let it fall, still clasped in his hand, onto the white sheets.

chapter 20

Using the small brass key, Matt wound the clock. One last click and it was done, and he hung the key on its hook on the side of the delicate frame. He lowered the glass dome over the works, silencing the faint whir of the spinning gears, and then used the old polishing rag to remove any trace of smudges or fingerprints from the glass. Chin in hand and elbows on his raised knees, he sat, watching the tiny wheels winking in the fading light.

"Matt," Charles said from the door.

"Hello, Charles," Matt said, without turning.

"I have something you might like to see," Charles said, coming into the office. "Do you mind if I turn on the light?"

"Not at all."

Matt slid the clock back over to the side of the bench as Charles set a package down in front of him. Flat and rectangular, about the size of a large serving tray, the air courier and customs clearance stamps almost obscured the label. The Fleigander Foundation. It must be from Klein. Matt had tried calling him after he had gotten home from the hospital, but the phone had rung, unanswered. That hadn't come as a surprise, for he knew the scientist traveled frequently, and had homes elsewhere. Matt opened the thick cardboard lid and then the lighter one inside, under a layer of bubble wrap, and lifted out a painting from the foam bed it was nestled in.

A swallow, its wings arched, rose into the sky. The delicate gray of the bird, the pillowing eddies of the cloud and the reaches of empty blue beyond, all had the liquid depth of oil paints, layered and glazed. But on a panel, not canvas.

"Aren't you pleased?" Charles asked, as Matt studied the picture.

"It's very nice."

"Very nice? It's the missing painting, the one you said would be there. The series is complete."

"Yes, I know."

"Doesn't that mean anything to you?"

"It's good to have them all together."

"Good," Charles repeated. "Matt, I don't know what to say. You've been back for almost a month. And all you've done, as far as I know, is wind your clock. Have you even been up to see the portrait? No. I didn't think so."

Matt didn't know what to say either. That his dreams were more real than his waking life? That somehow he had fallen down in a small room only to wake up—where? Here? Everything was so familiar, so much exactly the same, but it was as though none of it really existed. Even Charles, standing next to him. He could have been painted by Paolo Uccello, Matt thought, looking at him. His beard had taken on the tone of the silver Paolo had used, tarnished to a dark gray by time, and his figure had the same ageless solidity, a study in perspective. But it isn't just Charles, he thought. It's everything. Like a painting in reverse, the world around him was slowly, almost imperceptibly, losing color and form. And what did he remember? Not falling down. Nothing. Except his dreams, and the problem with them was not remembering, but escaping them. They had all the color and the vividness, like the painting Charles was holding—

"Let me see that," Matt said, and took it out of Charles's hands. He turned it around to see the back. Verso paintings, usually of a family crest or motto, were commonly found on panel portraits of the Quattrocento, and this one was no different. Three irises were tied together by a silver ribbon, and on the ribbon in the rich blue of true ultramarine, three words were inscribed: "Amor omnia vincit."

Matt looked at the flowers. He touched one of them, the paint soft and ribbed with brushstrokes under his fingertip. It had been real. It had happened. They were memories, not dreams, and now, set free, they came flooding back, like the sun burning away the mist that morning, long ago in Gubbio. Like the sun rising over the ridge across from the villa. He saw Anna's hand, saw her loading the brush, rolling the tip in the paint, descending to the panel. He saw the studio in the cloister, and the church and the garden, and the fountain in the sunlight with the villa up above. He heard the water splashing, and her voice, and he remembered what it was she had asked him, the last time he had seen her. Valor, wisdom, and faith—which was the most important? He was holding the answer in his hands. Faith.

Matt thought of Anna, day after day bringing the painting to life, and then when it was done starting anew on the back, finishing where they had, with the three simple words he had asked her to remember. And she had, but it had been an empty victory, for he had never come back. He had never returned from the hunt. The hunt. A shadow, a blade silver and black, the world spinning and darkening, the sound of the wolf, shutting everything out—

Matt turned the painting face up. He could hear himself saying it, his last words to her, "You'll do fine," and he had been right. Her hand was unmistakable in the graceful arch of the bird as it reached skyward, in the delicate shading of the clouds. She had mastered the use of oils.

"So this came from Klein," Matt said.

"It's from the Fleigander Foundation in Prague."

"That's Klein."

"Klein who?"

"The foundation," Matt said. "You told me his family set it up, or something like that. Come on, Charles. Klein. He brought in the other painting."

"Which one?"

Matt laid the panel back in the box, careful to protect the verso painting, and went over to the wall where the series of birds hung. "This one," he said. "You were here when he brought it. You came in for the folder on the Duccio Diptych, remember? He was standing right here."

"We got that painting at Christie's East, last November," Charles said. "A phone bid, from my office. It barely made the reserve."

"Johannes Klein," Matt said. "He paid for the restoration of the studiolo."

"Which one? The pope's?"

"No."

"The one in Urbino, then."

"Ours. The one downstairs. From Gubbio."

Charles looked away, but not before Matt could see the sadness and concern on his face.

"No," Matt said. He leaped to his feet, his chair spinning away behind him, and then tore through the office and into the stairwell, taking the stairs two at a time, holding the banister as he spun in midair around the turn and sailed over the last three steps. Bursting through the door, he almost knocked over two visitors in his haste to get to the small gallery. Entering, he came to a dead halt.

A guard who had caught sight of him from another gallery ran up, seizing his arm. "Hold on, sir. Mr. O'Brien," he said, seeing who he was. "Can I help you?"

"There's nothing there." Matt, shaking his arm free, walked up to the bare white plaster of the empty wall. No pilasters, no heavy carved oak doors, no elaborate lintel with the Garter incised in it . . .

"Sir . . ."

Matt stepped backward slowly. Anna. He turned and ran from the room, the guard following to the door and then taking out his radio. The crowd of schoolchildren in the hall of armor scurried out of Matt's way like pigeons on the sidewalk outside. Up the stairs, through the musical instruments, past the silent keyboards, and then through the galleries one after another until he reached the one he was looking for. Panting from the exertion, he stopped in the doorway. Anna. She was still there. He leaned against the wall, almost overcome by the wave of relief sweeping through him, and held up his hand to the two guards who rushed up to him, their belts jingling and radios squawking.

"I'm fine," he said. "It's nothing."

How many times had he seen her just like this? Her face was turned toward a small group of viewers, their backs to him as they intently read the lengthy posting on the wall next to her, and he thought of how he had once come upon her, greeting some friends of her husband from Venice, on their way to Rome.

Matt left. He pushed through the tall glass doors and stood at the top of the broad steps of the museum. Fifth Avenue stretched before him, the dark buildings rising into the mist and the rain. So he had gone back. It had not been a dream after all. And neither had been the studiolo. He remembered it perfectly, could see it, could see himself standing in it. Something had happened, he didn't know what, but there was no denying that he had stood in it. And the feel of the sun—the real Umbrian sun—he could feel it warming the back of his hand, molding the veins and lines into a map of the new world. "Ercole . . ." He could hear the voice, hear the hooves down below on the paving stones, echoing up. And then he had opened the door and stepped out into the library. The library of the grand duke Federico da Montefeltro— Klein. Klein would know. He might have vanished from Charles's mind, but he existed for Matt, every bit as real as the studiolo. But the studiolo was gone—

"Excuse me."

Matt glanced up to see a man approaching, his large, friendly face apologetic. Behind him Matt could see his family, smiling. After five years in New York, Matt recognized the look; they'd spotted a celebrity. He looked around to see who it was.

"I'm sorry to bother you," the man said to him.

Matt looked at him in complete surprise.

"You're the guy..." The man unfolded the magazine he carried in his hand and offered it to Matt, who saw his own face under a larger image of Anna, next to the headline LOST AND FOUND. "We just want you to know how impressed we are." Matt found his hand being shaken as a camera clicked, a flash of brightness in the gray rain. "Would you mind?" he asked, holding out a pen.

Feeling slightly ridiculous, Matt took the pen. A couple walking up to the doors gave him a quick glance, trying to place him, turning the ridiculous into the absurd. Matt folded the magazine and, about to scribble his signature, stopped, thought, and then wrote a brief inscription before handing the magazine and pen back.

"Amor omnia vincit," the man read aloud.

"What does that mean?" one of the children asked.

"Vincit," his father said. "Da Vinci. It's something about Leonardo," he added, looking at Matt for corroboration.

"He's right," Matt said. And he was, Matt thought, walking down the steps, although not in the way he had meant. There were many ways to be right. The quote was from the *Aeneid*, but Leonardo, in trying out a new quill, had inscribed the saying many times in the upper corner of his notebooks. Tell me if anything's been done, he also wrote, late in his life. Tell me if anything's been done. I'll find Klein, Matt thought. And I will return from the hunt.

chapter 21

Out of the subway, one block south, down the hill—how many times had he walked the same route? Rounding the corner the river came into view, dull gray under the overcast sky, with New Jersey beyond it, the color of car exhaust. Flanked by weathered granite, the stark simplicity of Klein's apartment house stood out like a destroyer among a fleet of ocean liners, mothballed at the end of the great age of ocean travel. The lobby, sleek mirrored glass and travertine marble polished to a high gloss, was reassuringly familiar to Matt.

"I'm here to see Dr. Klein," Matt said to the doorman, whom he recognized from his previous visits. What was his name? He tried to remember. "Is he in?"

"Who?"

"Klein. Seventeen F, the penthouse."

"You've got the wrong address."

"Klein," Matt repeated. "Seventeen F."

"No one here by that name."

"That's impossible," Matt said. "I was here just a few weeks ago. He must have just moved, then," Matt said, when the doorman didn't respond. "Can you give me his forwarding address? Dr. Johannes Klein."

"You'll have to talk to the building manager."

"Fine."

"He's not here."

"Is there a number where I can reach him, then?"

"Yeah. Hang on." The man went to the small office. Matt followed, waiting in the door as the man wrote down the information.

"Where did you get that picture?" Matt asked.

"Which one?" the man replied, looking up at the wall. The biplane rose from the sand, watched by a solitary figure, leaning forward with his hand extended. "It's always been there, as far as I know."

"I'll buy it," Matt said, taking out his wallet. "Here." He held out all the money he had.

"Get out of here," the man said. "Are you nuts?"

"Look, two hundred dollars," Matt said, counting the bills. "It's just a photograph. You didn't even know it was there. Who's going to miss it?"

The man hesitated and then took the bills.

Matt took the picture down. It was from Klein's apartment. He remembered the frame, thinking of it hanging in the hallway, next to the soldier from the Spanish Civil War and the strange series of shapes, the Faraday salt print.

"You don't remember me, do you?" he asked at the entrance on his way out.

"No. Hey..." the man added.

Matt, walking away, turned around.

"There is no Seventeen F. The building stops at sixteen."

———————

On the second floor of the ducal palace in Gubbio, in the southeast corner, was a small irregularly shaped room, barely larger than a closet. Matt had seen it, stood in it, taken a quick glance around the bare walls. The terrazzo floor was all that remained of the studiolo, but the room was still there, as it was on the floor plan of the palazzo now displayed on his computer screen. Matt opened the scan he had taken from a text on physics. It was the same series of twelve shapes he had seen in Klein's apartment, the early salt print of the Faraday magnetic fields of disturbance. The sixth was the one he wanted, halfway down the page. Faraday, Klein had answered when Matt had asked him who, in physics, had had the same transformational impact as the use of oils in Quattrocento painting. He could see the print hanging on the wall, next to two men, one watching an airplane balanced between two worlds, the other at the moment of death. Transformations and force fields. And a series of paintings, from tempera to oil.

Matt traced around the irregular shape and then, having cut it free, pulled it across the floor plan of the palazzo. After a brief moment of double image, it disappeared, merging with the outline of the room that had held the studiolo, leaving the spiky fringe he had noticed when he had first seen the photograph of the shapes in Klein's apartment. He knew, from the text, that it was made by iron filings on paper, showing the force fields of the magnets underneath. Remembering the vibration he had felt deep inside, just before the sound of the wolf tone and his losing consciousness, he wondered if that was why Klein had restored the room, to re-create the force field. It couldn't have been just to see it—Charles would have gladly showed him the stored panels.

A field, but generated how? It couldn't have been from the ground, some source deep within the steep hillside under the palazzo, for Matt had felt it resonate through him standing on the main floor of the Metropolitan Museum, on the other side of the globe from Gubbio. It had to be the panels. But, again, how? He had seen them laid bare on the workshop tables. The room was nothing more than wooden panels, glued together and held in place by nails. Iron nails, he thought. Hand-forged, thousands of them. Square, with flat heads, each one bearing the marks of a hammer. And he could see as though it were only yesterday Charles reaching for one and all of them rising from the box, clinging together like blue crabs tangled in a basket— magnetized.

But enough to create a magnetic field? The vibration he had felt had been overwhelming, like being hit by a wave. A wave, he thought, remembering Klein looking at the series of swallows—quantum birds, he had said; a bird in the sky, like the collapse of a quantum wave. But nails, even thousands of them, wouldn't be enough to create an effect like that. What else, then? Matt thought hard, drumming his fingers on the keyboard, but nothing came to him. Frustrated, he got up from the computer. He picked up the snow dome and shook it, the clown holding out his arms like a trapeze artist during an earthquake, his world suddenly topsy-turvy.

"What do you think, buster?" Matt asked. "Maybe it really was exhaustion. Maybe it was all just a dream."

Beats me, the clown seemed to reply, his arms wide; your guess is as good as mine. The red stars glowed on his cheeks, his bright yellow coat shone merrily. Matt set him down. The drifting notes coruscated in a rainbow of colors. Colors, Matt thought. Wood. Nails are magnetic, glue is a conductor, that leaves wood. Electric wood? Impossible. He felt like the notes, drifting aimlessly in the tiny world of the glass globe. Red and yellow, green and blue, a blizzard of color.

Colors. Minute pieces of wood, tens of thousands of them. All of them dyed, arranged in patterns. Charles had been very particular to analyze the dyes and re-create them as closely as possible for the replacement pieces. Matt had helped in the complex process. The source of the color, chopped roots or beets or even just straw, was boiled with water. The wood was boiled, too, but with lye to make it more receptive to the dye. Shaving soap, usually. And then came the most important part, fixing the color to the wood. A mordant was necessary for that, like flux in soldering. Zinc or tin chloride, or chrome, or ferric acetate—metal salts, chemists called them. And Faraday had already established himself as the leading chemist of the day when a friend had asked him to write an article on magnetism, turning his attention to physics.

Matt had used them all, the mordants known to dyers since ancient times. With gloves, for they were as corrosive, some of them, as acid. Acid and base, he thought. Metal salts carried heavy electrical charges. Alternating colors, alternating charges. Faraday's greatest discovery had been electromagnetism.

Magnetism in the nails, glue as a conductor, and wood electrically charged. The panels had been batteries.

And? So what? His elation quickly faded. It was still not enough. A battery was not an engine. Like a magnet, it was a force field, but a latent one. And the force that moved through him had been dynamic.

Something was still missing. What was it? There was something else, something hovering in the shadows just beyond the edge of memory. He closed his eyes and thought back to the day of the press conference. He had left and entered the studiolo. Walked around. There had been the drone of Petrocelli's amplified voice. The soft, barely felt whisper of the circulating air. He had reached the longer wall, was approaching the Garter and the vanishing point. His shadow had moved across the wall, finding the black circle of the inlaid shadow of the Garter. The vibration had begun, a slight tingle not in his feet but in his bones. Like an approaching train, sensed before heard, it had grown, swelled, thrilling through him, finally merging with the harsh dissonance of the amplified drone into the note, the wolf tone— And that was the last he remembered.

No. He had again missed something important. Back. Walking: the wall, the vanishing point, his shadow sliding along the wall . . .

The shadow, in front of him, and behind him . . .

Light. He had felt it, as faint as the touch of the

circulating air, on the back of his neck. Not from the window in the nook, which was the studiolo's main source of illumination, but a shaft of light from the high clerestory window. Not as strong as the Umbrian sun, but light nonetheless. Through a pane of glass.

The index of refraction, Matt thought. Was that what Klein had been trying to tell him with the glass rod? In his most famous experiment, Faraday had passed a beam of light through glass with a high index of refraction and discovered diamagnetism. A dynamic source of energy, light, interacting with a latent one, the electromagnetic field created by the intarsia and the nails. A force field.

The light hadn't been weak, though. Matt raised his right hand, studied it, turned it back and forth. I held it just like this, he remembered. When the wolf tone had stopped, when silence had flowed back into the studiolo, when the only sound was that of the dust drifting noiselessly through the square shaft of afternoon sun coming through the high clerestory window behind him, he had lifted his hand into the light. Feeling the weight of the sunlight, and the warmth as he turned it, he watched the shadows of the veins and the tendons, the creases of his fingers, the deep lines across his palm as it filled with light, spilling over the edge. From somewhere outside the open window there had come the regular clip-clop of horseshoes on paving stones, and then a high whinny. "Ercole," a voice had called from far below.

chapter 22

The blade, motionless, extended in front of Matt like a reflection of the moon rising over still water. Eyes fixed on the unwavering tip, he kept his breathing regular and deep, only the rigid muscles in his arms and shoulders betraying the strain of holding up the long broadsword. As the afternoon light faded into dusk, shadows grew and settled on the derelict equipment and unfinished projects left stacked around the walls of the old loft by the former tenant, a welder of abstract sculptures and heroin addict who had locked the door one day and never returned. Matt, when the landlord had said that it would be his responsibility to clear the junk out, hadn't told him that that was one of the main reasons he was taking the space. He had felt an immediate refuge in the abandoned world, with its air of time suspended, where only the shadows were alive.

"Forty-eight, forty-nine, fifty," Matt counted aloud, and

then slowly lowered the broad tip until it touched the rough concrete floor. He relaxed his shoulders, rotating them like a gymnast, and bent forward, leaning his forehead on the braided steel of the hilt, warm from his hands. It might not work; it might never work. He felt like a blind man trying to grope his way out of a maze. But at least now he knew that there was a way out. Anna had told him so. She had sent him a message of faith.

Matt, sifting through the detritus that had been left in the loft, accidentally bumped into a rusty steel bar leaning against an old lathe in the corner. Toppling to the floor, it had rung with a tone that resonated through him, a ghost of the last thing he had heard standing in the studiolo, and then again in the spinning shadow world of the forest. The wolf tone.

Hanging the bar from a hook in the ceiling, Matt found himself time and again in the next few days standing in front of it and tapping it. As he felt the vibration enter him he just let the vague image in his mind grow and develop of its own volition without trying to force it along. He knew he could read about Faraday and all the rest of the history of physics, but that would not get him a single step closer to understanding how he had gotten from a room in the museum to a world that somehow existed—where? In the past? Within the room itself? He was not a scientist, and never would be. From his reading, though, it became clear that there was only one fundamental law in nature, and that was that nothing was unique. In fact, no phenomenon or event he read about was accepted as being true until it had been reproduced. It was simple logic, then; he knew that what had happened to him really had happened—Anna had sent him the proof of that. Therefore, all he had to do was reproduce the conditions, and it would happen again. It didn't matter if he understood it or not. The studiolo might be gone, but what had it been? A set of conditions, and they could be reproduced.

The image in his mind at last resolving into a definite idea, Matt had set to work with increasing determination and sense of purpose until he was stopping only to eat or snatch a few hours' sleep when he could no longer stave off the need. And now it was ready, and so was he, if his plan worked as he hoped. The time had come.

Matt straightened up, raising his head from the hilt of the sword. He flipped a switch at the side of the door into the enclosure he had built out of plywood to the exact dimensions of the vanished studiolo, as he had taken them from the floor plan of the ducal palace, and then walked in and stopped on the exact spot where the orthogonals had once converged on the shadow of the Garter. The vanishing point. He stared at the wall, covered in squares of paper he had printed out, an image pixilated to the point that it was more an intimation—a wave not yet collapsed, made real, fixed in time. Vibration, Klein had told him; everything is vibration, a continuum that bridged the seen and invisible, the heard and the unheard, the known world and the infinitely vast cosmos of matter and energy, of which time was only one aspect, like the shading Anna had added to give the clouds substance and weight, to make them real.

Matt had quickly abandoned the idea of trying to re-create the intricate patterns and images of the original walls, knowing he would never be able to remember them in enough detail to be convincing. By the time the walls were built and he was ready to finish them with an image, the choice of what to use was clear; like the solution to an equation, there was an inevitability to it, as though it existed before the problem did. He had taken a scan of a painting of the swallow—he had chosen the one Anna had done for him, the one in oil on panel—and, having enlarged it on his computer, printed it out square by square to reassemble on the wall.

Clearing his mind, Matt stared at the wall. He felt the back of his neck grow warm from the August sun shining through the carefully cleaned part of the window, high up, that he had left uncovered when he had masked all the rest. It was like the hand of a friend, resting on his shoulders, telling him not to give up; a reminder that he was finding not a way out but a way back.

The timer ran down and the vibration began, generated through the walls and the floor by the induction transmitter Matt had attached to the steel bar. It slowly grew, climbing through Matt, branching out and suffusing him like water drawn up through a tree, and as it did, it slowly dropped in pitch, reaching its maximum intensity just as it found the frequency of the wolf tone. Matt, resisting the impulse to tighten up in anticipation, in hope or fear, forced himself to relax and let go, to let the vibration surge through him, as he focused on the suggestion of motion on the wall, of wings seen and not seen, of clouds there and not there.

Nothing. Matt felt the sun slip from his neck, the

vibration fade like a sunset, the warmth disappear. The image in front of him became a random collection of squares. It hadn't worked. He slowly walked out of the room, trying to rally himself from the disappointment that had taken the place of the vibration. He picked up the sword again, telling himself it would work, that he would find a way, and when he did, he would be ready. But his mind rebelled. Now, he thought, now, not tomorrow. There is no tomorrow, no future, there is no time to lose, nothing to wait for—and as the anger surged through him he lifted the sword and slashed at the bar again and again, taking a savage pleasure in watching it jump until it was thrumming with the blows. The wolf tone awoke, low at first, then growling louder and louder as he attacked, throwing every ounce of his strength into each vicious stroke, as though with each one he could cut the bar in two and force his way out of the shadowed limbo to the place he belonged. Again and again, harder and harder, until with one last terrible blow he staggered back, exhausted, the heavy tip dragging a pale line on the scuffed wooden floor.

Unaware, he bumped into a pedestal, turning just in time to see the old jar rock back and forth in slow motion and then, teetering on edge, topple over, sailing through the air to smash on the floor. The irises lay in a tumbled pile, their petals glistening blue and yellow in the light of the lamp and the last rays of the setting sun. Serves you right, he told himself, all his anger spent, and put the sword down to pick the flowers out of the water and broken glass. A pile of books between the pedestal and the old chair had also fallen over and now lay scattered in the puddle of water. He knelt down, taking the top one and brushing the water off the cover. Seeing they had all gotten wet, he grabbed an old shirt to wipe them dry.

He stopped, hand raised with the crumpled shirt in it, feeling a faint stir of air against his face. Suddenly alert, he focused all his senses. There, by the door—the scrape of leather on the floor. He stared into the concealing darkness. A shadow moved. Leandro, he thought, it had worked after all! With a convulsive lunge he kicked the books and flowers away, grabbing for the sword, scrambling to gain his footing in the slippery wetness.

"Matt?" Sally asked, coming forward into the fading light. "Are you . . ." Her voice trailed off as she stared at him.

Matt stopped, half up and half down, on one knee like a Knight Templar caught in his devotions. He began to laugh. The sword dropped with a clang as he settled back onto the floor, laughing even harder. "It's okay," he said. "I decided to be an artist. It's what you always said I should do."

"This isn't exactly what I had in mind," she said, awkwardly walking past him to look at the enclosure he had built. "You've let your hair grow," she said, coming back to him. "I like it."

"It's good to see you," Matt said, seeing from her belly, big and rounded under her open coat, why she was walking so heavily. On her finger was a gold ring.

"Charles called, he was worried about you. He said he hasn't seen you for over a week, and thought I might know where you were. I meant to call you when I got back from Japan, but I've been so busy, and my leave starts next week. There's just so much to get done before then."

"How did you find me?"

"Credit card."

"What?" he asked.

She shrugged. "Okay, so it wasn't strictly legal. A friend in our research department owed me a favor. He ran a check on you. So that's what you wanted all that plywood for. Twenty bucks, the delivery guy was almost willing to carry me up here."

"You're in the wrong line of work," he said.

"What do you mean? That's just called due diligence. I do it all the time, just not usually in East New York. You should keep the door locked, you know. It was wide open. Anyone could have walked in."

"So how are you, Sally?" Matt asked, turning back to the mess on the floor.

"I'm fine. What happened?"

"I lost my balance," Matt said. "Here," he added, handing her an iris. "Time is a flower."

"Oh, bullshit," she said. "The last of the romantics. You'll never change. Let me help." She picked up the rest of the flowers and then, looking around, found an old can to put them in. "Are you living here?" she asked, adding water from the tap of the tiny sink, heavily frescoed in splattered paint and resin.

"I've been working," Matt answered.

"On what?"

Matt didn't reply. He was looking at a book he had picked up that had landed facedown and splayed open when the pile had fallen over.

"What is it?" Sally asked. "Matt!" she pushed his shoulder.

"Sorry?" he asked, looking up. "Nothing. Just a picture."

Sally looked over his shoulder. "What is that? Some guys playing miniature golf? What kind of book is this?" She flipped to the cover, the book still in Matt's hands. *"The Copenhagen Group and Quantum Physics,"* she read aloud. "Jesus. Something light, to while away the time, huh? Isn't that Einstein?"

"Looks like him," Matt replied. A row of men in three-piece suits grinned up from the page, brandishing their putting irons like weapons of valor from days gone by. One of the men had a mustache and short hair, famously tousled but still jet black. "That one on the left watching the rest play is Heisenberg," he said, reading the caption. "Then Pauli, Bohr, and Gamow." He fell silent again.

"Matt?" Sally nudged him.

"I'd better get back to work," he said.

"Me, too, I guess. Well, I'm glad to see you're all right. I'll let Charles know."

"Sally," Matt said. "Take care."

"You, too."

Matt watched her go, thinking that he would never see her again, and wondering who it was she saw when she looked at him, what past they shared that he didn't even know about. He sat down and began to read the book he had found. Hours later, when he had finished, he looked back at the photograph. Einstein, Pauli, Gamow, most of all Bohr and Heisenberg: the men who had invented quantum mechanics. But there were two others in the background, unidentified. One, with the fresh, open face of a student, bore a striking resemblance to Kamal, as he might have looked, very young, and without a beard. It was the other one, though, that had stopped Matt. Almost hidden in the shadow behind the solid, phlegmatic presence of Bohr, in half-profile and slightly blurred as though he had been moving—still, there was no mistaking who it was. Klein. Klein, as Matt had known him, not a day older or younger.

chapter 23

Matt, waiting in line to pass through the metal detector at the
departure gate of the American Airlines terminal at Kennedy
Airport, thought about the encounter that had led him to be
boarding a plane to Istanbul instead of Prague. The photograph
in the book had taken him to its author and a Princeton
laboratory tucked into grounds so well groomed that Matt at
first mistook it for a golf course. The author, initially curt and
dismissive, had become more accommodating when Matt had
taken out his book.

"I have no idea," he replied, when Matt pointed to Klein
in the photograph and asked who he was. He had been much
more helpful, though, with the man standing next to Klein.

"That's Kalil," he said.

"You know him?"

"Yes, he was at the Institute for Advanced Studies when I got there. But that's got to be ... what? Thirty years ago."

"Do you know where he is now?"

"Probably pushing daisies. He's ninety, if he's still alive. The last I heard of him was a paper he published in the early eighties."

Through the paper Matt had traced Kalil to Birmingham, where he had been on the faculty, and then to CERN, the advanced nuclear research lab in Berne, Switzerland, and finally to the University of Istanbul, where he had served on the faculty until his retirement ten years ago. Discovering that he was still listed as professor emeritus, Matt had decided to take a chance and try to find him in person. He had no idea what he might be able to tell him, but he was standing next to Klein in the photograph, and just the chance that there might be someone else alive who had known his friend was enough for Matt to make the journey. If he couldn't find him he could always go on to his original destination, Prague, and the Fleigander Foundation, the address of which he had copied down from the box that had held the last of the swallow paintings. If it was indeed there; he had tried calling the number he had found listed in several Internet telephone directories, but, as with Klein's number, the phone had just rung, unanswered.

Matt, next in line, stepped through the gate. The high-pitched ring of the alarm began to sound.

"Please step back through and empty your pockets," the guard said.

Matt, having tossed his change and keys into the small tray, stepped back through the gate. The alarm went off again.

"Step over here, please," the guard said, as another joined them. "Do you have any metal plates from operations?" she asked, passing a wand over Matt's legs and then his arms.

"No," Matt replied.

The wand began buzzing as it passed over Matt's waist in his back.

"Please remove your coat, sir," the guard said, suddenly all business.

"My coat?" Matt asked, shrugging it off. It was his old tweed, the one he had worn for years.

A National Guard soldier in battle fatigues who had been watching them from his post nearby didn't return Matt's apologetic smile as the guard felt the hem of the jacket and then reached into one of the side pockets. "You've got a hole in your pocket," she said, and wormed her hand along inside the coat until she found what she was looking for. She worked her hand free. "That's beautiful," she said. "You don't want to lose that," she added, handing Matt a small pin.

Matt took the compresa, letting it dangle against his palm. The three irises, emerald and azurite, sparkled in their gold and silver setting. The coat, he remembered as the guard handed it back to him. He had been wearing it that day of the press conference, the day Anna had been unveiled to the world.

———

The plaintive summons to prayer of the muezzin, amplified, rose and fell across the dusty roofs and alleys of the ancient bazaar quarter of Istanbul, tumbling down the steep hillside from the Suleymaniye Mosque to the turquoise waters

of the Golden Horn, busy with shipping and ferries. Matt, after
an hour of threading his way through streets choked with traffic
and unending swarms of people, was relieved at the quiet he
found within the tall house when his ring was answered and the
servant had closed the door behind him. They stood in the
hallway, cooled by the tile floor and plastered walls and the fan
overhead, as Matt explained his intrusion, the woman's stoical
impassivity making him sound even to his own ears like a
traveling salesman making a pitch. All the way from New York,
tried to call but couldn't get through, the head of the
department of the university right up the hill had graciously
given him the address, hadn't he called? He had said he
would—Matt finally ground to a halt, realizing that her
expression was not one of skepticism but incomprehension. The
woman didn't speak a word of English.

Matt started to give her his name but stopped. "Johannes
Klein," he said.

The housekeeper disappeared into the recesses of the
house, leaving Matt to wait. When she returned, he followed
her along a passage, past rooms hidden behind dark screens of
carved wood, onto a long, covered porch overlooking a garden
that while small was large enough to shut out any traces of the
city outside the walls. The housekeeper led him down the stairs
into a miniature forest, a profusion of brightly colored
blossoms, red and yellow and a luminous purple, under the
arching fronds of palms and ferns. Dressed in a neatly pressed
linen suit, Kalil looked up at him from under the brim of a
Panama hat. The smooth face in the photograph, creased then
only by a smile, had weathered into a geology of a life. His

hands, one holding a cigarette that yielded a slight spiral of blue smoke, were brown and dry and deeply veined, but the black eyes that took in Matt shone with a concentrated vitality, like an oasis in the midst of the encroaching desert.

He listened to Matt's introduction of himself and then nodded to the chair next to him. "A cigarette?" he offered as Matt sat, and waved to the pack of Lucky Strikes, half-empty, on the table by his elbow.

"Thank you, no," Matt declined, struck at how the man had aged, realizing that he had expected that, like Klein, Kalil would still be the same age as in the photograph, taken almost seventy years before. But he had traced this man through the years, while he had only known Klein in the present, without a past to place him in. Or a future, as it was beginning to seem. "I have to apologize—"

"Not at all," the man said. "I wasn't expecting that you would be Klein. He was an old man when I knew him. But you used his name, obviously to get my attention. Why is that?"

Matt reached into the inner pocket of his jacket and took out the photograph he had sliced out of the book before leaving.

"Amusing, that I thought he was old," Kalil said, looking at the photograph through a magnifying glass that he had picked up from the table. "He looks so young now. Yes, I remember that day very well. Was it at Tivoli? I tied Bohr for the lead. He would have won but he was more interested in perfecting his swing. A singular approach to life, to concentrate your attention solely on the things you can't do and don't know, but that was his way." He chuckled. "He was a terrible teacher. He never wanted to talk about anything he knew, only those things he didn't. And there is dear Werner. Herr Doktor Heisenberg had no such problem. If he didn't understand it, it could not be understood. He was our bookmaker, kept a running assessment of the odds. You are a historian?" he asked. "Have I become a part of history? A footnote, I suspect."

"I'm interested in Klein. He was a friend of mine, and he's disappeared."

"He had a way of doing that. He was an interesting man to be interested in. He worked with Rutherford at McGill and later in Manchester. That is where he met Bohr, who was Rutherford's assistant at the time."

"I knew him in New York."

"Are you sure it was him?"

Matt thought. There was no question at all that Klein was the man he had known. But Rutherford had been a professor at McGill before the First World War, so for Klein to have worked with him, then Klein would have been over one hundred twenty years old when Matt met him. And yet Kalil hadn't said it was impossible. He had merely asked Matt if he was sure it was he. Matt reached into his coat and took out the other photograph he had brought with him.

"Klein was there that day," Kalil said, looking at the graceful biplane just taking flight. "He was a man of the most wide and varied pursuits I have ever come across. He had a degree as a medical doctor—a pathologist—and he was himself a photographer of no little merit, and a musician, too. He raced aeroplanes. He had one of those insane machines that were just flying engines, with the stubby little wings, that roared around and around in circles, scaring the living daylights out of those of us huddled in the stands below." He shuddered at the memory.

"I have to find him," Matt said.

"Mr. O'Brien, I'm afraid that I am fated to disappoint you. I do hope you have the time to buy a carpet while you are in town. A fine kilim, perhaps? I know just the man to see, and at least then I won't feel that I have completely failed you. But Klein"—he sighed and shrugged—"I haven't seen him since the war. The Americans got him, from what I heard. They didn't force him, you know, that isn't their style. I would suspect they thought that they had made him an offer he couldn't refuse, as they say. I've always found it amusing that the general wisdom is that it is typically nouveau riche behavior, to throw money around as though one had no sense of its value. I'm talking about the Americans. On an individual basis, perhaps this is so, but as a matter of national policy, it is actually diabolically ingenious. You might think it a strange inversion of the traditional way of exercising power, to enrich your subjects unnecessarily, when you could just waltz in and take what you want. After the war, who could have said no to the Americans? They could have taken anything they wanted. But outright taking produces resentment, the result of which, as we have seen without fail, is that sooner or later the victim shows up on your doorstep, ready to fight to take back whatever you might have made off with. But when the transaction is commercial, the act of submission is voluntary, and therefore completely emasculating. No, to pay for it is the perfect exercise of power; you get what you want, and your opponent, by his own act of complicity, is rendered powerless to object. But this is the sublime touch—by overpaying, you demonstrate that the money is essentially meaningless.

"In the case of Klein, though, any attempt to buy him would have been laughably unnecessary. Aside from the fact that he had no need for money, he would have gone anyway. Klein—how do you say it? He always went where the action was, and it was clear that the future lay on your side of the Atlantic. My apologies," Kalil added. "I forget that you are yourself an American. But now everyone, it seems, is becoming one. All of our aphorisms have become lines from movies. What used to be 'Plus ça change, plus c'est la même chose' is now 'I'll be back.'"

"You've been of enormous assistance, Professor Kalil," Matt said. "I can't thank you enough."

"If I might ask, Mr. O'Brien: why is it so imperative that you find our mutual friend?"

"Professor, do you believe in time travel?"

"Isn't that what we are doing right now? Traveling through time?"

"Yes, but I mean back, into the past."

"You traveled through time to get here. The world you left, New York, is six hours behind us."

"That is only a matter of convenience, though. If I called a friend of mine it might be midnight there and after dawn here, but we would be talking at the same time. We're still in the same world."

"Are you? Hang up the phone and where are you? Not in the middle of the night in Manhattan. It ceases to exist. You are here, regardless of what is happening there. Time is only one aspect of things. The least important. This notion of yours, traveling back and forth in time, is quaint, but completely misleading. If you want to have any understanding of what you experienced, you must leave behind this notion of time being sequential, like station stops on a railroad line."

"How do you know what I experienced?"

"Mr. O'Brien, please. I may be old but I have not completely taken leave of my senses. It is obvious from your question that you are the one to tell me about traveling between worlds."

"Yes," Matt admitted, and went on to tell him about the studiolo and all the events that had ensued since then.

"You see?" Kalil asked. "I haven't taken leave of my senses, and neither have you. But that is precisely our problem, that we are captives of our senses. It is what we wrestled with in Copenhagen: the behavior of matter at a subatomic level does not correspond to our experience of the physical world. Newtonian physics is perfect for us. We see a tiger coming toward us, we run away. My car hits yours, mine is bigger, you die. I shoot a mortar and the shell goes up and then it comes back down. But this has no relation to the way matter really behaves. What our senses tell us bears no relation to the way the world works or is constructed. Except for one, of course. Our sense of humor. That is the only direct apprehension of the real world we have.

"Matter is energy. It's a particle and a wave, all at the same time; it's everywhere and nowhere, it's everything and nothing at all. And the underlying reality is that there is not just this one world we know, but an infinite number, all existing simultaneously. That's not a theory, Mr. O'Brien, it's the true nature of things, independent of what we see or think."

"Like the Parthenon."

"If you like. But it would be a grave error to think of these worlds as parallel universes, like books on a shelf. They are the facets of a jewel. Each one distinct and equally real, but each refracting the same essential reality. A man walks along a street on a sunny day. He glances at a shop window—a large plate glass window polished to perfection. You have done this many times, haven't you? In it you see a world of infinite detail. Bright, as real as real can be. But then you notice shadows moving in the background. You adjust your focus, and suddenly the bright and sunny world that seemed so real becomes only a reflection, an illusion that you now see beyond to what is really there."

Kalil reached for the pack of cigarettes. He struck a match several times until it finally flared into life. He lit his cigarette and then exhaled, shaking out the match. "Air, Mr. O'Brien," he said. "The sea in which we swim. And like water to a fish, it's invisible to us. But think of the worlds to be found, right here." He cupped his hand. "What time is it?" he asked.

"Five o'clock," Matt replied.

"Ah," Kalil exclaimed. "Time for my show!" He picked up the remote control next to him and clicked it. As a wide-screen television blossomed to life in the verdant growth the familiar theme of the *I Love Lucy* show blared into the courtyard. Rapt, Kalil was soon shaking with laughter, trembling like an old tree in a windstorm. Matt, thinking that his audience was over, got up as unobtrusively as he could.

"Stay, stay," Kalil ordered. "Here," he said, handing him the remote. "Choose something you want to watch. A satellite dish," he confided, and then settled back into the wicker armchair as Matt reluctantly sat down again. "I don't even know how many channels there are. Go on."

Matt clicked the channel. A news show in Turkish was followed by a soap opera in Spanish. Scowling faces hectoring each other on politics came and went in a flash, replaced by a squad of men, in black and white, cautiously patrolling through a field of tall grass. Whales and dinosaurs and satellite weather images and then faster and faster he clicked, mesmerized, image following image with increasing speed until they all blurred together. He lifted his thumb and the blur resolved, like a slowing roulette wheel, into the random pattern of multicolored sticks and bars that stirred a memory before recognition settled in like the wheel coming to rest: the studiolo, the borders of the inlaid cabinets. The pattern dissolved into a scene of prosaic simplicity; a street, with carriages, and people strolling along the sidewalks. For some reason—the cafés, the streetlights, the paving stones—he thought it must be someplace in Europe. Scandinavia, perhaps, the way the light was so clear, or northern Germany.

Matt switched the channel. The same street, the same people. A streetcar turned the corner, a woman with a perambulator talked to a friend, the shadow of a cloud drifted across a façade. He clicked and again found the same scene; the streetcar was farther along. As he clicked, it moved along the street as though in an early movie, jumping slightly as the channel changed, otherwise exactly the same. Was it? He stopped. The woman with the perambulator. She was gone. He clicked back. She was there. He clicked back again; here was a man hanging on the streetcar, about to step off, who hadn't been there before. He clicked ahead and the man stepped off and walked away unconcerned right by the place where the woman had been talking—back and forth Matt went, channel after channel, comparing details. The light was different; not the time of day or the shadows, but the quality of it. The streetcar had reached its stop and come to a halt, passengers getting off and waiting to board, and at the café a waiter was clearing the table. Matt clicked ahead several channels, holding each just long enough for the image to form. Always the same street and the same scene, but slightly different each time.

Kalil's housekeeper reappeared, giving Matt a severe look as though he had overstayed his welcome. The old professor was sound asleep, folded back in his chair. Matt laid the channel selector on the photographs he had shown Kalil and then followed the woman up the stairs and back through the dark and quiet hallway to the bustling street.

chapter 24

The building was not what Matt had expected when he checked into the hotel and showed the address to the clerk at the desk. "This street is not far," she told Matt in careful English, tracing the route from the Hotel Europa on a map. "I think to walk there would be best, if that is fine with you." It was certainly fine with him. After the endless delays in what should have been a short flight from Istanbul to Prague, he was more than ready for a walk. As with Kalil, he didn't want to call ahead; if there was anything to be found at the Fleigander Foundation, then the best chance of finding out was in person. He felt, as irrational as it might be, that he was on the trail of the elusive scientist, who had been resurrected from memory to a blurred image in a photograph and now to a real person. Klein was somehow intimately connected to the foundation, and he was Matt's best hope of finding his way back to the Quattrocento. How, he had no idea, but Klein would know. All this had happened because of him. From the restoration of the studiolo to the completion of the series of swallow paintings, Klein had played a key role. The answer lay with him, and he was out there somewhere.

He stood on the quiet street on the south edge of the Nove Mesto district, past the green oasis of the park at Charles Square, and looked up at the plain white Cubist façade of the building, or as much of it as he could see behind the gauzy curtain of the scaffolding. The houses on either side were halfhearted Baroque pastiches in a pastel pink that in the flat light of a gray afternoon could be seen to be peeling and crumbling, like decorations at a party that has gone on too long. A directory in the lobby had Fleigander—just the single name, nothing else—on the top floor. Matt climbed the stairs, circling up around the central atrium, past doors of dark smoked glass that gave him back an attenuated version of himself and offered nothing else. The door, FLEIGANDER again alone on a small plaque to one side, opened when he tried the knob; he had half expected it to be locked, no one there. Inside he found a modern office, sleek tubular furniture and a desk behind which sat a girl whose hair, short and black, was dyed silver at the ends. She paused in her typing and looked at him.

"I'm here to see Dr. Klein," he said.

"Your name?"

"Matt O'Brien. We've met before," he said, remembering why she had seemed familiar to him. She was the girl who had been playing the harpsichord the first time he had been at Klein's apartment, when he had seen the Leonardo drawing.

"Have we? When would that have been?"

"A while ago," Matt said. When, indeed? A good question. Another lifetime?

"I'm afraid I don't remember. One moment," she added, and left through a doorway behind the desk.

Matt, waiting, looked about the reception area. Decorated with abstract monotypes on handmade textured paper, it might have been the office of a very successful and exclusive psychiatrist. On a table under one of the prints was a vase of irises, tall and fresh. The simple ribbed glass was the same, Matt realized, as the one that he had awakened to find in his hospital room.

"You asked for Dr. Klein?" A slender man not much older than he was, dressed in a somber gray suit with a handkerchief in the breast pocket as precisely arranged as his hair, approached Matt from behind the desk. The woman returned to her seat and began typing again.

"Yes," Matt said. He had seen this man before, too. At the reception for the opening of the studiolo, when he had mistakenly thought the man was Klein.

"May I ask what this is in regard to?" The man's demeanor was polite but noncommittal, like a banker interviewing an applicant for a loan.

"I'm from the Metropolitan. We received a painting from you."

"Yes. I trust it was satisfactory."

"It was exactly what we were hoping to find."

"Very good."

"And Dr. Klein?" Matt asked. A telephone began ringing on the secretary's desk, a soft double tone.

"He is unavailable," the man replied. The phone stopped in midring, unanswered.

"When might I expect to see him?"

"I can't say."

"I'd like to speak to him personally."

"I'm afraid that would not be possible."

"He's a friend. I know he would want to hear from me."

"Even so. Unfortunately, we have no way of contacting him."

"But this is his office, isn't it?"

"I wish I could be of some assistance."

"I know you do. And I thank you for all your help. But if he's not available, then he's not available. Oh, if I might ask you one more thing," Matt said, taking out the glass prism that had been hanging from his hospital window. "What do you think of this?"

"It's beautiful," the man replied, lifting it as Matt held the chain. "Excellent workmanship. It appears to be very old. Interesting touch," he added, fingering one of the curved rays.

"Isn't it? I thought you might have seen it before."

"No. Not to my knowledge."

Matt slipped the prism back into the inside pocket of his coat. "I've taken enough of your time," he said. "Thanks."

———————

Matt threaded his way through the crowds milling across the Charles Bridge, oblivious to the carnival atmosphere as he thought of what he had found and what to do next. Leaving the guitars and mimes behind, the soft choruses of "All we are saying is give peace a chance," and the fake Prada bags set out on blankets, he wandered into the narrow, twisting alleys up the steep hill on the other side of the river. He had run into a dead end. His interview at the foundation was added proof that Klein did exist, but how could he find him? There had been no Johannes Klein in the city directory, when he had asked at the desk, and none in the Czech Republic. But when he went back to his room and searched on his laptop through an Internet directory the drought had turned into a deluge, yielding hundreds across Europe. He could see himself becoming the Diogenes Rodrigo had mentioned in jest, searching not for porcinis but the real Dr. Klein.

Matt climbed the hillside as the light faded and the crowds thinned and vanished until only an occasional solitary figure passed in the shadows. Reaching the top he looked down on the city, shadowed in a dusky purple as the sun, which had come out from the clouds for a last moment of glory, touched the horizon. Impossibly real fairy tale spires reached up to the clouds hanging low over the city, their soft gray shining with a rainbow of colors, glowing in the last rays of the setting sun. Facets of a jewel, Matt thought, remembering what Kalil had said, and took out the prism. He held it up by the chain, the beveled glass sun with its flame-shaped points sparkling dully as the light, fading, was unable to break free in a rainbow of its own. He thought of Kalil's television, of all the different versions of the trolley and the street scene that he had switched through, all different and all almost exactly the same. But, like the captive colors hidden in the prism, they were all there, in the vibrating air that was all around him.

Kalil had been right, Matt thought, descending into the welcoming dark. He had spent all his time and energy thinking about how to get back. His mind couldn't help going from now to then. But wasn't that exactly what Kalil had said was not the case? There was no now and then. There was a world he belonged to, but it was not in the past. He was walking through it right now, if he could only see it. A longing came over him that was almost magnetic in its intensity, pulling at every atom of his being as though it would gather him up and dissolve him into the invisible air.

Time was a variable, Matt realized, but it was not all that mattered. If it did, then this was the best place to be. With streets that hadn't changed since they had first been built centuries ago, Prague at night was a city outside of time. The present retreated as silently as the tide, revealing the forgotten shore that lay beneath the reflected light of day where the past survived, unseen. He crossed the river in the pale light of the rising moon, almost full, the Charles Bridge to the north bathed in yellow lights like a stage set. On his meandering journey through the city he had passed through every age from the medieval to the Baroque, but none of them had pulled at him the way the studiolo had, or the portrait, or now with an overwhelming power, Anna and the Quattrocento.

Matt looked up, hands deep in his pockets. Without thinking, he had found his way back to the quiet street he had been directed to earlier in the day. Klein, he thought; I am lost. This is all happening because of you. Why? Where are you? Matt, counting his options, realized they had dwindled to none.

He couldn't allow this to become a dead end, for he had no place left to go. What was his next step? He thought of Klein and the quantum birds, how the arc was made of a series of steps, each separate and each inextricably linked to the one before and after, forming a single graceful unbroken line leading up into the sky.

With a gathered leap and a grunt Matt was up, resting on the wooden planks of the scaffolding that obscured the face of the building as he regained his breath. The rest was easy, and he was soon on the top floor. Hinged at the side, the windows were all securely fastened. Without a second thought now that he had made up his mind, Matt, one hand in the other, used his elbow as a battering ram. A solid rap, and the glass cracked; with another, more gentle, shards fell inside, and he could reach through and unlatch the window. From cleaning a picture to breaking and entering: not the career path he would have expected under normal circumstances, he thought, as he climbed into the office and stood, listening. But these were anything but normal circumstances. Would they ever be again?

Satisfied he was alone but still afraid to turn on a light, Matt felt his way through the black, navigating out the door like a deep-sea submersible exploring a sunken ship. A hallway led him to the large open space of the reception room, where the windows shone with the unobstructed light of the moon, casting a pale glow on the quiet interior. Matt saw the irises in the vase by the entrance. He went over and lifted the flowers, holding them carefully so that the water dripping from the long stems ran back into the vase, and felt around with his free hand.

It was there. His fingers closed around a slender glass rod. He pulled it halfway out and then let it drop, clinking against the side of the vase, before replacing the flowers.

The index of refraction, Matt remembered mentioning to Klein. That had been the first day he had met him, when Klein had brought in the painting. Matt had been talking about glazes, and how walnut oil had a higher index of refraction, allowing some pigments to disappear and become pure color. The way glass disappears in water, Klein had said. Disappear. Find the right world and become a part of it. Is that what Klein was telling him? Was the message even for him? It had to be; he never would have thought to look, if not for the vase in the hospital, and Klein had brought that for him. But why?

And why not. That was the real question, Matt realized, the one that he had been avoiding for too long. Ever since he had awakened in the hospital. He had found his world, but then lost it. He had been there and now wasn't. Why not? Can loss ever fully be explained or understood? Matt thought of Masaccio, and the drawings that Anna had shown him. The angel with his sword, the two figures being driven from the Garden. They understood only too well, he thought. That was why they were forced to leave—they had sacrificed innocence for knowing. I, too, was expelled, driven out, he thought, feeling again Leandro's hand closing on his neck, and the rising sound of the wolf tone. But now, in the shadows of the moon a world away from where he had begun and just as far from where he wanted to be, was the time for truth. And the truth, he knew, was that he had never fully been a part of that world he had found, for he had never entirely relinquished the world from which he had come. They had gained the knowledge that had lost them their world. He had never surrendered his.

Part of it was how he had gotten there, Matt thought. He had sought refuge in the studiolo. He had been running away. But a refuge could never be a world, and if he were to disappear like glass in water, he would have to become a part of that world, not hide in it. Not out of fear or longing, but because there was no place else for him to be. Knowledge would not help, thinking was a dead end. There is no knowing, he thought. There is only becoming. That was the wolf tone, the irrational that was there, an essential part of every world, the thing that in a strange way gave it meaning. It was the irreconcilable that must be reconciled.

Matt continued down the hallway past the reception office, in the direction the man had come from that afternoon, stopping at the door of the next office to the last. Different from the rest, it had the same window and desk but no computer, no file cabinets, no telephone console or organizer with paper clips and pens and photographs of the family. A blotter, edged in red leather, a single pen rising from a block of marble, an early Cubist lamp, a small book; the decor was spare and uncluttered, like Klein's apartment had been. There were no cabinets to search, not even a shelf of books, so he sat at the desk, wondering what to do next.

The problem wasn't a lack of options, it was too many. There was an entire office suite to be explored, sifted through in the dark, and then all put back. It was already past nine, according to the clock on the desk, the hands like shadows in the moonlight. That gave him eight hours, at the most. He

reached for the book at the side of the desk and opened it. A
calendar, there were entries on every page, in the same hand
but with a variety of ink from the spidery black of an old
dipped nib to a blue felt-tip. Holding it in the direct moonlight,
Matt riffled through the pages. September fourth through
twelfth had the same entry, Kitty Hawk. The eighth also had
Paris, lower on the page. Copenhagen, London, Paris again, and
then New York on several days in January, then again in March
and April. Every day was a different city, often two or three on
the same date. There were names, too, after some of the
places—Rutherford, Helmholtz, Atget, Bohr, Montgolfier,
Lavoisier, Seurat, Turner, Vespucci.

Matt checked the cover to find what year the book was
from, but there was none embossed; none on the flyleaf or title
page either. Berlin, São Paulo, London, all on the same date.
Tokyo and Siena, both on the twenty-ninth of February. It was a
book of hours, Matt realized, a lifetime of discovery and
exploration, collapsed into a single voyage around the sun.
Leafing further, a name caught his eye, and he stopped.
November. What was the date that he had first met Klein? Now
he knew. The fifteenth. There it was in black: NY MMA, Matt
O'Brien. He kept looking. Prague was there, a number of times.
After one notation of the city on October twenty-first, Klein
had written the names Mozart, da Ponte, and Casanova, and
then underneath, *Don Giovanni*, Stavovske Divadlo, eight-thirty.
Curious, Matt moved on to the current date. Prague and *Don
Giovanni* again, and the same theater and time. But instead of
the other names, Mozart and da Ponte and Casanova, was once
again his own: Matt O'Brien.

chapter 25

The soprano could be heard, muffled by the closed doors of the auditorium, as Matt walked into the deserted lobby of the theater. The box office was closed, a curtain pulled down behind the window. It was after the intermission, the opera already into the second act. One of the doors to the hall opened, held by an usher as a couple hurried out, the woman arranging an Hermès scarf over shoulders dark with a cruise-ship tan as her husband, a large, florid man with tooled snakeskin boots, propelled her along by the elbow.

Taking in Matt's plight with a quick glance, he reached into the side pocket of his green blazer. "You need this?" he asked, holding out his ticket stub.

"Thanks," Matt replied, not surprised that the man had assumed he was an American. Judging by what he had overheard all day the chances were better than even that anyone you spoke to would be an American, including the panhandlers and street musicians.

The usher bowed as Matt entered and then, reading the ticket, gestured to the stairs. Up one flight, Matt hastened along the curved row of doors. Finding the box empty, he slipped into one of the plush velvet chairs, angled toward the stage. Absorbed by the drama, no one in the boxes on either side even glanced at him. The lighting gave the painted drops of the long dining hall the dreamy feel of a late-evening dinner party, as though the audience were sitting at one end of the table with the rakish Don at the other. He bantered with his manservant, Leporello, enjoying his feast as a band entertained him.

The musicians could just be seen in the tiny pit, the silver buttons on their coats winking like coins. The theater was small, a jewel box of gilt arabesque against a rich olive gray. Four rings of balconies rose like terraces of a cake to a domed ceiling decorated with classical motifs just visible in the dark. Matt searched the audience, almost lost in the shadows reflected from the stage lights, his eyes sweeping the row of boxes across from him. He stopped at the sight of a woman intent on the opera, on her shoulder the hand of a man standing behind her, hidden in the shadows. Hair swept back in a French knot, with curls at the temples, she wore a dark blue dress that shone almost black in the dim light. The inclination of her head, the air of watchful repose as she listened—

"Anna!" Matt called out, rising to his feet, leaning on the balcony. His cry was drowned out. As a tremendous chord crashed out from the orchestra, a massed roar of strings and horns and timpani that surged through the hall.

"Don Giovanni," a deep bass intoned, insistent and overwhelming. Buffeted by the harsh chord Matt hung on to the rail as the Commendatore, tall and gray as death, appeared against a new backdrop of wintry black.

"Don Giovanni," commanded the imposing figure again. The chord rang out again, its dark cadence washing against Matt, sinking deep inside until it vibrated in his bones. Anna was still there, but only faintly in the darkness across the hall, but she was looking for him, she had heard his voice.

"Wait!" Matt called, but the chord sounded again. He held on to the rail as it dropped in pitch, flattening and slowing to the jarring discord of the wolf tone. Gathering his strength he struggled for the door. He had to get to Anna. And Klein; he knew that was Klein with her. Out of the box he forced his way along the hall, the chord resonating in the walls and the floor, boring into him from every side as it grew and grew. The hall was endless, the doors curving ahead of him as he fought his way forward. Hanging on to consciousness against the gravitational pull of the dark he grasped at a door, hoping it was the right one. As he forced his way into the box the chord died away, leaving a silence like that after a tremendous clap of thunder.

The box was empty, the theater pitch-black, silent. He felt his way forward into nothingness, stumbling against the chairs, and then his waist met the balcony. Beyond, in the blackness, he could sense a yawning emptiness. He held the rail, senses straining into the dark but finding nothing. The theater itself could be gone, he could be standing at the edge of the world, nothing left but a railing and a small piece of carpeting under his feet.

Matt turned and felt his way out of the box, suddenly aware of material around his neck, the feeling an unpleasant reminder of a hand clutching his throat, lifting him off his feet. The deserted hallway was close with the heat and waxy smell of the hundreds of candles in the sconces and chandeliers, their flames motionless in the still air. Matt, unsteady, as though the deck of a ship were falling away under his feet, crossed the hall to a mirror.

Around his neck was a white kerchief, wrapped several times and then tied in a wide bow, nestled inside the lapels of a long white double-breasted vest. Over it he wore a long black coat, with a collar turned high in the back and broad rolled lapels. His cream-colored breeches were buttoned and tucked into tall leather boots.

Matt ran down the broad stairway to the lobby and then out to the steps of the theater. He came to an abrupt halt at the sight of the throngs promenading along the sidewalk. Passing in and out of the pools of lamplight were men wearing powdered wigs and tricornered hats. Dressed in gaily patterned coats and breeches, they escorted women in wide skirts that took up half the narrow sidewalk. The din of shod hooves and iron wheels clattering over cobblestones and the ammonial stench of manure and sweat pressed against him as he walked down the steps of the theater. Which way? Right or left, he had no idea where Anna might have gone.

Matt fell in with the passing crowd, drifting along as he tried to grasp what had happened. The world he knew, already falling apart, was now completely gone. Kalil was right, he thought; time is not linear. But what comfort was that? He had no control over it. He was still in Prague, but in the eighteenth century, and he had no money and no friends and no idea of how to get where he wanted to be. Thinking might not be the answer, but what was he supposed to do now? Just go with the flow?

"Gott im Himmel!" a man cried out as Matt, preoccupied with his thoughts, ran into him. Staggering back, the man had his sword half unsheathed.

"I'm terribly sorry," Matt replied, his hands up.

"Watch where you go," the man replied, switching to a heavily accented English.

"Yes," Matt agreed, picking up the man's hat and dusting it off before offering it to him. "My fault entirely." He bowed, one hand over his chest, the other extended with the hat still in it.

The man glared at him as he snatched the hat. The woman at his side murmured in his ear, tugging at his arm, and he reluctantly sheathed his sword. He glanced around, sharp eyes taking in the crowd that parted around them, searching for any sign of an accomplice while feeling his pockets, satisfying himself that he still had all his effects. He settled the tricorner on his powdered wig and then stalked off, hand on the woman's elbow.

Matt, panicked by a sudden thought, drew into a doorway out of the flow of the pedestrians. Searching through the inside pockets of his own coat, his hand found the wavy spikes of the prism. It was still there. And so was Anna's compresa. He took it out and looked at it, just to be sure, and then put it back.

What would Kalil say now? Matt could see him in his chair, lighting a cigarette. "If you want to meet someone, Mr. O'Brien, what do you need? A time and a place." Matt felt a faint stab of hope. Perhaps this wasn't such a disaster after all. Yes, time is a variable, and one that he couldn't control. But the place—those were just coordinates, like a map, and he could set them. And if he did, then time might follow. But where? He could go to Gubbio, and try to retrace his steps to the villa, but he might never find it. Was it even a part of this world? And even if it had survived, the chances were that it would be changed, and he knew that to see it, so far removed from Anna and the world he had known, would be too sad to bear. He had to find a place that was as timeless as the studiolo had been, where he could free himself from the larger world. He was ready, he could see the land that lay beyond, he could taste it and smell it. He felt like the neophyte that Anna had drawn, the man waiting to be baptized in the fresco in the Brancacci chapel. The chapel—

Of those three, which is the most important? Anna's voice came back to him. Time was a flower, and the flower was an iris, and it stood for faith. The Brancacci chapel was where they had found each other, when he had taken out her drawings and together, looking at them, they had discovered the world that they shared. Time, and the changes wrought by time, were the varnish on top of the painting that lay beneath, unchanged and unchanging. The outer world, whether the one he had been born in, or this one of eighteenth-century Prague, even the Quattrocento, those were the facets—but the jewel itself was the world he had found with her, and it was there, in the Brancacci chapel.

Three balls over a shop across the street proclaimed a pawnbroker. Matt dodged between the carriages and entered the store, a space barely large enough for the man in a Turkish fez and a brocade smoking gown ensconced behind the counter, let alone the myriad of odds and ends lining the walls and hanging from the ceiling. Matt eased the ring off his finger, the first time it had left his hand since he had received it from his parents the day of his high school graduation. With reluctance he placed it on the green baize pad in front of the man, who watched him impassively. Before he could reach for it the ring was gone, scooped up by a brown blur.

"Bring that back," the man in the fez ordered, looking up at the elaborate swirls on the top of a rococo cabinet.

A monkey in a short red jacket chattered in reply, waving the ring like a trophy.

"Now, Farouk!" the man barked. "Have you already forgotten what happened to your brother?"

An even more animated reply from the tiny primate set the tassel of his own miniature fez swinging wildly.

The pawnbroker reached for a long stick with a metal tip next to him. Before he could touch it the ring was on the baize, the monkey back complaining from his perch. The pawnbroker picked up the ring, his fat fingers surprisingly quick and nimble, and examined it through a loupe. "Plate," he announced dismissively, "and look at this stone. Cut glass. Half a pistole. What am I saying? That is too much."

"I'm sorry to bother you," Matt replied, reaching for the ring.

The man drew it back. "Permit me," he muttered, making a show of examining it again. "The light," he said. "So easy to make a mistake, and my eyes are not what they once were." He sighed. "Six."

"Twelve," Matt replied.

The man made as to give the ring back but held on as Matt took it, their fingers meeting around the gold coils. "Nine," the pawnbroker amended. "I'm a fool," he added with a shrug. "I should know better than to bargain this late in the day. I always regret it."

"I need enough to get to Florence," Matt said.

"Four, then," the man cried with pleasure, and reached under the counter. He laid four gold coins on the green baize. "You rob me," he said as Matt just stared at him, but added five more to the pile. "I am a fool," he repeated, taking the ring as Matt scooped up the coins, but he was still rubbing it between his fingers as the door closed.

———

Matt woke as the coach lumbered to a halt. Getting out and stretching, he could see Florence in the valley below, the last glow of dusk illuminating the white ribbed helmet of the Duomo and turning the Arno into a silver vein in a piece of black marble. When the luggage for the passengers making the

penultimate stop at San Miniato had been taken down, Matt
and the other travelers climbed back into the creaking Berlin,
the large carriage springing under their weight like an ungainly
ship. It lurched forward, soon gathering speed down the steep
hillside as the horses sensed the end of their journey. The
interminable week suddenly seemed as though it had passed in
a blur. The coach entered the narrow streets of the city, the
thundering of the hooves and wheels almost deafening as it
echoed off the tall buildings crowding in on each side. The
driver went at a pace that had seemed to be crawling when they
had been in the open country but now was at breakneck speed.
Driving along the river, Matt could see the lights on the Ponte
Vecchio closing in ahead, the tall arches of the Uffizi barely
visible in the moonlight to the right.

"Stop!" Matt cried out, and seized the gold-headed cane
from the gaunt gentleman who had been staring at Matt since
he had changed coaches for the last leg of the trip two days
before, nodding whenever Matt met his gaze but saying
nothing. Matt vigorously thumped the roof until the carriage
ground to a halt.

"Che fai?" the driver snapped, but Matt was already gone,
racing back to catch the carriage he had just caught a glimpse
of as they made the turn onto the Ponte Vecchio. It had been
heading in the opposite direction, toward the Pitti Palace, ablaze
with lights just up the hillside. The large, open forecourt was
crowded with carriages drawing up, letting their passengers off,
driving away. Matt joined the crowd making their way up the
steps into the palazzo, faces all hidden behind simple black
dominoes or more fanciful masks. In the press at the top of the

steps Matt caught sight of the man he had seen in the carriage passing on the bridge. Dressed in a long dark blue coat, he had silver hair falling loose to his shoulders. Klein. As Matt fought his way through the crowd his friend disappeared from sight into the palace, listening to the man who had just greeted him.

As Matt hurried up the stairs, a hand stopped him. Looking up, he found himself in the grip of an immense landsknecht, one of two soldiers standing guard on each side of the grand stairs, dressed in uniforms with garish striped hose and puffed sleeves, their cuirasses of polished steel almost hidden under flowing white beards. The landsknecht leaned his two-handed sword, as tall as he was, against the wall and drew a domino from the bag at his waist. Wordless, he handed it to Matt before resuming his statuelike pose.

The ballroom was already packed with guests standing in tight groups or promenading around the grand space, two stories high and running the entire back of the first floor of the palazzo. At one end an orchestra played, the festive strains of the spring movement of Vivaldi's *The Four Seasons* weaving through the buzz of animated conversation that filled the room. Matt wended his way through the crowd, searching for the dark blue coat and silver hair as the violinist, who had been conducting the orchestra, turned to face the audience and launched into the solo. Klein was nowhere in sight, not in the ballroom or the smaller room adjoining it where many of the guests were intent on a spinning roulette wheel and the soft slap of cards dealt by men in Pierrot costumes and blank white masks.

"Cento luigi," Matt heard a man in a painted leopard

mask say, advancing a pile of gold coins. A spectator, feathered hat under his arm, inhaled a pinch of snuff from the back of his hand, sneezing violently as the card was slipped across the felt. Continuing on, Matt scanned the crowd at the far side of the ballroom. The tall French doors stood open, the long gold curtains barely stirring in the light breeze that did nothing to lessen the almost suffocating heat from the dozens of chandeliers and tall candelabra ranked along the walls that made the room as bright as midday. Matt saw a shadow on one of the balconies, black on black, silver against the dark.

"A beautiful evening, isn't it?" Klein asked as Matt came up next to him, his mask dangling from his hand as he leaned against the old marble balustrade.

"Johannes, what's going on?" Matt asked, taking off his domino.

"I think you know the answer to that."

"Do I? I know things are coming apart. Literally."

"It's the nature of things. The second law of thermodynamics states it clearly—disorder always increases."

"Thanks," Matt replied. "That's a real help."

Reaching into the inside of his brocade waistcoat Klein came up with a small coin, which he tossed out into the dark. The gold disk spun in a long arc up and then down, landing with a tiny splash in the still fountain. A faint grin deepened the lines in Klein's angular face.

"You know how to look below the surface of a painting," Klein said, "how to see the things that others find invisible. But that's only half the equation. If you have eyes to see and ears to hear. Isn't that how it goes? You must listen the way you look.

Music of the spheres or string theory, call it what you will—
there is a chord that is the sum of all things. A wave of
possibility that each of us collapses into the music of our own
world."

"The wolf tone. Is that what you mean?"

"In part. But don't confuse cause and effect. Musicians talk
about centering the note. A note might be in tune, but not
really ring. When it's centered, it comes alive. All the overtones
sound, all the harmonics. It becomes a chord, blossoming from a
single note, and within a chord can be found an infinity of
music, if you change the variable of time. An entire world, all
within a single note."

"But what does that mean?"

"Nothing," Klein answered. "Why does it have to mean
anything?"

"You're not even trying to help me."

Klein laughed. "Yes, you're right. I'm doing everything in
my power to stand in your way."

"Where's Anna?"

"I don't know. I'm not the answer man. The particular
harmony of your world is something you can only find yourself.
It's your chord, not mine. You have to unscroll it." He smiled.
"It seems so long ago, I had almost forgotten what it's like. Don't
worry, you'll get there."

"How?"

"I think you know the answer to that, too. What was it
that brought you to Florence? It wasn't me."

No, Matt realized, it wasn't. All the way down from
Prague he hadn't thought of Klein once. He had just happened

to catch a glimpse of his friend in a passing carriage, but he had been on his way to the Church of the Carmines. Which is where, he realized, he wanted to be now. There was one thing he did want to know, though, before he went.

"Why? Why did you do all this?"

"Me?" Klein asked in surprise. "Look to yourself, not to me. You're what got you from there to here. You and only you. Each step along the way presented you with a wave of possibility, but it was you that collapsed it into a particular course of action. It was your choice, always." He sighed. "But you're right. I did intervene. Why? I have to admit that as a scientist I found the situation immensely appealing. But it was more than that. You might call it the rules of the road: a traveler always lends a helping hand. There was really not much else I could do. Under the circumstances, it was my obligation. My pleasure, too, I might add."

"Good-bye," Matt said, holding out his hand. "And thanks."

"Best of luck, my friend."

chapter 26

Standing just inside the door of the church, Matt felt the deep
stillness gather and settle into him, the sense of quiet, of
timelessness, as familiar as if he had only just been there. But
something was different, something essential had changed. The
feel of the place was the same, the sense of space and the
paving stones underfoot, but the scent was different. The sweet
blend of incense and flowers and candle wax was gone, replaced
by the sharper smell of smoke and freshly cut stone and raw
wood. It was the fire, he remembered, reminding himself of
when, not just where, he was. The church had burned only
sixteen years ago, in 1771, a conflagration that had almost
completely destroyed it. Only the Brancacci chapel had
survived, although the paint had been irretrievably altered by
the heat. But had it survived?

Matt made his way in the almost complete darkness to the

right aisle and up the long nave, relieved to see that they, at least, were as he remembered them. He stopped at a side altar and took a taper, lighting it from the single tiny flame that glowed before a sorrowing Madonna, and then continued on toward the chapel, hoping against all hope that it was still there. As he approached, the walls of the chapel gradually took form in the wavering light, one of them partly obscured by a rough scaffold.

Figures appeared, Adam and Eve standing in the Garden. On the wall opposite, they were being driven from it, naked and sobbing, by an angel with a sword. Matt entered the chapel and turned, looking at all the panels one by one, his relief at finding the chapel intact overcome by the warmth of seeing old friends once again. Grouped in two tiers of panels, men were talking, listening, sleeping. He thought of the countless hours he had spent there sketching, studying, sometimes just letting go of all conscious thoughts as the forms and colors and people on the walls had come alive, suffusing him with their warmth. There was Masaccio himself, in the corner, reaching to touch the enthroned Saint Peter. And there, nearby, Alberti and Brunelleschi, architects of the age. Brunelleschi, Matt thought, who on hearing of Masaccio's untimely death at only twenty-eight had repeated over and over, We have suffered a great loss, we have suffered a great loss. We...

Matt turned to the wall opposite. There was Botticelli, looking out from the crowd of onlookers at Saint Peter's crucifixion. And there, at the very edge of the last panel, was Filippino Lippi, a questioning look on his face as though he were asking, Do you like it? Matt held the candle aloft. At the very moment that these figures had come to life, color flowing from Filippino's brush into the wet plaster of the new chapel, Matt had been with Anna. And there was the neophyte she had drawn, standing with the others on the shore of the river, uncertain and awkward, each waiting for Saint Peter to sprinkle water on his head. He was next in line, arms crossed, shivering, naked but for the smallest loincloth. Matt held the candle up, captivated by the man's expression. Why did I never notice him before? He has surrendered everything, placed himself at the mercy of an unknown future, but look at him: his face is alive with the radiant wonder of a man who has traveled to the ends of the earth and at last caught sight of the home he had thought he would never find.

The candle guttered out, the figures on the wall fading as the light died. Matt, exhausted from all he had been through in the past few days, thought of a chapel across the nave. Secluded, it had a broad stone bench along the wall where, unseen, he had often fallen asleep in the long afternoons. It might still be there. He crossed the nave in the dark, seeing it in his mind, finding the single step to the chapel. With a cry of pain he stopped, barking his shin on an unexpected edge of stone.

Matt limped back to the altar to get a fresh taper so that he could see what he had bumped into. It must be material for the reconstruction of the church, he thought, because the chapel had been empty when he had known it. Returning with a candle he found a family crypt, with a della Robbia glazed Madonna on the end wall and, in front of it, two sarcophagi carved of alabaster. An original della Robbia, he noted, not one of the garish confections churned out later by the workshop.

The large caskets had no family name incised, but the one on the left had the head of a lion carved in the stone, watching the church with sightless eyes. The lid on the right was inlaid with an intricate porphyry pattern of sticks and swirls, and above it—

Matt felt his heart grow still. Sculpted from the white stone were three irises, tied by a ribbon, the petals so thin and delicate that the light shone through them. He had found Anna at last.

How can this be? Matt thought. It was only a few weeks ago that I held her hand. She launched a tiny paper airplane. I folded it while I was talking to her—about what? What was it she had been saying? He remembered the paper, could feel how thick and stiff it was, how it felt to fold and crease it. He could see her next to him, feel her hand in his, even hear her laugh. But he couldn't remember what she had said.

This was Anna, Matt thought. This is all that is left. Dust and air. From a wave of possibility to a memory, and then to nothing at all. Everything fades and disappears, stolen by time. Time, not love, conquers all.

Matt touched the irises, as soft as the silk of the dresses that she wore. Eternally fresh and never to wilt, they might almost have been laid on the top last week. Faith. What good is faith now? The chord was eternal, but the music was not. It had a beginning and an ending, and he knew that here, under his hand, was the ending.

But something in him refused to accept the cold evidence before him, tangible and real as it was. He knew this was the ending, but what did that mean? Knowing was what lost me

Anna and the world I found, he thought. As he looked at the smooth white marble, the image of a drawing came to mind. He could see himself, lifting it out of the drawer. A drawing of a man. The penitent, waiting to be baptized. "That's mine," Anna had answered him, when he had said how good it was. But he had already known it was hers. Just as the same man, naked and cold, knew without knowing what he would find. A different kind of knowing.

"A man walks along a street on a sunny day. He glances at a shop window ..." Kalil's words came back to him. This is the window, Matt thought. Not the marble top, or the casket, but the church, the world around him. As real as it seems, what I see is no more than a reflection of what I know. Empty your mind of what you know, he told himself, and find the world that lies beyond.

Matt set the candle down on the marble lid. Going back to the altar he gathered up all the candles he could find and then carried them back, cradled in his arms, and piled them on the floor next to the sarcophagus. He took one and held it, the wick inches away from the steadily burning flame of the candle on the casket, and thought back to the day he had arrived at the villa. He could see it with perfect clarity—the large kitchen, the full table, Rodrigo bantering with Lisl. He felt the heat of the open hearth and smelled the pig turning on the spit and the herbs hanging from the ceiling and heard the crackling of the fire and then laughter, coming in the door, and there she was. And seeing Anna as he had that very first time, her gaze barely even touching him, he lit the candle and set it on the lid.

One by one, moment by moment and day by day, all the

different ways he had come to know her, he lit the candles until he had lit them all, standing them next to each other until there was a row and then another and another, a glowing sea of Anna as he knew her.

When he was done, Matt stood at the foot of the casket, hands on the lid. "I am a mountain lion," he said. "And I beg for mercy."

He climbed up on the other casket and sat, cross-legged, his coat draped around his shoulders. Beyond memory or thought, in a world even beyond faith, his being was filled with the presence of Anna, the woman he loved, in the constellation of flames dancing next to him, silent in the night.

———————

His cheek pillowed on linen, Matt woke slowly. Eyes closed, he luxuriated in the feel of the coarsely woven fabric, soft compared to the hard stone he lay on. Hard stone. He opened his eyes and raised himself on his hands. Aching and stiff, his body protesting, he looked down at his pillow, a folded blue coat. Next to it lay a long sword, the tooled scabbard attached to a woven leather belt, and a pair of leather boots, the soft uppers drooping to the side. His white linen shirt was secured by a braided silver belt, and on his legs were hose.

Matt swung his legs over and jumped down from the casket, hanging on to the marble until he could gain his balance. He stretched, willing his body awake. Candles gone, the bare marble of the casket next to him shone in the light from the stained glass window high up on the chapel wall. Swaths of red and pale yellow, green and purple, colored the marble, surrounding a patch that was still white. Long and wide, the whiteness was shaped like a sun with rays curved like fire.

Matt looked up at the window. He reached inside the folded doublet. The prism was there. The sunlight danced and shone inside the beveled glass as he laid it on the marble, a small sun inside the larger white one cast through the window by the strong light of the morning sun. With a heave and a grunt he dragged the heavy oak prie-dieu from its place in front of the della Robbia Madonna over to the tall window. Prism in hand, he climbed up and, balancing in front of the metal frame, rotated the glass sun until it slipped into place, clicking home into the surrounding frame of lead.

Matt jumped down and stood at the head of the casket, feeling the sun on his back, suffusing him with its warmth even through the stained glass. He watched the miniature sun, a glowing ultramarine blue surrounded by rainbows of fire, creep across the lid as outside the real sun climbed in the sky. The stillness of the church deepened, dust dancing in the motionless light, as the image of the sun slipped from the carved irises down across the inlaid porphyry, the random pattern of sticks and circles he remembered from the studiolo. As it reached the exact center the vibration that he had felt rising within him from the flagstones beneath his feet and the air around him inside him coalesced into a sound he felt rather than heard, a resonance beyond music, an infinite world of overtones and harmonics within the beauty of its one magnificent tone.

In the center of the glowing sun a line sprang to life, bright white, the blue of the sun canceling the blue of the inlay. The line was blurred, as though deep under water. The vanishing point, Matt thought, and he shifted to the side, his eyes on the line. Feeling something under the soft sole of his boot, he looked down. Scuffing with his toe, a gold sun came to light against the paving stones. Standing on it, the white line came into brilliant focus, connecting a chapel at one end to a villa at the other. Matt reached in, his hand passing through the chapel, the white line tracing its way across the back of his hand as he followed it to the villa. He tried to close his fingers around the tiny emerald irises glowing like a constellation inside, but they vanished when he touched them, leaving his fingertips stinging as though he had brushed the invisible tendrils of a jellyfish.

Just as abruptly as it had appeared, the scene vanished, the star moving closer to the irises carved in the lid. Leaning his weight on his hands on the marble, warm with the sun, Matt closed his eyes. It was there, burned on his memory, the path from the chapel to the villa. How long it would take he had no idea, but the way was clear. He stood up and stepped back out of the light, feeling the cool air of the church wash over him.

The nave, as he walked through it, was decorated with the rich trappings of the Carmines. Passing the Brancacci chapel he saw that the fresco of the crucifixion of Saint Peter was only half-finished, the unplastered part of the wall stenciled with the red drawing of the sinopia. A table laden with colors and tools stood in the center of the chapel, the floor by the wall protected by a rough drop cloth, splattered with paint and plaster.

Emerging from the dusk of the church, Matt was again dazzled by the brilliance of the morning sun. White on white, shadows slowly resolved, taking on substance, the vague form in front of him becoming an old woman, bent, sweeping the steps of the church. Without a cloud in the sky, it would be a hot day.

A young man walked up the steps. Long nose, narrow eyes under arched eyebrows, a lower lip slightly protruding with a strong chin to balance it and a sharp jaw, a red doublet and a shirt with a white collar, he passed Matt with barely a glance.

"Buon giorno, Madre Lisabetta," the man greeted the old woman.

"Giorno, Filippino," she replied without looking up, as she kept on sweeping.

chapter 27

Matt, walking through the night from the farm where the cart had left him the evening before, reached the place where the simple track to the villa left the main road north to Urbino. The air was clear and cool, soft with the rich scents of late summer, lavender and rosemary and ripening hay. As the black of the night turned to gray, pale colors appeared, filling in like light washes of watercolor. Rising above the ridge, the early-morning sun dappled the road with shadows as the cicadas, warming up, began to scrape one by one. The wood by the road soon resonated with birdcalls, answered from the tall stand of hay in the narrow field between the path and the hillside.

The morning breeze died, the trees and fields falling still until the only motion was Matt walking along the road, the supple leather of his boots white with dust. As the sun reached toward the meridian, high overhead, time seemed to slow to a halt, refracted by the glaze of the heat into the steady buzz of the cicadas, rising and falling like an ocean swell on a calm day. There was no past, no future, nothing but the world he walked through, as it was just then. What memories he had were of the morning, and the walk during the night, and the long cart ride and the day before. Frescoes, and a chapel, the city, and, ahead of him, the villa, and Anna. The rest was all a dream, fading under the hot sun like fugitive colors, crowded out by the scent of wild oregano and thyme and the beauty of the tapered cypresses that lined the dusty road, the curve of the hills against the sky.

Thirsty, Matt stopped at the sight of a trickle of water seeping down the hillside from the olive grove above. He scrambled up the steep slope to the welcoming shelter of the trees, a canopy of silvery green like a school of fingerlings against the sky above. Reaching the source of the stream, a pipe that had been driven into a rock ledge, he found an old cup, the majolica chipped and faded, hooked on a stick. He drank, enjoying the coolness of the water against his face as much as the wetness and the fresh, clean taste of it, and then put the cup back, careful not to disturb the frog willing itself into invisibility under the nearby fern, motionless but for the steady pulse in its sagging chin.

Matt walked farther up through the grove. Next to an old ladder leaning against a trunk several willow baskets lay tumbled together, ready for the harvest of olives ripening on the branches. The edge of the canopy was underlit by blue, as though the sea lay beyond the trees. A field of asters greeted Matt as he stepped from the grove, and he paused to enjoy the sight. An afternoon breeze had sprung up, rippling the sea of flowers and carrying a sound from far across the field, heavy, like a bear moving through the brush. Matt squinted, shading his eyes against the bright sun as he looked to see what it was.

Green scales coruscating, wings lifting like a hawk balancing itself, the manticore stepped sideways, arching its neck. From across the sea of flowers the beast watched Matt, its eyes opalescent in the sun, its head barely moving as the seconds became minutes. Finally it turned again, stamping its foot and twitching its tail, the forked end snapping like a whip, and then loped down the field and leaped up into the sky with a sweep of its powerful wings. Curving around low over the trees, forelegs held up, it gave a long harsh cry.

As if in echo, the faint silvery call of trumpets came to Matt from deep in the woods across the field, punctuating the high tenor yelp of dogs on the hunt. Each horn had its own note, sounding again and again, distinct but blending with the others. Like the scent of fire, the call aroused a sense of danger in Matt. Orlando, he thought. He must not waste time. He drew his sword and checked the edge, a sharp, unbroken line of silver, and then slid the blade back into its sheath.

Matt crossed the field, the flowers parting and then rejoining behind him, leaving no trace of his passing. Entering the forest the air was cool and fragrant with the resinous scent of hemlock. The yelping of the dogs, drawing closer, rose to an almost hysterical pitch, accompanied by the high whinny of horses and the heavy clump of their hooves on the ground as they forced their way through the underbrush. The shouts of men calling back and forth echoed through the trees.

Matt advanced as fast as he could, intent on finding what he knew was somewhere in the woods. Black and brown, gone so fast they seemed a trick of the light in the shadows, lean hounds slipped past through the brush. A man appeared, no more than a glimpse of bright colors against the green, a black stave slashing a bush aside. Seeing a lightening of the canopy off to his left, Matt angled across the forest. Crowns meeting far overhead, the trees opened to form a natural amphitheater, their black trunks surrounding it like mute spectators. Carpeted with leaves and grass, the clearing was no larger than a man could throw an ax. Matt emerged from between two trees and stopped at the edge of the grass.

The ring of his sword as he unsheathed it, loud in the quiet of the clearing, stopped the tall figure armored in black on the other side, his own sword in his hands. Beyond him Orlando lay propped against a tree, holding his leg, fear plain on his face as he looked up at the bronze eagle, wings raised and beak open in midcry, nodding down at him from the helmet framed against the leaves and the sky above.

The knight turned to face Matt and raised the blade, the point reaching toward the sky. He began to laugh, a low rumble that grew louder and louder as it echoed across the clearing, rising to the trees and filling the still air, resonating in Matt's ears after it had died away again to silence. The knight advanced across the clearing, an oncoming avalanche of polished black armor and chain mail, greaves and arm guards and armored boots and the empty black gash of the visor and, riding above, beak open and wings raised, the bronze eagle.

Standing his ground, Matt lifted his own sword high, as high as his arms could reach, and then sharply reversed it. He brought the point down as hard as he could, burying it deep in the ground. As the hilt quivered, he unfastened the belt around his waist and tossed it to the side. A quick turn of the pin fastening the silver belt holding his doublet and it was loosed, the coat falling open. He shrugged it off and threw it aside to land crumpled among the dead leaves and grass. With a firm pull the sword was free of the ground, the tip arcing around as he lifted it high in both hands, ready to meet his opponent.

Closer, step by step, the blade came on like a black line slashed into the green of the forest. Almost within striking distance of Matt it rose, the tip reaching higher, pausing like a hawk ready to fall from the sky, and there it stayed, the massive figure of the knight frozen as he looked down at his prey.

Three irises, precious stones set in gold and silver, shone in the subdued light against the whiteness of Matt's shirt. He raised his own sword high, angled to the right, the tip back over his shoulder, and then with all his might he lunged forward. His blade sliced through the air to land with a clash against the other, the steel of both ringing as his slid down, stopping only when it slammed hard against the hilt.

Without pausing, Matt's blade soared up, circled, and fell against the other once again, the clashing of the steel ringing out even louder, the note true and pure. The knight stepped back, uncertain, and then with a quick circling of his sword threw Matt's off and gathered himself to attack.

Matt, leg forward, braced himself against the onslaught, his arms giving only slightly as the knight's blade landed against his with a tremendous crash, the same note thrumming through his arms and torso as it filled the air. The knight seemed to hesitate again, as though confused by the sound. Wheeling back around, he attacked again and again, but Matt parried, held, crossed, met each slashing attack, always ready for the blade when it descended on him. Again and again it fell, the note ringing until it became one continuous sound in the air, and then the knight, a last furious assault spent, lurched away, sword dangling.

Matt paused, chest heaving wildly, throat burning as he dragged air into his lungs. He fought to hold on to his sword, his hands numb from the vibration still ringing in his ears. His eyes stinging with sweat, the leather against his skin slick and hot, he watched the knight stagger as he regained his balance and then turn back to him, raising his sword, ready to attack again. Not waiting, Matt charged forward, the silver edge of his sword high and gleaming with a rainbow of color in the dappled sunlight. At the last moment, he dropped the point of the sword and drove it straight into the black slit of the visor.

The force of the impact lifted the knight and threw him back, his arms spread wide, his sword tumbling to the ground. He hung in the air and then toppled over to land with a hollow clang on the ground. Matt, hands entwined on the hilt, stumbled forward, gasping for breath, the point of his sword still buried inside the helmet, the knight lying motionless and limp. Matt let go of the hilt and the sword fell over sideways to the ground as he sank to his knees, spent.

Matt rested, sitting back on his heels, as his breathing slowed, and then reached for his sword. About to clean it on the knight's sleeve, he stopped. There was no blood. The blade was clean.

Matt reached over to unlatch the visor, but the helmet fell away from his hand, rolling to its side, the eagle lying in the leaves as though it had fallen from the sky. Matt pushed the cuirass and then lifted it by the neck hole. It pulled free, the sleeves of the chain mail shirt slipping out of the heavy gloves and dangling like the shed skin of a snake. He tossed it aside and pushed apart the rest of the armor. Empty, the pieces lay scattered in the leaves like pieces of a forgotten dream.

———————

A giraffe, a hippopotamus, a lion and two cubs, the topiary menagerie stood guard as Matt passed. Down the short flight of steps, worn with age, to the lower garden, he followed one of the paths between the flower beds to the pool in the center, where a dolphin leapt, half in and half out of the water. By the side of the pool was a table, veined marble, and on it a majolica jug and glasses, one almost full, with a bright circle of thinly sliced lemon floating in it. Matt settled into one of the chairs and poured water into another of the glasses. Circling the rim with his finger, a note rose in the air, high and pure.

Asleep in the chair next to him, Anna stirred, but relaxed again as the note faded away. Her dress, damascene silk the color of ivory, fell in soft folds from the golden belt tied in a lover's knot under the bodice. A light blue cape, turned back to show the black lining, was draped over her shoulders, and holding her hair was a braided silver cord set with a single pearl mounted in gold.

Matt, as Anna slept, put aside thoughts of what lay ahead. At supper he would talk to Rodrigo about the project for the pigments, and there were other plans to be made, but for now it was enough just to enjoy the view out across the valley, the deep green of the hills on the other side infused with gold in the early evening light.

Anna stirred again, and awoke. She smiled at him, her eyes still filled with sleep. "You're back," she said. "Is it late?"

"No, it's barely evening. Have you been asleep long?"

"I don't know. After you left, I tried to work on the painting, but I was just so tired. I didn't get any sleep last night, you know."

"I'm glad you had a chance to rest."

"I had the strangest dream while I was asleep. I was in a theater and people were singing."

"What? 'Miracolo d'Amore'?"

"No." Anna laughed. "It was music I had never heard before. And you were there, too."

"What happened?"

"There was a storm, and it got dark. I couldn't see. The worst was the silence. But then—it must have been our talking about it at dinner—I saw the manticore. It was walking on the sea. And then I heard a trumpet. It was the most beautiful sound, like a rainbow."

"And then?"

"I woke and you were here."

"The hunt's over. The manticore got away."

"I'm glad." Anna leaned over and touched the compresa pinned to his shirt. "And Leandro?"

"There is no Leandro. He's gone."

"You had no way of knowing, and I couldn't tell you. The count died yesterday. That was why last night— I was afraid of what Leandro might do when he found out and knew his way was clear."

Matt put his hand over hers, still resting on his shirt. "I missed you."

"Did you?"

"Yes, I did," Matt said, and kissed her palm. He stood, and she rose, too, her hand still in his as he drew her close. She was light, as he put his arm around her and lifted her, and so was the kiss, as light as the sun reflecting off water.

"I want to have your portrait done," Matt said, his arm around her waist as they walked back up the path toward the villa.

"You can paint it."

"I wouldn't be able to do you justice. I think I'll stick to flowers."

"Who, then? Piero?"

"I was thinking about that Florentine, the one Rodrigo knows."

"How delightful," Anna replied. "He just painted my cousin Ginevra."